Wendy

Lady In Disguise

The Langley Sisters Series

Lady In Disguise is a work of fiction. Names, places, and incidents either are products of the author's imagination or are used fictitiously.

bookmark:Copyright

Published by Vella Ink Ltd

Cover by Seductive Designs
Formatting by Polgarus Studio
ISBN: 978-0-9922643-7-6

Also by Wendy Vella

Historical Romances

Regency Rakes Series

Duchess By Chance

Rescued By A Viscount

Tempting Miss Allender

The Langley Sisters Series

Lady In Disguise

Lady In Demand

Lady In Distress

The Lady Plays Her Ace

The Lady Seals Her Fate

Novellas

The Lords Of Night Street Series

Lord Gallant

Lord Valiant

Stand Alone Titles

The Reluctant Countess

Christmas Wishes

Contemporary Romances

The Lake Howling Series

A Promise Of Home

The Texan Meets His Match

How Sweet It Is

It Only Took You

Dedication

For Denise
A special friend who listened as I talked of endless plots and characters and who makes the best tea and cheese puffs in the world. You always knew I could do it.
Thanks for believing, my friend xx.

CHAPTER ONE

Lord William Ryder woke suddenly as he flew across the carriage to land face first on the opposite seat. Shaking his head in an attempt to clear the sleep-induced fog, he wondered what the hell Luke was thinking, pulling his horses to a halt so quickly. Slapping both hands on the seat, he levered himself upright.

"Stand and deliver!"

Hands still braced on the seat, Will shook his head again; surely he hadn't heard those words correctly.

"Those within the carriage step down at once or I will blow a hole in the side!"

In the past few years, Will had been shot, stabbed, held hostage and forced to leap from a burning ship, and now he had arrived, to what he believed the safety of his homeland, and within hours he was being robbed. If rage weren't nipping at his heels, he'd laugh.

"I will give you a five-count!"

"I'm coming!" he bellowed, reaching for the door. Pushing it open with enough force that it banged loudly against the carriage, Will stepped down. Cooler now that dusk had settled, he could smell the trees and earth of his homeland.

"No risks, Luke," he cautioned his driver quietly as he

looked at the riders before him. "Well?" he then questioned the two masked men, waiting for one of them to speak; curiously, both seemed almost unnaturally still. "Are you robbing me, or did you want to take tea?" His drawled words had the required effect, as one of them spoke.

"Throw your money over here, or I will shoot you!"

"You had better make that shot count, because you can be assured if you miss, you won't get a second one," Will stated calmly, looking at the two riders. Both wore black hats pulled low to cover their eyes and scarves hid the lower half of their faces. Pistols were pointed at him and his driver. They looked menacing, yet not overly big, he thought, eyeing the slender thigh of the one closest to him.

"The penalty for robbing a peer is death I believe," he added, reaching into his pocket and removing a money pouch.

"The penalty for starvation is the same, my lord!"

With the coin pouch now in his hand, Will looked at the man. His words were muffled, yet he could hear the desperation.

"You'll end up with your neck stretched by the hangman's noose if you don't rethink your choice of career, young man."

"Spoken like a cosseted nobleman, Lord Ryder. Now throw me that purse and we shall be on our way."

Will paused, holding the highwayman's gaze, and then slowly threw the purse in the air, the coins making a chinking sound as they resettled in his palm.

"It appears you have me at a disadvantage, sir. You know who I am, yet I am at a loss to remember you. Of course, that could be because you have your face covered and a pistol pointed at my head."

Will watched the horse lift its head as the man's hand tightened on the reins. Interesting. It was dark, and the moonlight was weak, but the highwayman had recognized him immediately, if that reaction was any indication. He'd seen the worst life could offer, yet it saddened him that someone who had crossed his path would need to steal to survive.

"This is not a social call, Lord Ryder. Just hand over the pouch and we shall leave you to continue your journey."

"And if I say no, will you kill me where I stand?"

"We don't want to kill you!"

"Then turn your horse around and leave," Will said, his voice now low and menacing. The gun wavered and then steadied as the man transferred the reins into the same hand as the gun, the empty one he now held out to Will.

"Throw me that pouch."

"No." He watched the two highwaymen look at each other after he spoke. A suspicion formed in his head as the leader raised a shoulder in a gesture that looked far too feminine for a man.

"I will shoot your driver."

Will had not survived the last few years to be shot just miles from his home, and he realized that a young, desperate man aiming a gun at his head was a situation that could get out of hand quickly.

"Here." He threw the bag at the leader, who caught it easily.

"Now go, before I decide that you two need to be taught a bloody good lesson in manners," Will added, scowling at them.

They turned their horses and began to leave.

"I'll stop them!"

"No, Luke!"

Too late, Will watched his driver's knife sail through the air and lodge itself in the shoulder of the lead highwayman. The scream that filled the air told him his original guess had been incorrect. They weren't youths; in fact, they were women. He took a step towards her as she lurched sideways in the saddle, but she saved herself by gripping the horse's mane, and soon they were gone from his sight.

"Christ, I just stabbed a woman, Will."

"Just a flesh wound, Luke. She will recover." Will waved a hand at his friend. "Now shift over, I'll drive from here." Throwing a final glance in the direction the riders had taken; he then climbed up beside Luke and took the reins, eager to get home.

Forty minutes later, Will brought the horses to a halt on the rise; passing the reins to Luke, he then jumped down.

"Five years is a long time, Will."

"Aye, Luke." Will felt something ease inside him as he walked forward to take in the sight below. He had carried this place in his heart for so long, often believing he would never see it again.

Built by his ancestors, the gray stone walls of Rossetter House rose proudly up into the night sky. A flag fluttered from the turret that one of the previous dukes had built to add grandeur to the home. He knew every inch of the crest that was embroidered on that flag; two lions for dauntless courage, and a cross that was added for faith and service in the Crusades. Blue for truth and loyalty. In this, Will had fallen short; at the first test of loyalty, he had failed and fled.

A light twinkled in the turret room, and Will wished that he would find his mother in there spending time in her favorite room. Filled with light from sunrise to sunset, she had claimed it for her music. A cold wind ruffled his hair as memories assaulted him, memories that, until today, he had chosen to keep locked inside.

He saw his little sister crying, begging him not to leave as he stormed from the house with his brother's angry words resonating in his head. Joseph had called him a leech on the dukedom, demanding to know when he would become the man his parents had raised him to be. Will had remembered those words. They had motivated him to become the man who stood here today.

"How can so much time have passed, Will, yet there Rossetter sits the same as it always did?"

"Its history binds it to the earth as it has for hundreds of years, Luke. It would take more than the two of us to change that."

Would his sister and brother forgive him for his desertion?

His eyes followed the path that led to the lake, the water glittering in the moonlight. There, he had kissed Olivia Langley, the only girl to ever touch his heart, and he had walked away from her without a word too.

"It is hard to believe we are really here."

"You forgot to add finally, Luke."

"So I did."

It was time for William Ryder to go home, time to heal the wounds that had driven him away. Returning to the carriage, he once again pulled himself up onto the driver's seat. Taking the reins, he urged them down the driveway.

"It's bloody freezing."

"There is not even a flutter of snow, Luke. Don't let your siblings hear you speak of it being cold. They'll think I've turned you into a Molly."

"We need to acclimatize, so Freddy told me," Luke said, blowing on his hands.

"I hope your mother forgives me for allowing you to come to India with me."

"As I've told you many times, there are eight of us,

Will." Luke's words were mumbled from the depths of his scarf. "I should imagine she was dead chuffed when I left."

Luke Fletcher and Will had grown up together. His father worked in the Duke's stables and when he was old enough he had worked there too. He had seen Will storm from the house that day and when Will had told him he was not returning to Rossetter, Luke had asked to accompany him. There had never been a moment in the past five years that Will had regretted the decision to take him.

"I've never said this before, Luke, but I'm grateful to you for coming with me. It would have been harder had you not been there," Will said, pulling the carriage to a halt in the circular driveway. "To have my closest friend at hand, should I need him, was worth more than all the money we made."

"It was an honor, Will," Luke said gruffly, about as comfortable with sentiment as the next man.

Giving his friend a last look, Will then jumped down. Running a hand through his hair, he noticed his fingers were unsteady. Dragging in another deep lungful of cold air, he looked up the stone walls to the corner window on the third floor that had once been his bedroom. Was it still his, or had Joseph moved his belongings somewhere else?

"I'll take the horses to the stables and then head home."

"Good night then, Luke, and give my regards to your family. I shall call upon them soon."

"There is no need—"

"As I was the one to lure you away, there is every need. I have no wish to be at odds with your family, my friend."

"And yours will be happy to see you've returned, Will. I promise you that."

"Perhaps," Will said, feeling suddenly nervous.

He watched Luke until he was out of sight, taking those precious seconds to steady himself. Realizing the carriage would have been heard, he approached the front door. Lifting one hand, Will took hold of the iron knocker and banged it three times. Standing back, he waited. The sound of footsteps arrived several minutes later and light spilled through the door as it opened.

"May I help you?"

"It's only been five years, Alders. Surely I have not changed that much?" Will watched the faded hazel eyes before him widen and a huge smile crease the face of his family's oldest servant.

"Welcome home, my lord. Welcome home!"

Leaning forward, Will gripped Alder's shoulder and gave it a squeeze. The butler wrapped one gnarled hand around his forearm and returned the gesture with surprising strength.

"Do you never age, Alders?"

"I have not yet found the time, Lord Ryder," the butler said, stepping to one side to usher him in.

"Come, my lord. Your family have just finished their evening meal and are reading in the gold parlor. They will be pleased to see you."

"Lord, I hope so," he muttered, walking over the threshold. Stopping just inside, he looked around him. Growing up here, he realized now, he'd taken its beauty for granted.

To the left and right, three stone arches defined the long entranceway, and each was carved with intricate patterns of knights, lions, and stories of history that he had never taken time to study. Above hung tapestries and paintings in hundred-year-old gilt frames. Tilting his head, Will looked up to the cream ceilings from which hung a chandelier.

"I hope they don't still have you cleaning that, Alders?"

"I send the younger staff up there now, my lord."

Each floor had a gallery that looked down to the entrance where patterned carpets covered the huge floor area and drew the eye to the sweeping staircase at the end.

"Is everyone well, Alders?" Will said quietly.

"They are, my lord."

He felt some of the tension in his chest ease as he followed the butler down the carpet to the stairs. Walking up slowly, Will trailed his fingers over the polished banister he had slid down many times in his youth. Looking to the top, he studied the pictures of his parents, immortalized in canvas, smiling at each other as they had in life and down on all who entered their home.

"God, I still miss them, Alders."

"As do we all, my lord."

Their feet were muffled as they turned left at the top and continued along the hall to the gold parlor. Will feared his heart would give out, it beat so loudly. Alders didn't stop at the door, just opened it and walked inside, leaving him no choice but to follow.

"Lord Ryder has returned home, your grace," Alders said in somber tones.

Will stepped into the room and paused. Joseph, his brother, had turned to face the doorway. His features looked as if they had been chiselled from stone, cold and emotionless. Thea, his sister, was standing, one hand pressed to her lips the other braced on top of the piano before her. Joseph's wife, Penny, stood beside her with a tea cup in one hand. Will took this all in within seconds—the longest and slowest seconds of his life.

"Will?" Thea's voice was a hoarse whisper as she slowly began to move towards him. "Is it really you, Will?"

He couldn't speak; something had lodged in his throat as he watched his little sister. Tears rolled down her cheeks as she kept repeating his name and then with a sob, she launched herself at him. Will caught her and wrapped his arms awkwardly around her trembling body. She had grown so much in his absence. He breathed in her sweet scent and felt the burn of tears behind his own eyes as she sobbed. He hadn't been this close to another person in years, and had forgotten what it felt like to be held by someone who cared about him.

"Sssh, Thea. I'm home now."

Will felt her breath heave with a sigh, then she simply laid her head on his chest and wrapped her arms around his waist. She gave him the strength to lift his head and look at his brother.

Will now saw the gray hairs and lines on the face of Joseph Henry Edward Ryder, sixth Duke of Rossetter, that had not been there before he had left England, but he could discern nothing from his blank expression. Still standing where he had been when Will entered, the only thing indicating the Duke was less than his composed self was the clenching of his large hands into fists.

Their eyes met and held, neither moving, the only sound in the room the small hiccups coming from their sister.

"So, you have returned."

Will's arms tightened briefly around Thea then eased as his brother spoke, the deep controlled words sounding unerringly similar to the late Duke's.

"I have, your grace."

Will hadn't meant the words to be an insult; he had simply not known how to address his brother after so many years. They had never been close. The bonds other brothers shared had been lost under the responsibilities forced on his brother from a young age. Yet, he saw instantly that Joseph had thought the formal use of his title an insult, his body growing more rigid, eyes narrowing.

"One hopes the years have changed you for the better, William."

Will would not have stood passively while his brother made a statement like that before leaving England, but the years had changed him. He had learned that strength came from remaining in control at all times.

"I believe I have."

The brothers once again looked at each other, the gap between them only a few feet, yet to Will it was the width of the ocean he had just crossed.

"And are you to stay with us or is this a fleeting, yet long overdue, visit?" Anger sharpened the Duke's words.

"For a while, if that is acceptable?"

"Of course it's acceptable, Will," the Duchess said, pausing to glare at her husband before stepping between the brothers. "You have a nephew to become acquainted with."

"A nephew," Will said, shocked as he looked into the pretty face of his brother's wife.

"He is two, Will," Thea said with a last sniff as she eased out of his arms.

"And thoroughly spoiled by everyone here," the Duchess added, moving forward to kiss his check and give him a surprisingly sturdy hug.

Petite with red hair, the Duchess might appear angelic, yet she had a backbone of pure iron when required. She loved her husband and family passionately and Will was relieved to see no censure in her eyes when she looked at him.

"His name is William, but everyone calls him Billy," she added.

"William? Did you doubt I would return?" he questioned her, yet it was directed at his brother.

"It is a dangerous world out there, Will, and we had no idea in what part you resided or if, indeed, you lived or died. Joe and I wanted our son to carry your name in case you did not return."

"I'm sorry," Will said. "It was never my intention to hurt you, any of you."

"And yet you walked away from here without word, William, and stayed away for years, never once sending so much as a note to let us know your situation."

The words were spoken quietly yet Will heard the anger in them. His brother had no intention of forgiving him any time soon for his departure.

"I have no defense against your words, Joseph, everything you say is true."

Surprise flashed across the Duke's face briefly, he had expected Will to argue with him.

Penny squeezed Will's hand before going to her husband and slipping her arm around his waist. Joseph unbent enough to do the same, pulling his wife closer.

"It is late now, and Thea needs her bed. Therefore the reunion will wait until the morning, William," Joseph said.

"Oh, but—"

"Go to bed, Thea. We will talk tomorrow." Will kissed the top of his sister's head and then urged her from the room.

"Alders will have your room ready by now. Therefore, I bid you good night, William."

He watched the Duke and Duchess leave the room, the latter throwing him a final wave before passing through the door ahead of her husband.

"Goodnight, Joe."

Will knew his brother heard him, as his footsteps faltered briefly, but he did not stop.

CHAPTER TWO

Olivia Langley gritted her teeth as Jenny, the family's housekeeper, poured something that burned like fire over her shoulder.

Dear God, she'd robbed William Ryder!

Lying face down on her bed, Livvy gripped the blanket with both hands. Desperation had forced the Langley sisters out into the cold tonight in the hopes that they could steal enough money to survive, and of all the people who could have stepped down from that carriage it had been Lord William Ryder, the man she had once loved.

"I should have put a stop to this foolishness before it began!" Jenny said.

Livvy heard her sister, Phoebe, soothing the housekeeper as thoughts tumbled around inside her head. She felt numb; even the chill from hours spent outside could not penetrate it. They had stolen money from an innocent man and no matter how dire their circumstances, Livvy didn't think she would ever forgive herself.

"It had to be done," Phoebe said, reading her thoughts.

"I know we had no other choice, Phoebe, yet I still struggle with the guilt."

"And the shock of who we robbed, sister. I know seeing

Lord Ryder after so long has upset you."

It had upset her because Livvy always believed that when she saw him again she would be prepared, Yet, how could you prepare yourself to see the man you loved while pointing a gun at his head?

"Tis wrong for gently-bred young ladies to go about dressed as hoydens brandishing pistols!"

"We've talked this over, Jenny." Livvy sighed, suddenly feeling older than her twenty-two years. "Phoebe and I believe this was the only course of action open to us. After our cousin sent that letter stating he would no longer support us financially, everything changed."

The sisters had sold anything of value in the house over the past few months, even their father's precious hunting pictures, but the money had soon gone.

"The tonic Bella needs to ease her pain is expensive, and now that you've told us her leg is worse, we must find the money to get her to Scotland for treatment. This is the only way we know how." Seeking a diversion, Livvy found the miniature of her mother that sat on the small table beside her bed. The mirror image of Phoebe with her blond locks and pretty face, she could have done with her soothing presence now.

"Thieving from people is the only course of action open to you?" Jenny demanded. "Have you written to your cousin again? The new Viscount Langley, explaining how dire your circumstances are now that he has withdrawn his assistance? Surely, he has obligations to you all."

"I have written to him many times telling him of our struggle, yet he has not replied. We are out of options, Jenny. You must see that." Frustration and fear made Livvy's voice sharp.

"Jenny is only trying to protect us, Livvy. After all, this step we took was a dangerous one and goes against everything we've been raised to believe in."

Livvy closed her eyes as Phoebe spoke from behind her. "You think I don't know that? That I haven't spent days thinking about how our parents would feel if they knew? Believe me, it is only desperation forcing us along this path. I will not see Bella suffer because she does not have the proper care. And I will not have our name blackened, and therefore both yours and Bella's chances of happiness hindered, because our cousin will not fulfill his obligations and support his family."

"And your happiness, Livvy?" Phoebe added.

"We cannot even afford the most basic necessities at the moment and even if I could find work, it would only produce enough money to stave off disaster. Nothing further." As the eldest in her family it was Livvy's responsibility to secure her sisters' future happiness, not her own. She had long since cast aside her dreams of handsome men and happy ever afters in favor of reality. "I have not been back to the village since Mr. Bailey inquired when he could expect payment for the outstanding meat bills."

"Yes, that was a horrid moment," Phoebe agreed. "Until then, we had no idea that our cousin had stopped paying them."

"A Langley has always lived in the village of Twoaks and we will not be the first forced from it. Our parents were well respected and I will do nothing to change that."

"And yet if we had been caught tonight, our name would be sullied beyond redemption," Phoebe added. "And if we continue with this, we could be imprisoned."

"This was your idea, Phoebe. I just worked out the finer details," Livvy reminded her sister.

"I merely said 'Why don't we steal the money we need to pay our debts'. How was I to know you would actually take my suggestion literally? Although, in all honesty, it's a good plan because who would believe genteel Lord Langley's daughters capable of such a deed?"

"Had Lord Langley cared more for his genteel daughters, he would have ensured they were provided for before his death," Livvy snapped.

"He was a good father who loved us all very much, but he was not in his right mind towards the end," Phoebe said softly. "Grief over mother's death and the pain of his injury changed him; furthermore, he did not know he was going to die."

Yes, he did, Livvy thought, but kept it to herself. How their father died was a secret she would never share with her sisters.

"I fear that you will be shot by someone."

"We will do this only a few times, Jenny," Livvy soothed the housekeeper, hearing the fear in her voice. "Just until we have enough money for Bella's treatments and some of the household bills. I have no wish to become infamous for the wrong reasons." Livvy heard the door open and close behind her as she finished speaking and knew it was her youngest sister.

"Does it hurt terribly, Livvy?"

"You should be in your bed, Bella. This does not need to concern you." Livvy wanted to shield her little sister from tonight's events. Wriggling, she tried to look over her shoulder, but could only see the faded blue curtains that were closed against the cold night air.

"Stop moving, Miss Olivia!" Jenny scolded.

Submitting, she rested her cheek on the backs of her hands and concentrated on taking slow, deep breaths.

"Don't try to protect me, Livvy. I am part of this family. Therefore, I insist on knowing what is taking place within it," Bella said.

"You are in pain," Livvy whispered. "And I do not want you upset further."

Bella's sigh was loud enough for everyone to hear.

"As I told Jenny, I have been in pain lately with the cold

weather, but my tonic helps. I am not about to die, Livvy."

"Well, I am pleased about that, little sister; however, we did just rob a carriage at gunpoint on the strength of your illness. A whimper or two will ease my conscience," Phoebe said which made Bella giggle, as she had intended.

Livvy knew Bella was lying. Jenny would not have told them her leg was worse had it not been the truth, but she said nothing further.

"I have no wish for you both to do this just for me," Bella said as she softly rubbed Livvy's foot in comfort.

"It was not just for you, Bella. We need the money if we are to survive."

"Yes, Livvy, I understand that. However, it is also because your pride will not allow anyone to see our circumstances. Could we not simply ask for help?"

"An excellent question, little sister," Phoebe said.

"I have asked for help from the only person capable, our cousin, and he will not give it. Therefore, we are forced to steal," Livvy said, her words muffled in the pillow she had buried her face in. "And I will speak no more on the matter."

Livvy knew by the silence behind her that her sisters and Jenny were giving each other pointed looks; thankfully, however, they chose not to continue the discussion.

"Does it hurt?" Bella asked again.

"No," Livvy lied. Closing her eyes, she tried to push the pain aside, but instantly her head was filled with visions of him, William, Lord bloody Ryder. Why did he have to return now of all times, when the pain of his leaving had finally begun to ease to a dull ache?

"Isabella is sixteen, not stupid," Phoebe said. By the clink of coins, Livvy guessed she was now counting the money they had stolen from Lord Ryder.

"A little sympathy if you don't mind, Phoebe. I am in some

degree of discomfort, you know."

"Don't be such a baby. It's only a small wound."

Livvy felt the bed dip as Phoebe delivered these heartless words, and then her face appeared before her as she crouched beside the bed.

She was the beauty in the Langley family. Delicately arched brows rose as deceptively soft, sleepy, brown eyes studied Livvy. Long, dark lashes brushed her cheeks as she blinked. If only all those men who worshipped at her feet, spouting badly-written poetry knew what she was really like, Livvy thought, eyeing the innocent look in her sister's eyes with trepidation.

"If you're too pathetic to get out of bed, then I get to eat your supper."

"Witch!" Livvy spat as Jenny set in the first stitch.

"Oh, come now, sister, surely you can do better than that?" Phoebe scoffed, her perfect lips forming a pretty pout.

"Were there any justice in this world," Livvy hissed, "your face would mirror your shrewish temperament!"

"And yet here I crouch, still the muse to many a man." Phoebe looked anything but contrite as she flicked a golden brown curl over one shoulder. "I would also like to point out at this stage, sister, that we have stolen a nice amount of money tonight, which will see us in food for quite some time and get us halfway to Scotland.

"Really?" Livvy said.

"Really, and there is enough to pay some of our bills. It seems Lord Ryder carries a great deal of money on his person when he travels."

"Lord Ryder? Was it he you robbed?" Bella gasped. "Dear Lord, he must have been returning home from his travels."

Livvy groaned and buried her face in the pillow once more. They had robbed him and he had only just arrived in England. What must he be thinking? Not that she cared, the cad. He deserved some suffering for the pain he had inflicted upon her.

"Yes, it is not an auspicious homecoming, I'll give you that," Phoebe said. "Still, I'm sure a few coins will not see him in the poorhouse."

"Ouch, Jenny! Must you torture me so?" Livvy cried as the housekeeper stabbed the needle, with some force, through her skin.

"If you kept still it would hurt less," Jenny said, sounding unsympathetic.

"Was Luke with him?" Bella asked softly.

"I think so, but it was hard to see in the dark. However, if it was him driving, then it was probably he that threw the knife," Phoebe added.

"How did you feel upon seeing him, Livvy?" Bella appeared beside Phoebe so their eyes were level.

Livvy could see the pain Jenny spoke of now. The pallor of Bella's hollowed cheeks and the dark smudges beneath her green eyes told their story. The weight of responsibility suddenly felt heavier as Livvy chastised herself for not seeing what was before her.

Bella had grown up over the last year and lost the last traces of youth. She was maturing into a young woman and should have the love and support of her mother and father, not her elder sisters, as she navigated the treacherous journey into womanhood. Livvy would do everything in her power to make her well again; even if she had to rob every bloody night to ensure it happened.

Phoebe met Livvy's eyes and knew they shared the same thoughts. The elder Langley sisters were feeling guilty for what they had not seen.

"Who, Luke?"

"No, Lord Ryder, silly."

"It was a shock seeing him of course, Bella, but no more so

than had it been anyone I had not seen for a number of years," Livvy said.

"But you did not love just anyone, Livvy, you loved him," Phoebe said.

"I did not love him!" Livvy swiftly denied the claim.

"Oh, please, both Bella and I heard you wailing into your pillow for weeks after he left without a word."

"I did not!"

"Of course you did. We used to watch Mama and Papa decide which one of them would comfort you that night. When it was decided, Jenny made the tray and filled it with tea and cakes and then whoever was designated would go into your room and sit with you. Bella and I were quite envious."

Livvy remembered those nights. She had cried long and loudly into the comfort of her parents' arms. She had not realized that her little sisters were listening, however.

"Could you not have just left me with my pride? I believed neither you nor Bella knew."

Phoebe laughed. "Livvy, you used dance around the house, sighing and giggling and hugging yourself after you had spent time with Lord Ryder. It was fairly obvious."

"Yes, and when you and he were together it was as if everyone else ceased to exist." Bella sighed. "I had always believed he felt as you did, Livvy."

"Apparently not, as he left without a word." Livvy tried to keep the bitterness out of her voice.

"I'm sure he had his reasons, sister. Lord Ryder may have been a spoiled, indolent nobleman, yet he was always a gentleman with you," Phoebe stated.

"Well, it matters not, as all that is behind me now," Livvy said briskly. "We are both different people since last we met."

"He looked more handsome, though, don't you think?" Phoebe added and Livvy wanted to stuff something into her sister's mouth to get her to stop talking. "Bigger and more distinguished," she said, using the bedcovers to mop up the tears that Livvy hadn't realized she was crying. "In fact, it appears the black sheep of the Duke's family has returned, and looking nothing like the spoiled nobleman who left so suddenly five years ago."

"He wasn't spoiled," Livvy protested. "He was just misguided and misunderstood."

"He was a spoiled brat, who got into many disreputable scrapes that caused his family no end of angst, Olivia. You just couldn't see his faults through your love-dazed eyes," Phoebe added.

She had been blinded by love, Livvy conceded, yet that would no longer be the case. After kissing her, he had walked away and she would never forgive him for ripping her heart from her chest and stomping on it. When he had stepped from that carriage at her urging tonight, Livvy had nearly fallen from her horse. She had recognized him, of course; after all, he was the first, and possibly last, man she would ever love.

"Do you remember that day when Lord Ryder told Livvy she was uglier than old Mr. Boswell's one-eared, toothless dog?" Bella laughed, which made her look like the carefree young girl she had once been.

"Yes," Phoebe giggled. "She had walked straight up to him and jumped into the air and punched him on the nose, and from that day forth they had been inseparable. He resembles his brother the Duke more now," Phoebe added. "Especially that fierce scowl."

"We shall have to be careful to keep Livvy away from him until she is healed," Bella said. "As they were very close before he left."

Yes, they had once been very close; so close that Livvy had believed he would one day be the father of her children.

"He will not connect a highwayman with the Luscious Langley Ladies."

"Don't use that name, Phoebe. It makes us sound like women of loose morals," Livvy scolded.

Even her laughter was appealing, Livvy thought sourly as Phoebe giggled.

"Oh, to be sure we are not woman of loose morals, sister, merely dashing highwaywomen who will fleece the rich to give to the poor… namely us."

"Is it just me?" Livvy said, looking at Bella. "Or is she getting more annoying with age?"

"I like being a Luscious Langley." Phoebe pouted. "It suggests we're not boring like most of the other women of our acquaintance."

Ignoring her sister, Livvy patted Bella's hand. "I'm sure we shall see nothing of Lord Langley, Bella, don't fret." She sincerely hoped that was the case because, for some reason, from the day she had been old enough to take note of Lord William Ryder, he had drawn her like a moth to a flame, and although she believed her heart now healed, the flutter in her chest when she had seen him had unsettled her. It had been shock, of course, Livvy reminded herself. She would never allow herself to love him again.

"Almost done now, Miss Olivia," Jenny said, pulling Livvy from her thoughts. She would have to make sure to keep away from Lord Ryder in the future, and not because, like Bella had said, he would connect her to the highwayman. She would keep her distance because his sudden departure from her life had nearly destroyed her, and she never, ever, wanted to feel that kind of pain again.

CHAPTER THREE

"I hope I am not imposing on you," Mrs. Popplehinge said, settling herself in a chair in the Langley front parlor, which was the only room in the house Livvy took great pains to keep tidy. It had the best drapes and pieces of furniture collected from the other rooms so that no one would suspect the household was, in fact, struggling for money. Windows ran along the entire wall and let in plenty of light, even on a gray winters day like today. A fire blazed in the hearth and Jenny kept the flowers fresh and the rugs swept, and even to Livvy's critical eye it was a lovely room.

"Not at all, Mrs. Popplehinge," Livvy said, placing one hand over the small rip she had just noticed in the skirt of her dress.

Dabbing her lips with a handkerchief that wafted a sickly scent around the room, Mrs. Popplehinge turned to glare at Phoebe as she and Bella entered.

"You know I would not ask if I were not in desperate need."

Livvy gave Phoebe a look that said silently, *Behave,* as Phoebe sat next to Mrs. Popplehinge and then made a great show of yawning loudly.

"How can we help you, Mrs. Popplehinge?"

The woman was head of every committee in the area and her long-suffering husband was, by silent vote, the mayor of

Twoaks. Mrs. Popplehinge had called unexpectedly and thrown the Langley sisters into a spin as they had been clad in their oldest dresses and outside feeding the animals.

"Let's just present ourselves like this," Phoebe had said, to which Livvy ordered, 'Get up those stairs and tidy your appearance at once.' Phoebe had poked out her tongue and dragged a giggling Bella behind her. Livvy had then hurriedly scrubbed her face and hands in the kitchen and asked Jenny to re-tie her hair before she brushed out her skirts and ran to the front door to let Mrs. Popplehinge in.

"Thank you, Jenny," Livvy said as the housekeeper came in with a tea tray.

"I need someone to do the flowers and look after the church while I am in London, Miss Olivia, and as there are three of you here with little to do, I had hoped you could take on the task."

Mrs. Popplehinge was a tall, stick-thin woman who spent the majority of her days delving into people's lives. Her bright red hair was pulled into a severe bun that was so tight, her eyes tilted up at the corners. She dressed in dark colors and always carried herself very upright, mouth pursed in disapproval.

"Of course, I know I can rely on you and Miss Isabella, too," Mrs. Popplehinge said, glaring at Phoebe who fluffed her curls and smiled insolently back.

The mayor's wife had hated Phoebe since she had turned down her son's marriage proposal. Bernhard Popplehinge had made a fool of himself for months, calling on Phoebe and sending her gifts. In fairness, she had been gentle with him at the start, thanking him but offering him no further encouragement; but he had been persistent and finally he had asked her to marry him. Horrified that she would dare to refuse him (his mother, rightly or wrongly, had instilled in him a great deal of self-worth), he had demanded to know her reasons for the refusal. That was when everything turned nasty, as Phoebe was never one to hold back when provoked. She had used words like ferret-faced and weakness of mind until Bernhard had stormed from the house. He had then fled to London and married another woman within weeks.

"I had a letter from dear Bernhard. He and his sweet-tempered wife are expecting their first child in a few weeks, and that is why I must travel to London to be at her side at this trying time."

"Has she no mother of her own?"

Livvy narrowed her eyes as Phoebe spoke, but of course she just smiled sweetly and batted her eyelashes, looking angelic. Appearances, Livvy thought, were deceiving.

"Of course, darling Margaret has a mother, you foolish girl!" Mrs. Popplehinge stormed, flushing red, which clashed terribly with her hair.

"I wonder why she will not be at her side, then," Phoebe mused, her face a picture of innocence.

"I am going to support my Bernhard!"

"What a wonderful mother you are, Mrs. Popplehinge."

"Yes, well," Mrs. Popplehinge said, not realizing that Phoebe was mocking her. Eugenie Popplehinge was a literal creature. "Children who are without parental guidance tend to lack the respect necessary to participate in society, and often find themselves cast out due to misguided behaviour."

Seeing the storm clouds brewing in her sister's eyes at this pointed reference to herself, Livvy quickly said, "Indeed. Well, you can rely on us to look after the church in your absence, Mrs. Popplehinge. We shall look forward to the task."

"Of course," Bella added.

"Excellent. Since the Reverend's wife passed, the burden of the church's interior has, I fear, fallen heavily upon me. Therefore, I shall enjoy the rest from this chore."

Livvy and Bella mumbled the appropriate response. Phoebe

remained silent and stone-faced.

"Before I leave, I must tell you the marvelous news," Mrs. Popplehinge said, getting to her feet. "Mrs. Fletcher told Miss Lindsey this morning that her son, Luke, has returned with Lord Ryder."

"Oh we knew that."

Mrs. Popplehinge looked crestfallen as Phoebe cut her off.

"But thank you, anyway," Livvy added, ushering the woman out of the parlor. Walking back minutes later, she was relieved to hear the wheels of Mrs. Popplehinge's carriage rolling out of the driveway.

"Children lacking parental guidance," Phoebe mimicked, and then she and Bella collapsed in a fit of giggles onto the sofa.

"That woman is dangerous, Phoebe, and taunting her only makes her more so." Livvy picked up her tea and took a mouthful as she walked to the windows. She wanted to be sure that Mrs. Popplehinge did not return unexpectedly.

"She's a meddling busybody who loathes us as much as we loathe her," Phoebe stated.

Relieved the driveway was now clear, Livvy returned to the table to pick up the tray, wincing as her shoulder pulled. The bite of pain made her angry. Why was she the only one who understood how precarious their situation was? Slapping the tray back down she watched their best tea things bang together and was relieved when nothing broke.

"Do either of you understand how perilous our position is at the moment? If word gets out that we cannot meet our bills, or that our father left us penniless, then we will be received by no one. We will be pitied and shunned and left to bloody well starve. Every door to every social occasion will shut with a resounding bang, and you two will have to live with me for the rest of your lives because no man will want a penniless wife, even if she is pretty!"

"I don't know which I shudder at most," Phoebe mocked. "The door slamming or being forced to live with you."

Normally, she would have laughed as Bella was doing, because that was Phoebe's way. She poked fun at everything, especially anything serious. But today she couldn't. Today, Livvy was feeling raw and exposed after seeing Will again. Her shoulder ached and she was fearful of their future and, more importantly, she was fearful that she did not have the strength or courage to see this charade through to its conclusion. Bella was sick, they were penniless, and she was terrified that she would crumble under the weight of responsibility and guilt of what she was forced to do.

"You won't be so cavalier, sister, when you no longer have your looks to rely on, and you can be sure your beaus will not follow behind you like lovesick swains when you have nothing else to recommend you!"

"One day, I will find a rich husband and save us all, so you can stop venting your spleen, Olivia. I know where my duty lies," Phoebe said calmly.

Before her parents' deaths, Livvy had also been known for her volatility. She would pout and cry when thwarted or angered and say the first thing that popped into her head. Now, she no longer had the luxury of such behaviour. As head of the family, she had to remain in control at all times; however, some moments were harder than others.

"Do you believe that I want that for you, Phoebe? To see you in a loveless marriage just so our futures are secure?"

"You expect me to believe the thought has not crossed your mind, Olivia, when it would be the answer to all our prayers?"

Had Phoebe slapped her, the impact would have been less devastating.

"Dear God, how can you believe that of me? I want to make sure both you and Bella have your pick of men and can find the one you love. I want happiness for you both, joy and laughter. It would be torture to see you sold to the highest bidder."

"Livvy, there is no need for this, I assure you. I have no wish for a love match; therefore, I shall marry the richest man who asks me and we shall be saved."

Phoebe's laugh was hollow and her eyes glittered with anger. Livvy knew she was being cruel deliberately. Lashing out because she, too, was feeling the strain of the life they were now forced to live. Yet even though Livvy knew the reasons why, it hurt no less. Looking down at the patterned rug beneath her feet, she willed herself not to cry.

"I'm sorry if the person I have become led you to believe that I want such a match for you. But everything I have done, and am doing, is for you both. Please never doubt that."

"Livvy, wait!"

She didn't. Ignoring Bella's words, she turned from her sisters and left the room. Hurrying through the house, she made her way along the hall past the dark squares on the wall where her father's cherished hunting pictures had once hung, and down the stairs and into the kitchens. Jenny hummed softly as she walked through, but Livvy didn't stop. Lifting her old cloak off the peg, she toed off her slippers, put on her boots and hurried out the back door. Using her good arm, she swung the cloak around her shoulders as she walked.

It was cold, but she enjoyed the chill against her cheeks as she headed down the garden and opened the gate that would take her to the cemetery. Looking back as she closed it, she noted two faces pressed to the glass in the parlor. Turning away, she lowered her head and started walking.

She wasn't sure what hurt the most, that her sisters believed her capable of such insensitivity or that perhaps the person she had become could be that insensitive. Shooting a last look at her home, she noted the windows were now empty.

Willow Hall had been a real home for the first seventeen years of her life. It was big and rambling with many rooms, most of which now stood empty. It had been filled with love and laughter for years, but all that had changed with the death of her mother.

Viscount Langley had accompanied his wife and youngest daughter to visit a neighbor, and on the return journey the horses had spooked and bolted, causing the carriage to collide with a tree. Their mother was killed instantly but Bella had her leg trapped and their father, his arm. The doctors had amputated it that day, and after that he had suffered with terrible pain and simply lost the will to live, and not long after he had passed away. Livvy had gone to take her father his lunch and found him dead, slumped backwards in his chair, his eyes staring sightlessly at her as she had run to his side.

"And I understand how you suffered and that you took your life to be freed from the pain of your body and heart, Papa. Yet you left us alone without a penny," Livvy whispered, still feeling the ache deep inside her from his death.

Their family had revolved around the strong and loving Lord Langley. The man who had adored his wife to distraction, and his daughters equally, had strode around the house and lands with a daughter usually hanging off one arm as he talked endlessly of his love for this place he called home. To watch him wither and die had destroyed Livvy and her sisters, and no matter how hard they fought to retain the good memories, they were left with the ones created in the last days of his life. The dull, pain-filled eyes and gaunt, hollow cheeks of a man who no longer wished to live.

Livvy tried not to wonder what her parents would think about the decisions she had made for her sisters as she walked along the worn path through the woods. How they had taught her to always be honest and fair in dealings with people. But what other choice was there? Her father's will had left no provisions for them; everything had gone to their cousin. Livvy had believed that this meant the new Viscount Langley would pay their bills; therefore, they had continued to order from the village. It had been mortifying to realize that this was not the case. They owed several proprietors money and were just lucky that, due to the history they had in Twoaks, they were not being hounded for it. At least they still had a home; for some reason, the new Viscount Langley had allowed them to remain at Willow Hall.

Leaving the woods, she started up the hill and was breathless by the time she arrived at the little cemetery perched high above the village. Her shoulder was throbbing and her gloveless fingers were chilled as she opened the gate and then made her way along the rows until she found the two headstones that sat side-by-side. Bella had been here, Livvy realized as she saw the fresh flowers. Her little sister liked to place them here every few days. The effort of walking up the hill must cause her pain, yet she did it because their mother had loved flowers so much.

"It's all such a mess," Livvy whispered, walking to the graves of her father and mother and then dropping to her knees between them. Placing a hand on each, she lowered her head. She felt close to them here, close to the people she remembered and loved.

"I'm stealing from people because we are in desperate need of money, and my pride will not let anyone know that we are poor. I cannot, even if Phoebe and Bella don't understand why I am doing this. I will not have shame brought down on this family or on the names of you both. I will not taint our name and thus ruin their chances of a future," Livvy vowed. "Perhaps the task is too great and we will fail, and perhaps no one but me understands why I'm taking these risks, yet I have to at least try." Feeling the hot sting of tears behind her eyes, Livvy slumped onto her father's grave and wept.

***

Will threw a stick for Gilbert and watched as he took off after it. At least his Labrador, like his sister and Penny, had forgiven him for leaving.

He had woken in his bed this morning and found himself smiling; even the prospect of facing his brother could not dampen his pleasure at being home. Before leaving, he had felt only unrest at Rossetter, yet now it represented the roots he had missed so much in his travels. He knew the changes in him would mean he could not stay here for long. He and his brother could never live under the same roof again, but he would not think of that today. Tomorrow would be soon enough.

An early riser, Will had washed and found the breakfast parlor only to find his brother there before him. Stunned to hear singing, he had entered to find a small, pink-cheeked, fair-haired boy being jostled on the Duke's lap. The boy was giggling and tugging handfuls of his father's hair as Joseph sang. His brother's face was softened in a smile as he looked down at his son.

Will had cleared his throat and the smile had fallen, to be replaced by the cold look of the previous evening.

"I trust you slept well?"

"Very well, thank you."

"This is your nephew, Billy," Joseph then said.

Will had never been overly fond of children, possibly because he had never met any; However, Billy was his blood, and having lived without family he knew how important it was for his nephew to know he was there for him if one day he should need him.

Moving closer, he had crouched and held out his hand. The boy had taken one finger and squeezed it hard, offering him a wide smile that showed off two small, white teeth. Rising, he had kissed a soft cheek and then seated himself at the table. The brothers had not spoken again; however, Billy's noise had been enough to make the meal bearable.

Pulling his overcoat tighter, Will skirted an icy puddle and wished he'd taken Penny up on the offer of a pair of Joseph's gloves. Living in a cold climate once again was going to take some getting used to. Walking up the path cut in the side of the hill, Will made his way to the cemetery that overlooked the village of Twoaks. His parents were buried here and he had visited them rarely before he left; however, upon waking this morning he'd known he needed to come.

Passing through the small gate, Will entered the cemetery and looked around him. Nothing appeared to have changed overly much; the older graves were at the rear and in need of a good weeding, while the newer were closer to the front.

"I wish you were here, Mama."

Looking over the headstones to where that voice had come from, he saw a lady sitting beside a grave. Her head was uncovered and lowered. Red-gold hair hung in a long, thick, plaited rope down her spine. Will felt his heart skip a beat as he stared at the back of Olivia Langley's head. She was the only woman he knew that had hair the color of sunset. Her mother must have passed away sometime in the last five years. Will felt a twinge of sadness for the vivacious lady who had always had a smile for him whenever they met.

"I promised you I would look after them. Do you remember, Papa? When you died, I came up here and said I would do whatever it takes to give them a safe and happy future."

He should not intrude on her grief; he should go, turn around and walk away before she saw him, but he couldn't get his legs to move.

"But I didn't think it was going to be so hard."

Christ, she was crying, soft sobs that tore at his insides

because they were the sound of someone whose heart was broken. His feet carried him forward and soon he stood behind her.

She was on her knees. One of her bare hands clutched a headstone and her head was bowed in defeat. Will read the two stones and realized that both Lord and Lady Langley had died since his departure.

Will had thought about Olivia a lot since he had left, about the days they had spent walking over the hills of Twoaks talking of everything and anything. With her, he had always managed to drop the façade he had erected to shut everyone out. With her, he had been a man who had nothing to prove, a man happy with the company he was keeping. Looking at her ring-less fingers, he had the answer to one of the questions that had plagued him, and knew he had no right to feel pleased about her unmarried state.

"Olivia, don't be alarmed. It is I, William Ryder."

His words had been spoken softly, yet Will watched her fingers briefly clench around the headstone, the knuckles turning white before releasing it.

"Please accept my sincere condolences for the loss of your parents. They were lovely people."

Still she didn't look at him, but sat back on her heels, her hands now in her lap, head lowered.

"I lost my parents, as you know, many years ago, yet still I miss them. It is almost as if the world is in some way depleted with their passing. Of course, I had you to thank for helping me through their deaths, Olivia. You walked endless miles over these hills listening to me talk as I tried to come to terms with the grief."

She was listening to him. He could tell because her cries had stopped. There was just the occasional hitch in her breathing.

"To say it eases would lessen what they meant to us, Olivia, yet given time we learn to live with their death."

She seemed so small, huddled in front of him, worn black cloak hanging behind her. Eyeing the patches around the hem, he wondered just how hard Olivia Langley was finding things. The sad little figure before him was a complete contrast to the delectable young lady who had once brought him to his knees with just a look.

"Come, take my hand, Olivia, and we shall sit on the seat above the cemetery and look down at the village of Two Oakes while we become reacquainted."

He heard her sniff.

"I-it seems you have been gone too long, my lord, if you now pronounce the village's name like an outsider." Her voice was thick with tears.

"I had just come to that realization, Olivia, hence my return home. Now come, you need to get up off this cold ground," Will added, putting his hand under her elbow. She gave a sharp hiss of breath.

"Are you hurt, Olivia?"

"No, my lord, you just startled me."

Placing his hands on her waist, Will simply lifted her to her feet when she made no move to stand. She was light as a feather and he could tell she had lost some of the soft curves that had once tormented him, and he wondered again how hard Olivia Langley was finding life.

"Thank you," she said, turning to face him and then dropping into a curtsey.

Five years ago, Olivia had been seventeen and a young lady who was beginning to understand the hold she had over men, most especially him. She had made him feel like one minute he was standing on his head and the other on his feet. But more importantly, she had become the one person in his life who had understood to him.

"Hello," Will said, looking into her sad, red-rimmed eyes. She was still beautiful; in fact to Will she seemed more so. She had lost the roundness in her face and every bone was now defined, from the line of her cheeks to the curve of her jaw. Her face was pale and dark smudges under her cinnamon eyes told him she was not sleeping well. She appeared fragile and vulnerable, both words he would previously never have used when describing the luscious Livvy Langley

"Good day, Lord Ryder." She looked at him, her eyes expressionless. "How long have you been back from your travels?" Her voice was distant, as if they were strangers.

"I arrived home last night."

"Your family must be pleased to see you."

"Some of my family are pleased, Olivia."

"Surely your brother's reaction does not surprise you, my lord. You walked away without a word."

Will smiled but she did not respond. "How did you know it was Joseph?"

"Thea talked of you constantly and always with longing, Lord Ryder, I doubt she would have been anything but happy to see you."

The wind caught at her hair, pulling a lock free, and she brushed it aside impatiently.

"And you, Olivia? I walked away from you without a word. Do you forgive me?"

"It matters not how I feel, my lord," she said, dropping her eyes, which told him it did matter a great deal.

"Yes, it does."

She didn't know what to say to that so she fell silent, another surprise. The Olivia he had known had no idea how to be quiet.

"I know my apology is late in coming, Olivia, yet I will tender it all the same."

She glared at him then. "I have no wish to hear your

apologies, Lord Ryder. They are of no consequence to me."

Realizing that now was not the time to pursue this topic any further, he instead took her arm. "Will you walk with me to my parents' graves and then sit with me on the seat overlooking the village? I need to catch up on the gossip and the Langleys, if my memory serves me well, always knew what was going on in Twoaks." She didn't respond instantly, although her fingers curled into fists at her side. Will knew she was going to refuse him, so he steered her along the row of headstones and down the next before she had a chance.

"Release me please, my lord. I need to return to my home."

Ignoring her, Will continued on to where his parents were buried in a special, raised area to the rear of the cemetery beside their ancestors. He walked to the headstones with Olivia and stood silently, reading the words.

"I miss them still, even more so now I have returned," he said quietly.

"I always make sure to visit them when I come here."

"Do you?" he queried, wondering why.

She shot him a defensive look.

"I'm sorry if you do not feel I have any rights to visit with them, my lord, but I knew them well, especially after they rescued me when I was six years old and had gotten lost in the woods"

"I am not censuring you, Olivia." Will looked down at her; she was studying the headstones, thus avoiding his eyes. "Dare I ask what a six-year-old was doing alone the woods?"

"It matters not, my lord. I was merely explaining why I visited them."

She was bristling like a hedgehog. They had once been friends, very close friends, but now he realized she thought of him as anything but.

"Surely you cannot leave me hanging like that, Olivia. To

hear something new about a parent, who has been long passed, is a treasure no one could resist."

She chewed her lip for several seconds while waging some kind of war within herself and then finally, with a small huff of breath, she spoke.

"My father had told me that there was a family of tiny people living in the woods at the bottom of Willow Hall. They only came out when they were sure no one would see them because they were fearful that their secret would be discovered."

"You mean they had other secrets besides the fact that they only reached your knees and lived in the woods?" Will teased.

"Six-year-olds are literal creatures, my lord. My interest was purely in the secret, not the viability of the story. And, of course, I also once believed everything my father told me."

Will heard the pain in her words. She obviously still felt her father's loss keenly. Releasing her, he touched the headstones of his parents and whispered the words, "I'm home now, rest easy," before he once again took Olivia's arm and led her out of the cemetery.

"I should return to my sisters, my lord."

"Please finish your story, Olivia," he said as they climbed the rest of the path to the seat. Lowering her onto the wooden bench, he took the place beside her. She shuffled aside, putting several inches between them, and then perched on the edge. The old Livvy would have never moved away from him; in fact she would have settled her skirts, making sure to let her fingers brush his thigh.

"It does not look as if much has changed down there." Will looked at the village that lay below them. Small and bustling, it was a hive of activity as carts, carriages and people scurried about. From this distance they resembled a colony of ants.

"Change is inevitable, my lord," she said in a flat voice.

"Tell me the rest of the story, Olivia."

"I slipped out of the house when no one was looking and ran to the woods. I walked and walked, lifting leaves and branches, kicking aside dirt but I could not find the little people. When I grew tired, I looked around and realized I was hopelessly lost and could not find the path home."

Will remembered her as a six-year-old skipping down the aisle in church; she had been beautiful even then.

"I could always wail louder than anyone else," she added with a small tired sigh that tugged at his chest.

"Your parents were out riding and overheard me. Your father picked me up and asked why I was out there alone and I told him that I was trying to find the little people who make the best sweets out of lemon and honey."

Will laughed. "So that was the secret."

"Yes, and to their credit your father and mother never laughed at me. In fact, your father said that he was sorry to be the bearer of bad news but he had heard that the lemon and honey people had moved on to Inverness in Scotland."

Will couldn't remember the last time he had laughed like this. If only his servants could see him now; all of them believed him a serious, unsmiling man.

"Your father lifted me up into your mother's arms and then they took me home. They sang songs to me all the way and then stayed to take tea with my parents. I worshipped them from that day onwards. I was devastated when they passed."

His laughter slowed and this time it was he who sighed.

"They were the very best of parents, Olivia. Thank you for sharing your story with me," he said, looking at her. "However, I find it hard to believe I am only just hearing this story now, when we spent many hours together talking of anything and everything in the past."

"I have no further time to sit and converse with you, Lord Ryder." She quickly regained her feet thereby, in her mind, ending the conversation. "I must leave you now as my sisters will start to worry if I am overlong."

"You once called me Will, Olivia," he said, standing.

Ignoring his words she dropped into a quick curtsey and then winced upon rising.

"What is wrong with you? That is the second hiss of pain since I arrived."

"I am pleased that you are home safe, my lord," she said, again ignoring his question. "I am sure we will see nothing further of each other so I bid you good health and good day."

Frowning, Will watched her leave. Why would he not see her again? Was she not going to London for the season and would she not be attending any functions in the village or surrounding countryside over the Christmas period?

"I'll walk you home," he said, striding after her.

"There is no need, Lord Ryder; I am quite capable of making my way home and have been doing so for many years. Please stay and enjoy the view as I prefer my own company."

Well, she couldn't have made that any clearer, Will thought. She did not want to spend any time with him.

"You're hurting and upset. What sort of gentleman would allow a woman in that state to walk home alone? Not to mention that the lemon and honey people could attack at any moment."

She stopped at the gate and looked up at him. It wasn't a glare, as such, but pretty close to his mind. Excellent. She still had some fighting spirit. Keeping his expression pleasant, he reached around her and pushed the gate open and then motioned for her go through.

***

Livvy had realized one thing when she looked up into Will's eyes for the first time in five years; he was still the most handsome man she had ever met. Her heart thudded in her chest, her palms grew damp and her stomach was doing silly little flutters. He'd always had that effect on her, only now she resented him for it.

He still unsettled her and at that moment in time she wanted to slap him, hard. She hated that he had the freedom only a man could have and that he was supported by the comfort and wealth of his family, but more importantly, she was angry because once she had loved him and he had walked away from her without a backward glance. She could not lay the blame for what happened to her family at his door, yet when she had needed him most he had not been there for her and she would never forgive him for that, no matter how unreasonable she was being.

Looking away from the intensity of his gray gaze, Livvy realized that while he had been handsome before, in a boyish way, he was even more so now. His once long, black curls were cropped short, and although his face did not have the classic elegance of some, it was commanding, with high cheekbones and a long angular jaw that seemed more prominent than she remembered. His skin was tanned and he had lost the look of the idle, pampered nobleman. Even his body was now solid and muscled, his broad shoulders defined by the lines of the jacket. There was an aura of strength about him that had not been there before.

"You said we would not see each other again, Olivia, yet surely you will attend the Twoaks Derby and the social events over the next few weeks? And what of the London season? It is due to start in a few months. Are you not in attendance this year?"

His long strides easily kept up with her as she walked down the hill and into the woods below. *Be nice, Livvy. Speak calmly and this will be over shortly. You had to see him some time, now is as good as any.* Once this meeting is over then she need never see him again, or at the very least she could take steps to avoid him.

"Yes, of course," Livvy muttered, not wanting to discuss the fact she had never had a season in London.

"And are you backing Jaccob Bell in the Derby again this year, Olivia?" The breath left her body as he lifted her easily over a fallen stump and replaced her gently back on the ground on the other side.

"Please don't touch me." Lord, she was breathless from that brief contact. She needed to get away from this man. He was far too disturbing.

"Once, you liked me touching you."

"Once, I was foolish and gullible. I am far from that now!" Livvy snapped and instantly wished she hadn't, because she had no intention of alerting him to her feelings towards him. "I will, of course, back Jaccob, my lord; however, I also ride in the Derby now," she added, quickly changing the subject.

Livvy didn't instantly realize that he had stopped until she took a couple more steps and noted his disturbing presence was no longer at her side. Turning, she searched for him. Surrounded by tall trees and shadows, he looked like a god of the forest who could call together his minions and drag her into his dark world. Not that he would, she reminded herself, because he cared nothing for her.

"Is there a problem, my lord?"

"Surely it is too dangerous for a woman to ride in such a race?"

"Women have competed in the Derby before, and I am a good rider and have managed to ride the previous two years without incident. In fact, even with my limited intelligence, I manage to ride astride."

His smile started in his twinkling gray eyes and finished on his lips which he opened, revealing large white teeth. It made her stomach flutter again but she kept her expression passive.

He means nothing to you any longer.

"And there is the tempting, mouthy vixen I left behind," he said. "I was worried that she had vanished under the weight of responsibility you now shoulder, Olivia."

What did he know of her responsibilities?

"None of us can stay as we were, my lord, and it would be unrealistic and childish to suggest otherwise." Livvy tried to shuffle backwards as he moved closer. Damn, her words had sounded panicked and he knew it, the rogue. The smile still flirted around his mouth. "I would also ask that you not address me so familiarly and now call me Miss Langley, as we can no longer lay claim to being friends."

That stopped him; he stood just an arm's length from her, staring intently, his head tilted slightly to the side, as if trying to read her thoughts.

"We will always be friends, Olivia, and you will always be Livvy to me, even if I am no longer Will to you."

"Friends do not abandon friends," Olivia whispered, and then could have cut out her tongue. She hadn't spoken without thought in years, in fact since this man had left England, and now she had told him how much his departure had affected her. "Not that I cared. It was just impolite of you," she added, cringing inside at how silly her words sounded.

He closed the distance between them until his chest blocked her view of the forest.

"I'm sorry that I was not here for you when your parents passed away, Olivia, and I will say again that I'm sorry if my departure hurt you, but at the time I believed the only option open for me was to go. I was angry and confused, and did not think much about the impact my departure would have on those I left behind."

"You did not hurt me, my lord. I was seventeen and,

therefore, quite happy to move on to the next source of amusement."

Livvy stepped backwards but her escape was thwarted by two large hands cupping her elbows.

"Yet your demeanor would suggest you are angry with me; therefore, I must have hurt you in some way."

"I have no wish to discuss this any further."

He was silent for a while, and Livvy could feel his eyes on her face while hers looked over his shoulder.

"I missed you, you know. Missed the way your hand would fit inside mine as we walked through sun-warmed meadows on a clear day. We would seek out the largest tree and lie beneath it and you would sing to me."

Livvy closed her eyes as one hand cupped her cheek. She willed herself to stay rigid and shut out the memories his words were forming in her head.

"I used to hear the sound of your laughter some nights while I struggled with the need to come home. I could see your face and the way your eyes lit from within when you smiled at me."

She stiffened as his fingers trailed over her mouth.

"I have never seen a more beautiful smile to this day."

His voice had always mesmerized her, the smooth deep tones like heated honey, but she was no longer the naive girl he had left behind. The pain of his departure had taught her one thing— never trust him again.

"I have no wish to hear any more of your ramblings," Livvy said, struggling to get away from him; she winced as pain shot through her. "Therefore, I insist you release me.

"But this, Livvy," he said, his breath brushing her ear as he inhaled deeply. "I have never smelled your scent on another."

Dear God, she could smell him, too, and it made her knees tremble as the memories swamped her.

"I wonder if you still taste the same."

"The same as what?" Livvy whispered.

"That kiss we shared." He pulled her closer. "Your first kiss, if I remember correctly."

"H—how conceited of you to suggest it was my first kiss, my lord, or that I would remember it." Livvy placed a hand on his chest and tried to push him backwards. He, however, simply placed his larger one on top. Around them the woods suddenly seemed quiet, and she could hear the soft rasp of her breathing as he lowered his head.

"You remember," he whispered. "Just as I do." And then he was kissing her.

She had relived that kiss a thousand times, but memories, she realized, fell short from reality. His hand moved up to cup her chin; the other held her waist as he drank from her lips, a slow, sensual onslaught that made Livvy's body heat all over in seconds. Slumping forward, she landed on the hard wall of his chest as he pulled her closer.

"I have missed you, sweet Livvy Langley."

All rational thought fled with the first taste of his mouth and Livvy would have stayed here in his arms surrounded by nature had his fingers not brushed the knife wound on her shoulder and jolted some sense into her.

"Ouch!"

"Olivia, are you all right?"

She couldn't look at him. Sanity had returned with the searing pain and she was mortified that she had behaved in such a wanton manner, especially with him, of all men.

"Olivia?"

"No!" she said sharply as he reached for her again. "Just stay away from me in the future, Lord Ryder. There will be no more sun-warmed meadows. Those days are gone forever, and I would thank you to remember that." Picking up her skirts, she turned and ran from him as fast as her shoulder would let her.

Reaching the gate at the bottom of her garden, she hurried through. Turning, she saw him behind her. He lifted a hand in farewell, which she ignored; walking up to the house, she did not look back even though she wanted to.

CHAPTER FOUR

Will made his way home, deep in thought. There was no refuting the fact that, like he, Olivia Langley had changed. Losing her parents had obviously thrust her into the role of looking after her sisters. She had made it more than clear that she wanted nothing further to do with him and he couldn't blame her for that. Yet Will realized that he wanted to see her again, and he wanted her forgiveness.

Whistling to Gilbert, he heard the dog's excited barking as he splashed along the shallow stream towards him. Will waded across to the grassy bank opposite. Walking up the driveway to Rossetter House he knew he needed to talk to someone about the Langley sisters and, more importantly, Olivia, and what had happened to them in the five years since he had been gone. Minutes later, he was striding through the house in search of his sister.

He found Thea in the turret room murdering a piece of music that he thought may be by Mozart, yet was not sure. She had grown so much in his absence, now a young woman. He felt a pang in his heart for the coltish girl he had left behind. Sun filtered through the windows, lighting her raven curls, and he was awed at the beautiful lady she had become. Slipping onto the seat beside her, he placed his fingers over hers.

"Perhaps if you did not draw blood every time you played you would achieve a better result."

She giggled and then kissed his cheek.

"I'm so glad your home, Will."

"So am I," he replied, kissing the top of her head. He was not a man comfortable with emotional gestures; however, perhaps now he was home that, too, would change.

"Now the trick with playing the piano is to caress the keys, not bash them into submission, sister."

"I hate the piano but Joseph makes me practice. He says I need to be well rounded, not just a simpleton like so many of the other debutantes."

"Did he now? Well, I believe in this, he could be right. So how about I give you a few lessons to see if we can stop everyone running for cover when you are asked to play?

"Ouch!" He grimaced as she thumped him on the arm. "A well-rounded debutante would never strike a respectable peer."

"Respectable, you?" she scoffed.

"I'm sorry I left you here alone with Joseph," Will said, running his fingers over the keys softly.

"Joe is a good brother, Will, and has cared for me as a father would. I know you believe he has no feelings for you, but that is not true. He was so worried when you left, he paced these halls for days, muttering about going after you and then one day he just stopped and never mentioned your name again."

"We have always been brothers in name only, Thea. Don't make more of it than there is," Will said, wondering why the words hurt so much when spoken aloud.

"I believe you're wrong, Will, and if you were to apologize to him as you have to me, I think you would be surprised."

Would he? Or, more importantly, could he apologize to his brother?

"I was so angry with you when you left without a word. I

even hated you for a while," Thea said. "But over time, I realized that you needed to do what you had and that staying here would have destroyed you, Will, and possibly Joe too."

"I didn't know how to come back until now," he said as she studied him, her eyes running over every detail of his face.

"You're different now, aren't you, Will?"

He nodded but remained silent. Thea threw her arms around him and hugged him.

"I love you."

"Love you, too," he whispered, holding her close. For so long he had hurt deep inside, but now he could feel himself starting to heal.

"I just went to visit mother and father's graves and met Olivia Langley there." Will brushed a kiss on her forehead before releasing her.

"Livvy! Oh, how was she? I do not get to see Phoebe and Olivia very much since their parents died. Bella still visits occasionally, but I rarely go there anymore."

"Why don't you go there anymore?" Will picked up one of her hands and laid it on his as he began to play. "Feel how lightly I touch the keys, Thea."

"Because everything changed when their mother died." Thea looked at him, her eyes solemn. "Viscount Langley lost his arm in the same accident, and Bella hurt her leg and Livvy and Phoebe had to nurse them both and then the Viscount died and suddenly they were all alone."

Will knew how much he had relied on Olivia and his siblings during his parents' death; he wondered who had supported her.

"Is Bella's leg all right now?" he questioned.

"No, she suffers terribly, but they have found a clinic in Scotland and Livvy is hoping to get Bella there to have some treatment one day soon.

He remembered the youngest Langley as being a happy

young girl with blond curls and bright green eyes. The thought of her injured and in pain did not sit comfortably with him.

"I don't think everything is as good as they say it is for the Langley sisters, Will." Thea frowned down at the keys.

"How so?"

"Livvy never had a season and she said it was because she was in mourning and that she needed to stay here with her sisters. However, Bella said that it was because she wanted to wait until Phoebe had hers and they could come out together."

"That seems fair." Will swapped their hands and guided Thea's up and down the keys.

"Yes, but Livvy is twenty-two, Will. Her hopes of finding a husband are diminishing every year she does not enter society. Of course, Squire Melnock has offered for her, but she will not have him."

"Squire Melnock!" Will roared, feeling the bite of anger. "He's old enough to be her grandfather."

"Olivia is always so evasive with me now," Thea added, ignoring his outburst. "And once, I called in on her unexpectedly and she was scrubbing the walls in the parlor in an old dress."

"Why is that unusual?"

Thea looked at him before speaking.

"Viscount Langley was a wealthy man, Will, with several homes and lots of money. They always had new clothes and plenty of servants, and not once did Bella ever mention doing household chores."

"You say that as if it were a foul word sister."

"Don't get moralistic with me, brother, I know how to do chores. Penny and Joseph make me do the gardening twice a week, and I have to go into the kitchens once a week to learn how the household works."

"Apologies tendered, sister."

"Accepted, brother."

They played for a while before Thea spoke again.

"The thing is, Will, the Langleys were always my friends, but they were atrociously spoiled and earned quite the reputation as flirts.

"And now?" he queried.

"And now, they are quiet and dignified. They rarely raise their voices or laugh. Phoebe still has a tongue that could slice a man in two, yet even she rarely wields it anymore."

"You're worried about them?" Will ran a finger down her check.

"They are my friends, Will. And I miss them. Livvy and I used to have long talks before Penny came along. She would counsel me on all sorts of things and I could ask her anything, but now…"

"Now?" he prompted.

"Now when she thinks no one is looking at her, she appears so sad and alone and it breaks my heart."

Will knew what she meant; he had seen the sadness and vulnerability that sat beneath the surface of Olivia Langley today, and he had not liked it either.

"I voiced my concerns with Joseph and Penny and they went to visit with them, but upon their return they said that everything seemed all right. However, they offered their assistance should it be required."

Will couldn't imagine Olivia Langley's pride allowing her to take Joseph up on that offer.

"We shall keep an eye on them, Thea, and if they need any help, I shall step in. Now I'm going to ask you something, and I would rather we kept this conversation to ourselves."

"I promise," Thea said solemnly.

"How did Olivia react to me leaving England?"

Will watched her closely so he would know if she was hiding

anything from him. Thea had always been open book.

"I went over there the day after you left because I believed she needed to know about your departure from a friend. I asked her to walk outside with me," Thea said quietly. "I told her that you had gone and that we had no idea where to or when you would return, and do you know what she said, Will?"

"No," he whispered. "Tell me."

"She took my hands and looked at me. I could see the tears in her eyes as she said 'Thank you for telling me, Thea'. She then said she was sure you would return one day soon and that I was not to fret as you would stay safe until then."

"So she wasn't too upset then," Will said, and for some foolish, twisted reason this disappointed him.

He was subjected to a look from his sister that had his toes clenching inside his boots.

"I was never in doubt that you had broken her heart, Will, and the months that followed did nothing to change my opinion."

"She spoke of me often?" He felt like a fool for asking the question, but knew he must.

"No, she never mentioned your name again in my presence, but Bella said she could sometimes hear her sister crying in her room late at night."

Will played softly while he thought about his sister's words. Olivia had loved him and he had probably loved her, yet he had been too caught up in himself to want to act on that love.

"Promise me you will never hurt her again. I fear she can take no more pain in her life."

"I promise," he vowed.

They sat in silence for a while, both lost in their own thoughts, until Will became aware of the butler standing in the doorway.

"What is it, Alders?"

"A Mr. Frederick Blake has arrived, my lord, and is asking for you."

"Well, he made good time," Will said, regaining his feet and urging his sister to hers. "Come, I want you to meet this man, Thea. He saved my worthless hide and kept me safe numerous times over the past five years."

"But who is he, Will?"

"A friend, and the man who runs my life," Will said as they left the room.

They had reached the hallway that led to the stairs when he heard Billy squeal somewhere up ahead, and then the little boy appeared with his harried nursemaid at the rear.

"Hello, Billy. Are you going somewhere?" Thea said, holding out her arms as he stopped before him.

Tilting his head back, the boy studied Will, ignoring Thea's question. His expression was intent as he looked at his new uncle. Will wondered if it was possible for a child so young to read a person's character, because it felt exactly like what his nephew was doing, and then, to his surprise, Billy lifted his arms.

"He wants you to pick him up, Will."

"I might drop him." He couldn't take his eyes from the boy.

"You won't."

Bending at the waist, Will placed his hands on either side of the soft little body and lifted him high.

"Settle him against your shoulder. He likes that best."

Doing as his sister instructed, he tucked Billy into his shoulder and felt a small arm wrap around his neck. He heard Thea tell the maid that they would watch the boy for a while and then she put her hand on his back and urged him towards the stairs.

"He is a robust little fellow, Will. He won't break, I promise you."

"I've never carried a child before."

She didn't comment on the husky timber of his voice, instead following him down the stairs.

Three carriages were lined up in the entrance way as they arrived outside. A well-built man in a neat black suit was directing people in a loud, booming voice. Joseph was standing beside the first, looking bemused.

"I believe these are your carriages, William?" the Duke said, looking from his brother to his son who babbled something indiscernible at him.

"Freddy, come over here!" Will bellowed, stopping beside his brother.

"My lord." Freddy smiled as he took Will's hand and pumped it several times.

Not overly tall, Fredrick Blake's personality more than made up for his lack of inches. He had sparkling blue eyes, eyelashes a woman would die for and a smooth, shiny bald head. His mouth was usually curved in a smile and he was the most intelligent, shrewd man Will had ever met besides his brother. He had refused to call Will by his first name, but he classed him as a friend all the same.

"Fredrick Blake, this is my brother the Duke of Rossetter, and my sister, Lady Althea Ryder," Will said. "Billy, don't pull my hair," he added to his nephew who ignored him and continued doing exactly that. "And this is my nephew, who has a long title that is far too weighty for one so young; therefore, he is just known as Billy."

"He's got the look of you, my lord," Freddy said, studying Will and Billy after he had greeted everyone.

"God save us all," the Duke muttered.

"I'm sure you will ensure he does not follow in my footsteps, your grace,"

Joseph sighed at Will's curt tone. "I'm sorry, that came out wrong," he added, shaking his head.

Stunned, Will looked at his brother. "Good God, did you just apologize?"

"I've apologized to you before… surely?"

Will shook his head.

It was the Duke's turn to look stunned. "She was right."

"Who was right?"

"Penny."

Will had no idea what his brother was talking about. Joseph looked suddenly uncomfortable, as if he had just realized something that he would rather not have.

"Will you come to my office, William, if you can spare the time? I would like to talk to you, please."

Will gave his brother a searching look, but could read nothing further on his face, so he nodded and then handed Billy to Thea. He did have things to say to his brother and perhaps clearing the air between them sooner rather than later would at least make his stay here a more harmonious one.

"Are you hungry or tired, Freddy?" he then questioned before moving to follow Joseph.

"Not a bit of it, my lord," his man of affairs said, looking bright-eyed as he took in the house and surrounding gardens.

"Alders," Will said to the hovering butler. "Please assist Mr. Blake in unpacking the carriages while I discuss something with my brother.

"At once, my lord."

"I shall see you soon, Freddy," Will said before following Joseph inside.

Joseph's office had been their father's and grandfather's before that. It was big, impressive and smelled of leather and books. Thick rugs sat on polished floors and the furniture was expensive and sturdy. It was a man's domain, and before he left Will had hated the room and all it had stood for. Located at the front of the house, it had a huge arched window overlooking the driveway so its occupant could see anyone coming or going.

Will watched his brother sink into the high-backed chair behind the desk and then took the one in front. The last time he had been in this room had been the day he and Joseph had argued, the day he had left the house for London.

"I am pleased that I can now put that memory to rest," Joseph said.

"Pardon?" Will wasn't sure he had heard those words correctly.

Joseph leaned his head back on the chair and looked at him, his eyes steady as they searched his face.

"The memory of our last argument here. I can now put it to rest."

The man seated before Will seemed suddenly different from the harsh, unyielding duke he'd always known. He noted the laughter lines around his mouth, and even his posture was less rigid.

"Penny talked at me for endless hours last night about you. Demanding I unbend enough to actually have a conversation with you, William. For some reason, she believes we have never communicated with each other, and that this is the time to start and more importantly I, as the eldest, must be the instigator. She fears that you will leave again if I do not and… I do not want that."

Will just stared at his brother. He had expected a lecture and harsh words, but never this.

"Well, say something," Joseph said when he remained silent. "Or must I beg?"

"Beg for what?"

"Your forgiveness."

"But there is nothing for me to forgive, Joseph. I was at fault, not you."

The Duke braced his elbows on the desk and then put his head in his hands in a very un-dukish manner.

"I do not like speaking of emotions and have trouble articulating them as do most men, but I will try or my wife has informed me she will sleep in my son's room until I do."

Shaking his head, Will wondered if he was actually hearing these words.

"I would pray every day that you were not in any danger and that your horse would appear so I could take those words back."

"I thought you would be relieved to see me go. At the time, I was fairly certain you were not overly fond of me."

Snorting, Joseph shook his head. "I wanted to place my fist in your jaw, but that did not mean I didn't care for you, Will. You are my brother, and while I did not like the man you were turning into, I believed you could be saved or I would not have bothered to try."

Had he been wrong in believing his brother wanted to control him? Had Joseph only wanted to help guide him on the right path? If Will had truly taken the time to look, would he have found the big brother he'd always wanted?

"When I realized you were not coming back, I sent a man to London to find you. When he returned saying that he had found evidence that you and Luke had boarded a boat bound for India, I knew I could do nothing to bring you home."

Will remembered Thea's words. *He was so worried when you left, he paced these halls for days, muttering about going after you and then one day he just stopped and never mentioned your name again.*

Climbing to his feet, Will began to pace. "I truly didn't believe you cared at the time. I was so consumed with anger and frustration over what I believed to be the wrongs inflicted upon me that I did not take the time to see how my departure would impact those I left behind. It wasn't until I was away from here that the guilt grew. I wanted to send you a letter many times, but I never knew the right words to say."

"'Joe, I'm well, please don't worry. I will return one day'."

Will snorted at his brother's drawled words.

"For the first few months after leaving here I felt free, and the pressure inside me eased, but it did not take long to realize what I had left behind and to understand how atrociously spoiled I had become."

"Why didn't you return sooner, Will?"

Will rested his forehead on the cool glass of the window. Did he even know why he had stayed away so long?

"I never fitted here, you know. Not really, Joe. Our father was the Duke and you were in training to be his heir, but what was I?"

"A son and a brother who was loved very much."

"Perhaps." Will looked out the window. "But I wanted more and never had the strength of character then to go searching for it, so I settled on being rebellious."

"You were certainly that," Joseph said.

"The more trouble I created, the angrier you got and a part of me relished in your rage. I wanted your perfect life to have a chink in it, and that chink was me." Will felt the shame that always came when he remembered his behavior. But he needed to say these things; they were five years overdue. And he would not leave this room until he had at least cleared the air with his brother.

"But why wait so long to return?"

"I wanted to make something of myself, be someone who the both of us could be proud of, Joe. It just took me so long to find that person and even longer to find my way back home. I'm sorry that in doing so I hurt so many people."

Will heard the clink of a glass.

"Penny says the problem is that we never really formed a bond, Will. Before Father died, I was always taking lessons or behaving like Father expected me to and after he died I became your parent and was no longer your brother. I'm sorry for that."

"Everything you said to me the day I left was true, Joe." Will sighed. "And I should have supported you after our father died, not made your life difficult."

"And maybe if I had asked you for that support instead of trying to do it all myself, then things would have been different."

Will was silent for a while as he thought about what he wanted to say next.

"I came to understand a bit about the pressure you were under and probably still are, when I was away."

"Tell me about yourself, brother, so I may now know the man you have become?" Joseph asked.

Will couldn't seem to stand still so he walked around the office touching things. He had never been good at baring his soul, and doing so while facing his brother, the one man he had never really spoken to, was not easy for him.

"Come, Will, talk to me," Joseph coaxed. "I don't believe we have ever really conversed on any level."

"When I had packed my things, I left the house and stormed to the stables. Luke was inside and asked where I was bound. I told him, and he asked to accompany me," Will said, remembering that day.

"Yes, his mother arrived on my doorstep the following morning informing me that if anything happened to her boy it would be me that she came after, especially as it was my irresponsible brother that had led her Luke astray."

Will snorted. "Luke is no longer that boy, Joe; he is now a man with his own mind and income and a surprising aptitude for making money. He has the remarkable ability to do calculations quicker than anyone I've ever met."

"Really? I can imagine that could come in handy," the Duke

said, and then waved his hand for Will to continue with his story.

"The boat we secured a passage on was headed for India, and that was where I met Freddy. He, too, was leaving to seek his fortune, only unlike like us he was a man who had experienced a little of what life can throw at you without the protection of your family. He saved us from some men whose intent was to rob Luke and I and no doubt slit our throats, and has stayed with me ever since."

Joseph didn't speak, but Will saw his fingers clench around the crystal decanter as he reached for it.

"We talked for what felt like the entire journey to India and worked through a plan between us that would benefit us all. I had the title and some money and Freddy and Luke had the intelligence and were not afraid of hard work. Once we arrived in India we started to implement it."

"Please sit, Will."

Taking the glass his brother held out to him, Will sat and sipped the contents while watching Joseph do the same. He swallowed his smile; his brother would need the cognac's fortifying powers shortly.

"I put up the money and we purchased our first shipment of silks, which we then sold to anyone who wanted them. Eventually, we moved into other things, like spices and furniture, and soon we were able to buy our first ship.

"Ship!" Joseph spluttered. "You own a ship?"

"Three of them, actually."

"Good lord!"

Will laughed at his brother's stunned expression.

"Freddy began to accompany the shipments back to England and then he started buying warehouses to store the goods in."

"And you never thought to accompany him?"

Will held his brother eyes. "The time was not right then, Joe, as it is now."

"So how rich are you?"

"Extremely."

Joseph laughed, a great rolling sound that filled the room, and Will couldn't remember the last time he had heard such a noise coming from his brother.

"Richer than I?"

Will nodded.

"And what do you plan to do, now you're back in England?" Joseph questioned when he had himself under control.

"I will continue to bring shipments into the country and there are a few other things that I would like to look at investing in here in England. Firstly, however, I had thought to purchase some property nearby."

Not much silenced the Duke, but silenced he was.

"Stunned, brother? I hope in a good way," Will said, wondering why he suddenly felt uncertain.

"In a good way, brother, I assure you. Mother and Father would be very proud of the man you have become, and I am only sorry that I doubted you for so long."

"I gave you no reason to believe in me, Joe. I hope that has now changed."

The Duke nodded. "Do you know how many times I have longed to just say the word brother and know it was you I was talking to, Will?

Will nodded, because he had felt the same, too many times to count. He knew their relationship would take time to grow, yet for the first time in many years, he believed that he and Joseph would one day become friends. Slowly the pain inside him was easing, the tightness in his chest loosening. He was home, and home is where he would stay.

***

The Langley sisters put on their warmest stockings and best walking dresses and boots, then bundled into their outdoor clothes and set out for the church at a slow stroll. Bella had assured her sisters that with the aid of her walking stick, she could make it the short distance to the village and back. Livvy would find a ride home for them if she tired.

Mrs. Popplehinge had left strict instructions as to when the flowers should be changed, and what flowers to pick from the small greenhouse at the rear of the church; therefore, Livvy was determined that they do exactly as she had directed. She would not give the woman reason to complain.

"How is your shoulder, Livvy?"

"Much better, Phoebe, thank you," Livvy said as they made their way down the road that led to the village. "You will let us know if the walk gets too much for you, Bella?"

"Yes, Livvy."

"I wonder if walking to the village on such a cold day is healthy?" Phoebe said, looking at the gray sky.

"It will do us good. Because of my shoulder, we have been inside too long and I, for one, need some fresh air." That was not, strictly, true; Livvy had stayed inside because she did not want to see Will again, yet there was no way she would ever admit that.

"Can you believe it is nearly Christmas, and still we have had no snow?" Bella said, leaning on her walking stick while she swung her basket with the other hand. She looked pretty in her dark green, velvet cloak. A matching bonnet was nestled on her curls, with cream ribbons tied beneath her chin. Seeing the color in her cheeks and slight weight gain reinforced to Livvy that what she and Phoebe had done had been the right thing to do, even though the guilt of their actions was never far away. They had paid bills and subsequently ordered more supplies, and

Bella looked much healthier for the change in her diet.

The Langley sisters lived a charade when they left their house. Dressed always in their finest clothes, they acted as if the most pressing concern in their lives was choosing new trim for a bonnet when they were in the village of Twoaks, and so far the façade had worked. Livvy had serious doubts it would do so for much longer.

"Will you ride, Harvey, in the Derby this year, Livvy?" Bella called over her shoulder.

Harvey was Phoebe's horse, and she had ridden him in the race last year and placed third. She had hopes of winning the prize money the Earl of Dobberly put up this year.

"Of course she will ride Harvey. He is far swifter than her slug, Boris," Phoebe said, offering Livvy a soft smile. Taking the two steps to bring them together, she took her sister's hand in hers and squeezed it.

"Thank you, Phoebe, and although Boris is not as swift as Harvey, he is certainly no slug and I shall thank you not to mention it in front of him."

"Perhaps slug was harsh." Phoebe laughed. "And I'm sorry for what I said to you the other day," she added so only Livvy could hear.

"I'm sorry we argued, too."

"The thing is, Livvy, I spoke without thinking and hurt you and that was not fair of me. Bella and I are very aware that you are sacrificing your happiness to ensure we one day find ours."

When she let her guard down and showed the real person beneath, Phoebe was actually very sweet.

"Having both of you settled will be enough happiness for me, Phoebe. Don't you realize that?"

"But what of your happiness? Don't you want a family and husband of your own?"

The pale blue velvet bonnet framed Phoebe's pretty face and

Livvy hoped that one day a man would love her for what lay beneath the beauty.

"I don't want that for me. I'm going to be a wonderfully indulgent aunt to the nieces and nephews my sisters give me. Besides, loving someone is painful and hurts when you lose them."

Phoebe frowned. "Why would you lose them?"

Livvy looked away in case Phoebe saw what she was not saying.

"We lost grandfather and then father and mother. I don't cope with grieving very well."

"That is utter rot, Livvy! You are not a coward. How dare you give up your hopes and dreams just because you have lost loved ones? Many people lose family, husbands and wives, and go on to love again. If you won't be honest, then I will. You don't want to risk loving again because Lord Ryder hurt you."

Ferocious Phoebe was back and she was right. The pain Livvy felt when Will left had been unbearable, and she had no wish to ever experience that again.

"I do not want to discuss him, Phoebe. Furthermore, how do you know what it's like to love someone that way?"

"I don't," Phoebe said, flashing a wide smile. "But I have spoken to many people about this, Livvy, and all say that love is something you do not plan for and cannot halt once two people meet who are fated for each other."

Livvy swung her sister's hand for several steps, mulling over the words as they walked down the narrow, windy lane.

"Perhaps you are right, but the pain is something I have no wish to ever experience again, Phoebe. Therefore, I have a feeling no man will meet my exacting standards and fall at my feet declaring his undying adoration and love. No, I shall pin all my hopes on you and Bella receiving just such a declaration."

Thankfully, Phoebe didn't say anything further as they had

reached the village. She just harrumphed as the sisters walked over the bridge and down the main street.

Twoaks was a lively village, not too big yet not too small either, with neat stone cottages and shops that were usually bustling with activity even on a brisk winter's morning.

"Step to the side, sisters," Livvy directed as two carts being pushed by men involved in a heated debate rumbled by.

"Don't step in that!"

"I see it, Livvy," Bella said, limping around a large pile of horse manure.

"Good day, Mrs. Casey!" Phoebe called to the elderly lady who was sitting on her porch, as she had every day for as long as Livvy could remember.

Being born and raised close to a village was both a gift and a curse as far as Livvy was concerned. She loved being part of the community and sharing the highs and lows of those she knew. However, it had been hard, since their father's death, to hide their situation from people who knew them so well. Livvy hated lying, yet she had become skilled at it and that saddened her.

"I think we could make that with a bit more ribbon. Red, I think," Phoebe said, dragging Livvy to look in a shop window. Pressing her face to the glass, she studied the bonnet on display. "You have that bonnet with the hideous gray ribbon that makes you look insipid, Livvy. It will do perfectly for what I have in mind."

Livvy thought of the coins they had stolen and the few she had in her reticule. "I think we can manage a piece of ribbon," she said, ushering her sisters through the door. "However, I protest to looking insipid in that bonnet. In fact, I will go so far as saying I look fetching.

Phoebe snorted. "Fetching? You look bilious, and that is on a good day."

As they were now inside the shop, Livvy could not answer so she hissed instead.

"It seems something is hissing inside your shop, Mr. Todd," Phoebe said loudly to the proprietor as he came forward to greet them.

"Hissing, Miss Langley?" he said, looking alarmed and quickly glancing around his shop for anything that could make such a noise. "I cannot think what it would be."

"Good morning, Mr. Todd. Don't worry, I believe the noise was outside," Livvy reassured the proprietor while sending her sister a dark look.

"I'm sure you're right, Miss Olivia." He gave the door a final look. "Are you looking for anything in particular?"

"Red ribbon," Phoebe said promptly.

The shop was a riot of color. Braids, buttons and ribbons covered every inch. There were trimmings in every shade and size.

"I will show you all we have," Mr. Todd said, beginning to lay ribbons before them on the counter.

"I think this is too thin." Bella pushed one aside.

"Too red," Phoebe said, pushing another aside.

"How can something be too red?" Livvy looked at the offending piece of silk.

"Blood red, military red, and rose red—there are many shades, Livvy, and that is not the one we want," Phoebe said, discarding another.

"I had not realized that selecting ribbon was an art form, sister."

Phoebe merely flashed a blinding smile at her that encompassed Mr. Todd, who instantly flushed and stuttered that all the red ribbon in the shop was on sale today. *Of course it was,* Livvy thought as her sister continued to flirt with the man.

"I do believe you could murder someone and never face the consequences with that smile, Phoebe," Livvy stated as they left the shop minutes later with more red ribbon than they needed, and a length of blue because Mr. Todd had insisted the blue was beginning to fray and he could no longer sell it.

"Let us hope we never have to test that theory, Livvy. And now I'm hungry and because I saved you money on the ribbon, I think you should buy me a cinnamon bun."

"I concede the blue ribbon will look nice on your dress for the Assembly," Livvy stated, following her sisters down the street once more. "And I imagine all that manipulating would make a person hungry."

"It was not manipulation. It was coercion, sister, there is a subtle difference," Phoebe said, laughing. "I have been running through our dresses for the Christmas season, sisters, and I believe with a bit of trim here and seam letting there we will once again set everyone back on their heels."

"You are a miracle worker, Phoebe!" Bella cried.

And she was, Livvy thought. Their dresses were designed by Phoebe and Jenny, who had found all their mother's old gowns and spent hours transforming them into the current styles.

"That she is," Livvy said quietly, as she followed her sisters down the street. She felt a small measure of calm steal over her as she watched them laughing and chatting together. For today, she would push their worries aside and enjoy spending time with Phoebe and Bella. The precious coins she used to pay for ribbons and buns were a small price to pay for a few snatched moment of happiness.

"If a man smelled like that," Livvy loudly sniffed the cinnamon-scented air as they drew near the bakers. "Then I would have no trouble finding love."

"I would gladly wear cinnamon cologne, Miss Langley, if the result was you declaring your undying love to me."

And suddenly, with those drawled words, Livvy's small measure of calm fled. Of all the men in Twoaks, why did Lord Ryder have to be the one to hear her say that?

CHAPTER FIVE

Will had accompanied Freddy into the village after his man of affairs declared his intentions this morning of purchasing some gloves and a warmer hat. They had taken the carriage because Freddy couldn't sit a horse and he was not going to walk anywhere in this *'bleedin' weather'*. Directing him to the appropriate shop, Will had then visited Luke and his family. Mrs. Fletcher had at first scowled at him for several seconds before unbending enough at her son's urging to greet him politely and thank him for returning her boy to her safely.

"I see where you get your pleasant demeanor from, Luke," Will said as they left the Fletcher house to stroll down the street so he could reacquaint himself with the village.

Luke snorted. "Ma's always been hard on everyone, it's just her way. She cuffed my ears when I first walked through the door, as if I were still a boy, and then hugged me for a good five minutes all the while sniffling into my collar."

"I can understand your mother's motives. There have been plenty of times I've wanted to cuff you but—" The words died in Will's throat as Olivia and her sisters walked out of a shop ahead of him. Today she was dressed in an elegant, long, dark blue coat that fell to her ankles and there was not a patch in sight. Maybe things were not going badly for the Langleys after all.

"It's Bella!"

Will looked at his friend and saw the stunned expression on his face as he spoke. "Is there a problem, Luke?"

"My mother told me of her accident and I had thought—"

"Yes?" Will prodded his friend.

"I'd thought she would not be quite so beautiful now," Luke said softly, his eyes still fixed on the youngest Langely.

"You thought she would be ugly because she has a damaged leg?" Will pressed.

Luke visibly shook his head, as if to clear it. He turned, and his blue eyes held anger. "Bella could never be ugly, but I thought she would look pale and sickly, yet she looks"—he stopped again before adding—"wonderful."

There was a note in Luke's voice that Will had never heard before, almost as though he was awed by seeing Bella again.

"I didn't know you and Bella were friends. She would have only been eleven, like Thea, when we left surely?"

Luke's eyes were fastened on the youngest Langley, as if he could memorize every detail of her.

"She used to follow me around as a child and I looked out for her because she had no brothers and was always hurting herself or falling into some kind of trouble. And then she grew up—"

"Eleven is hardly grown up, surely?" Will protested.

"She was becoming a lady." Will had seen the closed expression his friend now wore many times before, and it usually heralded an argument between them.

"So you turned your back on her because she was a peer's daughter, and therefore above you, even though you were friends?" Will questioned.

Luke Fletcher had grown into a man since leaving England. He stood tall with broad shoulders forged from years of hard work. He had thick brown curls and pale blue eyes that drew women to his side with ease. His loyalty was unquestionable and he was possibly the most honorable person Will had ever known. They were friends that had shared much, but as far as Luke was concerned, there still lay one thing between them that could never make them equals, and that one thing was the source of all their arguments.

"Leave it, Will. She was eleven and turning into a young lady. It was just better that way."

"Better for whom?"

The blue eyes glared at him. "I said leave it, Will."

"And do you still believe you're beneath her, even though your wealth now outstrips most of the noblemen in England?" Will said with a calm he was far from feeling.

"Don't you ever stop?" Luke snarled.

But Will would not stop; he would speak his mind on this matter until it got into Luke's thick head.

"Just because you are not of noble birth does not mean you cannot have Bella as a friend, nor must you live life as a servant, Luke. There are plenty of wealthy untitled men in this country making their mark.

"Being a servant was what I was raised to do," Luke said stubbornly.

"You can call me Will, yet you still drive my bloody carriage. You lived as my equal for years, yet now we are back in England you cannot make the acquaintance of a young lady who was once your friend? You, Luke Fletcher, are one of the best men I know, but you're a bloody coward." Will fought to hold his anger at bay. The main street of Twoaks was not the place to lose it.

"I have no wish to live a different life," Luke said, his anger now boiling below the surface, as Will's was.

"And I say that's horseshit!"

"Of course that's your right, my lord." Luke's tone was lofty as he used Will's title to taunt him.

"And what of your money? Will you not use it for your family or yourself?"

"My family don't want it, and it's of no use to me so you use it," Luke snapped.

"And what of Bella? Will you run and hide before she sees you?" This time it was Will doing the taunting.

Luke glared at him, but Will stood his ground.

"Excuse me, I shall retrieve the carriage and collect Freddy."

"I have one of our men driving it, Luke, so there is no need," Will said as he turned away.

"I am one of your men now and also your driver, and I'm fairly sure that you'll end up in a ditch if I'm not holding the ribbons."

The words were delivered slowly through Luke's clenched front teeth.

"Stubborn fool," Will said, watching his friend stalk away from him. Sucking a large, cold breath of air into his lungs, he pushed Luke from his head. He would deal with him later. For now, he was going to follow the Langley sisters.

"I know where you wander, Miss Langley," he whispered as they turned towards the baker. In minutes, he was lengthening his stride to intercept them.

"Good morning, Olivia, Phoebe and Isabella," Will said, sweeping off his hat and bowing deeply to the three pretty ladies before him.

"My lord, how wonderful to see you again."

Why did he think Olivia's greeting lacked enthusiasm?

"Again, Livvy? Surely you have not seen Lord Ryder since his return?"

Will watched Phoebe shoot a frantic glance at her elder sister and wasn't sure why.

"I saw Lord Ryder at the cemetery a few days ago, Phoebe. I forgot to tell you."

"Oh, well, that explains it then." Phoebe gave him a wide smile.

If Phoebe Langley ever tired of being a lady, she could easily take up a career as a courtesan. Even at fifteen she had exuded naughtiness, from the tip of her head to the soles of her satin slippers. Now she was a sultry woman, all curves, pouty lips and creamy complexion, and the look in her brown eyes suggested she knew exactly what a man was thinking when they looked at her. There was no doubting that she had grown into an exceptionally beautiful woman, yet he would not be joining her admirers; it was the eldest Langley sister who drew his eye.

"It is a pleasure to meet with you again," Phoebe purred, lowering her long lashes.

Will guessed that flirting to Phoebe Langley was like breathing to every other woman.

"Hello, Isabella. It seems not just Thea has blossomed in my absence," Will said, moving to take the youngest Langley's gloved hand and kissing the back. Luke was right, she was beautiful, and like his sister she, too, was now a young lady deserving attention. Isabella had soft green eyes, two dimples in her cheeks and she was a close rival to her sisters for beauty; however, if one really looked, they could see the pain etched deep inside. He noted that she was leaning heavily on a sturdy walking stick and felt a tug of sympathy that so much had changed in her life since he had left.

"Thea must be very happy you are home, my lord," she said.

"Yes I believe she is, Isabella, as am I."

"May I ask how Luke is?"

The look of yearning in Isabella's eyes when she mentioned Luke was the same as his had been when he'd spoken of her.

"He is well and I'm sure you will see him soon," Will said, determined to make it so.

"We are just about to purchase some of Mr. Evan's

cinnamon buns," Phoebe said, interrupting them.

"Are you?" Will sighed. "I dreamed of those buns for years."

"They are still Livvy's favorites," Phoebe said, which made Will once again look at Olivia. The cool air had put a flush in her cheeks and she looked as every young lady should today: happy and trouble free. Well, she had looked that way before his arrival. Now a line had formed between her eyes as she scowled at him.

"We shall detain you no longer, my lord, as I'm sure you have much to do." Her voice was cold enough to dissuade most people. However, he was not most people.

"Actually," Will said, walking beside Olivia as she continued on to the bakery, "I am waiting for someone, and I can think of nothing I'd like more than eating a cinnamon bun with old friends to pass the time."

Taking her elbow, he maneuvered her around a horse that was stomping his hooves in agitation.

"We will not be stopping to eat them, my lord, as we are charged with tending the church flowers in Mrs. Popplehinge's absence." Olivia quickly moved away from his touch to clutch the door handle of the bakery.

"Surely, you do not expect me to stand idly by when pretty ladies are in need of nourishment?" Will placed both his hands on Olivia's waist. Lifting her off her feet, he set her down beside her sisters who stood silently watching him. "Wait here with your sisters and I shall return shortly with the buns," he added, winking to Phoebe and Isabella, who dutifully giggled. In seconds, he had disappeared inside the shop.

"You have to admit, that was neatly done," Phoebe said, her eyes on the now closed bakery door. "Perhaps between us we could simply lift Livvy out of the way when she becomes trying."

"The idea has merits," Bella laughed.

"H—how dare he handle me like that!"

Phoebe peered under the brim of Livvy's bonnet. "You sound like one of the heroines in Bella's books."

"I—I have no wish for him to buy us food," Livvy stammered.

"Three of Mr. Evan's buns are hardly that, Livvy. You are overreacting to Lord Ryder's kind gesture, and that is not like you, especially as you have already declared you no longer have any feelings for him. Now hush, because here he comes."

"They had a new flavor called the plum bun, so I got a few of those as well." Will joined the Langley sisters once again with a large package balanced in one hand. Phoebe and Bella took one each. Olivia, however, stood with her hands at her sides.

"Take a bun, Olivia." He could tell that she wanted to say no, so he lifted them closer so that she could smell them. "Take one."

"Thank you." Will swallowed his smile as she reluctantly gave in.

"Would I be imposing on you lovely ladies if I accompanied you to the church? It has been many years since I entered its hallowed walls and my black soul is well deserving of a good cleansing."

"I don't think you will enjoy—"

"Of course!" Phoebe and Bella cried over the top of their sister, who had been about to refuse him. Both then struck out in the direction of the church, leaving her with no choice but to walk beside him.

Taking a large bite, Will moaned. Swallowing, he then took another. He had been right. They were the best buns in the world. His mouth was alive with the taste of cinnamon and currants. Beside him, Olivia was daintily nibbling on a piece she had pulled off her bun. She briefly closed her eyes as she swallowed, a small smile played around her lips. The tip of her pink tongue appeared to lick a bit of sugar from the corner of her mouth and Will felt lust bolt through his body as he imagined that tongue licking him. Studying her bun, she then tore of another piece and repeated the entire process. Will had been propositioned in several different languages in some very imaginative ways; however, watching Olivia Langley eat a cinnamon bun was the most arousing thing he had ever witnessed.

"I must thank you for the buns, Lord Ryder."

Pulling his eyes from her mouth, he looked at the back of Isabella's head and felt his ardor cool. One did not lust after a woman when her two younger sisters walked before them.

"That wasn't so hard, now, was it?"

"What wasn't so hard?" she questioned, looking up at him. Hell, she had a sprinkling of sugar on her bottom lip. Memories of that lip beneath his nearly dropped him to his knees.

"Thanking me," he said gruffly.

"I am not so rag-mannered that I would not thank you, my lord, even though I had no wish for you to purchase us buns."

Will tipped his hat as a carriage carrying an elderly couple passed by and then looked down at Olivia once again. Thank God the sugar had gone.

"You had no wish for me to purchase you buns, or had no wish for anyone to purchase you buns?" he queried.

She tore off another piece and popped it into her mouth, making a small humming noise of appreciation.

"Tea is the best accompaniment to have with cinnamon buns, my lord," she said, ignoring his question. She was good at that.

"I loathe tea."

She looked at him, lifting one delicate eyebrow.

"Englishmen do not loathe tea, Lord Ryder."

"This one does… passionately. I developed a taste for coffee when I was away."

"Lord Ryder, do wait up!"

Will looked up as the loud voice reached him and saw several women hurrying towards them.

"Don't look now, my lord, but three of the town's most eligible young ladies are bearing down upon you," Phoebe said. "I'm afraid escape is impossible at this point," she added, her eyes alight with laughter.

"Dear God," Will whispered as the women smiled and waved at him. Leaning closer to Isabella and Phoebe he said, "I purchased you buns, therefore you owe me a favor, and I call in that favor now."

"Oh, this should be good," Phoebe said.

"I am begging you, do not leave me alone with those women."

"I'm sure you will cope admirably, my lord. Considering your past record with women, these three should not present you with any problems," Olivia said, her tone prim.

"If you stay, I shall have a dozen cinnamon buns delivered to you by sunset."

"Done!" Livvy said promptly. Will then watched as she turned to greet the approaching women.

"Lady Hemplewaite-Brown, Miss Chillervy, and Miss Smythe, how wonderful to see you again."

She changed before his eyes into a giggling, chatting young lady. She was even fluttering one gloved hand around, mimicking the others. He remembered this Olivia, the fun loving, sweet temptress that had once enthralled him.

"It's so seldom I see Livvy that way anymore, it always takes me by surprise," Bella said, looking at the group of women that now included Phoebe.

"Why do you not see her like this anymore?" Will questioned, feeling his stomach tighten as Livvy giggled; the sound was sweet and clear.

"It won't work, though," Bella added, ignoring his question just like her older sister often did.

"What won't work?"

"They won't be deterred for long, especially by Livvy and Phoebe."

Pulling his eyes from the soft skin at the base of Olivia's neck, Will looked at Isabella.

"Why?" he questioned. She, however, just raised her brows and looked steadily back at him. Turning to the women he studied them closely, and immediately understood what Isabella was getting at.

The Langley women could wear flour sacks and be beautiful; it was in their soft skin and the way the carried themselves. They were bone deep beautiful and that would not sit well with other women. He turned back to Isabella,took her arm and placed it through his.

"Your beauty rivals your sisters, Isabella, never forget that," he said, leading her slowly forward until they, too, stood in the chatting cooing circle of women.

"Lord Ryder. At last you have returned to us!"

"Ladies." Will offered them a bow as he removed his hat.

He only had a vague idea of who all three women were as they could only be seventeen or eighteen at the most—making them considerably younger when he had left England, thus not someone who had caught the attentions of a selfish rake.

"Are you attending the social gatherings during the Christmas season, my lord, starting with the Assembly here in town in three days' time?"

"Ah, Assembly?" Will said, looking at Olivia who just smiled back at him in that smug sort of way that suggested she was enjoying this—him, caught off guard. Well, it may have been a few years since he had faced English society misses, yet he had socialized in India and remembered what was required of him.

"Here in town," the blonde one, who he thought was named Miss Chillervy, stated.

"I can think of nothing that would give me more pleasure, Miss Chillervy, than attending such a gathering surrounded by, undoubtedly, England's most beautiful ladies."

"Amazing how quickly he transformed back into a rake," Phoebe whispered to Olivia, which of course Will heard, as he was meant to.

The three women all tittered and batted their lashes at him. The three Langleys, however, rolled their eyes. Surprisingly, it was their gestures that made him smile.

"I understand, dear Miss Langley, that Mrs. Popplehinge has charged you with care of the church flowers," Lady Hemplewaite-Brown said smiling, although the gesture never reached her eyes, especially when they turned from Olivia to Phoebe.

"Indeed she has and, as you can imagine, we are honored," Olivia said smoothly, although Will had the distinct impression she and her sister were in fact anything but impressed with the honor, especially Phoebe, who looked like she'd swallowed something vile.

CHAPTER SIX

"And are you visiting the church today, Miss Langley?" Lady Hemplewaite-Brown questioned.

"Yes. As you can imagine, my sisters and I are eager to see to the task Mrs. Popplehinge has set us." And that, Livvy thought, was her cue to leave. She would not stand around while these women fawned all over Will, nor did she want to listen to him flirt back with empty compliments that tripped with ease off his tongue. He had once complimented her in the same way; however, now she realized that those words had been insincere, and she had been thrice a fool for believing them.

Bloody man. He had strolled up telling her he would wear cinnamon for her love, looking like a hero in one of Bella's books. Tall, dark and absurdly handsome in a long overcoat with his hair curling over the brim of his black hat, he appeared far too disturbing for her peace of mind, especially as the last time they had met he had kissed her.

"If you ladies will excuse us, we must attend to the flowers," Olivia said, curtseying. Moving towards Will, she then did the same and, upon standing, took the remaining buns out of his hands before he could react. His gray eyes narrowed.

"You promised," he whispered.

"Surely you know that promises are made to be broken, my lord."

Livvy knew she sounded terse but could do nothing about it. She'd suffered when he'd left her, her emotions raging between pain and anger at his desertion. Eventually, she'd forced those feelings down deep inside, but seeing Will again had made them resurface. She needed to stay as far away from this man as possible if she was to keep her emotions under control.

"That was mean," Isabella said as Livvy took her arm.

"He can look after himself, Bella. Did you not hear him ladling on the charm just minutes ago?" Livvy would feel no shame for leaving him.

"You sound jealous, sister," Phoebe added, taking another bun before looking over her shoulder at Lord Ryder who was glaring at them.

"Don't be ridiculous! I just don't have the patience any more for all that simpering and mindless prattle."

"Well, I like him. He's funny and handsome, and if he wasn't old I would fall in love with him," Bella declared. "I was too young to really know him well before he left, but to my mind, anyone who buys me a cinnamon bun is someone worth my time."

Livvy and Phoebe stared at their youngest sister. She was rarely outspoken, especially over someone she did not know well.

"He's not old," Livvy felt moved to say.

"Old or not, you should be nicer to him, Livvy, especially as you robbed him on his first night back in the country."

"Sssh, Bella," Livvy hissed, looking around her. They were reaching the end of town, but there were still people about. "And I do not have to be nice to him at all. He is nothing to me. We are no longer friends.

"You will have to forgive him one day, Livvy."

"There is nothing to forgive, Bella, as I am well over Lord

Ryder and have no wish to continue discussing him; therefore, this will be the end of that subject, if you please."

The Langley sisters fell silent as they concentrated on consuming the remaining buns and walking to the church. Wiping the last of the sugar off her hands, Livvy opened the small white gate as they arrived and headed down the path that led around the back of the old stone building to the small door at the rear.

"Do you know, Phoebe, I am beginning to realize we were not very nice people before our parents died," Livvy said, lifting the latch and opening the door.

"Well, I'm sure this conversation does not include me as I am loved by everyone," Bella said, following her sisters inside. "So I am going to sit for a while and watch you two do all the work," she added. Limping towards the back of the church, she then settled herself in a pew, turning so she could stretch out her leg on the bench.

"We should not have let her come." Livvy looked at her youngest sister. "She's in pain."

"She wanted to, Livvy, and after a rest she will feel better," Phoebe said. "Now, tell me why you think we were not nice people?"

"Because of the way some people react to us. Old Mr. Bramble even said the other day that I was quite a pleasant wee thing now."

Phoebe thought about that while Olivia walked around the church, retrieving the vases and placing them on the floor beneath the table in the small annex at the end of the room. She then opened the cupboard and collected Mrs. Popplehinge's apron. Removing her bonnet she slipped it on over her coat.

"I suppose it could be true. We were terrible flirts even when we were younger, and you used to be quite cutting. Sometimes even I was in awe. However," Phoebe added, "most of the women in Twoaks have always disliked us, and each other for that matter, due to the fact that we are all competing for the few decent noblemen there are in this area."

"True," Livvy agreed.

"I'll go and cut some fresh flowers from the greenhouse," Phoebe said, picking up a basket and heading back out the door.

"I'll be back soon, too. Bella, you just rest," Livvy called to her sister as minutes later she followed Phoebe with an armful of dead flowers.

"I thought we had a deal?"

Livvy shrieked and dropped the flowers. "You scared me!" she gasped, clutching her chest as she looked at Lord Ryder. His gray eyes held a decidedly hostile glint as they stared back.

"Serves you right for abandoning me."

Heart thumping, she dragged her eyes from his unrepentant gaze and bent to retrieve the dead flowers she had dropped.

"You appeared more than happy with *'those women'*, Lord Ryder. In fact, I would go so far as to say you were comfortable with all the adoration," Livvy snapped when her tongue worked again.

"I would be more comfortable had I fallen into a bramble bush," he muttered, dropping to his knees beside her."

"I have no need of your assistance, my lord. Therefore, please return to your business." Livvy refused to look at him as she snatched a dead flower from his hand and then hissed in pain as a small splinter stabbed her.

"Let me see."

Livvy ignored him and tucked the hand into her skirt, but he was stronger and soon held it clasped between his.

"It's a tiny splinter, nothing more and there is no need-"

"What are these from?"

Livvy shivered as he ran his thumb over the calluses on her palm.

"Chopping wood," she said without thinking.

"Why are you chopping wood?"

He was just too bloody disturbing, with his handsome face and flashing white teeth, even if he was scowling at her. She shouldn't have said anything; now he would know that she had no one to chop wood for her.

"None of your business," Livvy snapped, tugging her hand back. "Now go away. I can manage very well on my own and have done for years."

"You were always such a sweet-tempered young lady."

He was taunting her, of course, and she shouldn't respond.

"Yes, well, one cannot stay the same forever, and now, as I have stated, I have no need of your assistance, my lord, so please leave."

"Unlike you, I still have the manners my mother continually hammered into me from a young age, and as you still appear to be in some kind of pain, the gentleman in me cannot allow you to carry anything that may inflict further discomfort."

"Oh, for pity's sake." Livvy glared at him. "We merely left you surrounded by silly young ladies. How bad can that have possibly been for you? Five years ago, you couldn't get enough of that sort of universal adoration."

He regained his feet in a fluid gesture as she picked up the last dead flower, and then she felt his hands around her waist and suddenly she was standing.

"Please don't do that, my lord!"

"Do what?" he said, looking as if he had no idea what she was talking about; however, Livvy was fairly certain he did.

"Pick me up," she snapped.

"I was merely assisting you, as your arms were full."

Livvy was not fooled by his innocent look. "Do not toy with me, my lord. I am no longer a simpering young maid who will worship at your overlarge feet."

He sighed, a long weighty one that started at his toes.

"I have apologized for leaving you without a word, Olivia, yet still you are angry with me."

"As I have stated, Lord Ryder, I neither care that you left nor that you have returned, but if I did, then a handful of words carelessly spoken would not make up for the hurt that you caused. Not to me, you understand," she rushed to add. "I have no need of your empty apologies, but your family, I'm sure, deserve more from you." Livvy drew a breath hoping it would steady her.

He looked at her, eyes solemn.

"And yet I say again that your attitude towards me would suggest I did indeed hurt you, Olivia, and you insult me by suggesting my apology was empty."

"Then you can take your leave, my lord, as we have nothing further to say to each other," she added, walking away from him.

"Leave? When the company I am keeping is so delightful? Surely you jest," Will said, following her for no other reason than he couldn't seem to get himself to leave. She halted again, her cinnamon eyes looking up at him. Will had to clench his fists to stop himself from touching the bruises beneath. She was tired and worried and he wanted to know why.

"Don't flirt with me, Lord Ryder. I am no longer available for your amusement."

"Are we flirting?"

"We are not flirting. You are flirting. Please note the difference."

Will held her eyes for several seconds and he saw another change in her. She was stronger willed than she used to be—however, so was he.

"I thought we were talking as old friends often do."

"As I have already explained, my lord, we are no longer friends, merely acquaintances."

"Would an acquaintance know about your love of butterflies and that your favorite book is the "The Aurelian" by Moses Harris, and the butterfly you most wish to see is the Purple Emperor?" Will fell in beside her as she began to walk away with the flowers. "Or that you cannot roll your tongue as I can and—"

"I have no wish to discuss the past," Olivia interrupted him, her voice sounding shrill. "Go and meet whoever it is you were meeting, Lord Ryder. This is not work for men and certainly not a lord."

Will thought about that as he trailed along beside her.

"So because I am both a man and a lord I am therefore exempt from carrying flowers?"

Her teeth snapped together so hard he feared they would shatter.

"Men do not traditionally do the church flowers, Lord Ryder, as you very well know."

"Is the Derby still run on the 21st of December, Olivia?" he said, changing the subject because it was a foolish one. She was walking fast to try to outstride him, which was ridiculous because his stride was two of hers.

"Yes."

"Excellent. I shall be settled by then and look forward to an entertaining day, especially as you are to compete."

"You are leaving Twoaks, then?"

She wasn't looking at him, so Will couldn't tell if she was happy or sad about the prospect. He thought, perhaps, the earlier.

"No, I'm looking to purchase a property nearby."

"Oh," was all she said as she threw the flowers, with what Will thought unnecessary vigor, onto the mound of other dried clippings and then turned to march back to the church.

"I think the Earl of Dobberly is to be praised for his forward thinking, Lord Ryder. After all, it shows a strength of mind, does it not, for being bold enough to continue to allow a woman to compete in his race, especially as there are many who would try to persuade him otherwise."

"I believe I am firmly put in my place, Olivia."

They had reached the church once again; the old stone building looked unchanged from the last time he had stepped inside its hallowed walls.

"Here are the flowers, Livvy," Phoebe said, joining them and handing the laden basket to her sister. "Hello again, my lord. I tried the plum bun but still believe the cinnamon ones superior."

"There you have me at a disadvantage, Phoebe, as I have yet to try a plum bun because your sister stole them from me."

"Well, perhaps you could stop and get another on your return journey," Phoebe added, looking from her sister to Lord Ryder, sensing the tension between them.

"Excellent idea, sister, and as I'm sure the buns will all be sold soon, you should take your leave at once, Lord Ryder." Olivia threw him a false smile of encouragement; her eyes, however, told another story.

"I couldn't possibly leave without going into the church; after all, I could walk out a better man."

"To the best of my knowledge, my lord, the last miracle performed here was two hundred years ago," Olivia muttered.

"Livvy!" Phoebe laughed.

"Your sister has lost her sweet nature since my departure, Phoebe."

"Not without provocation, my lord."

"Care to enlighten me further?" Will questioned Phoebe.

"No, she does not!"

Phoebe gave her sister a steady look then said, "I shall be in the glasshouse if you need me."

"Allow me," Will said, reaching around Olivia to take hold of the basket. She held fast so he tugged and she had to yield or give in to an undignified tug of war. Silently they walked into the church.

The interior was dark, the only light spilling in through the large stained glass window directly above the front door. The smells were the same, beeswax and the sharper tang of scented candles. Will looked to the large cross that was suspended above the altar at the rear.

"You found us, my lord!"

Searching the church for Isabella, he found her sitting in a pew resting her leg.

"Not a terribly auspicious task when you told me where you were going, Isabella," Will said, following Olivia with his eyes as she started arranging flowers. He didn't want her lifting anything heavy seeing as she was still injured in some capacity. He missed the small, knowing smile Bella gave him as he quickly walked to where Olivia was hefting a large vase onto the table.

"Can you not ask for help?"

"I would if I needed it." She grunted as the vase landed on the bench.

"I don't remember you being this stubborn five years ago," Will said, lifting the two others into place. "In fact, I remember men running hither and yon at your behest and you merely batting your eyelashes in gratitude."

"Things other than physical appearances change in five years, Lord Ryder, as I'm sure you are aware."

She looked at him briefly and then returned to fussing with the flowers. She was hiding secrets behind those eyes. Will knew it, yet he had no idea how to get her to trust him enough to share them.

"Do you and your sisters get support from Lord Langley?"

Taking several big glossy leaves she then forced them into the back of each vase.

"I hardly think that is your concern, my lord."

"Do you want for anything, Olivia, anything I can help you with?" Will persisted.

She crushed a leaf in one hand before speaking. "I will tell you what I told the Duke and Duchess, my lord. We are not their subjects, or in need of charity, and are more than capable of looking after ourselves."

Will grabbed her arm as she reached for another flower. He pulled her to face him and her eyes widened as she took in his anger.

"That is insulting to both you and my brother, Olivia. Joseph has never thought of you as his subject, or anyone else for that matter," Will said softly. "We are friends, Olivia, of long standing. I hope I can offer my support to you without you taking offense, especially after the loss of both your parents."

She tugged her arm free and began once again to arrange the flowers, her long elegant fingers twisting a stem or leaf until she was happy with the result. He couldn't see the emotions that undoubtedly flitted across her face, only the side profile of her cute little nose and full lips and, of course, the stubborn thrust of her chin. He wondered why he hadn't noticed that before. She then sighed as she took a step back to look up at him.

"Please accept my apologies, my lord; it was not my intention to insult you."

"It certainly sounded like an insult."

"I have apologized, my lord. It is not only men who have pride," she muttered, tweaking a petal. "Thank you for your concern, but we are quite well and have no need of your assistance. Now I have work to do, so please do not let me detain you further."

Will studied her face and realized he had yet to see her laugh like she once had, with unrestrained abandon; it had been one of the things he had loved about her.

"There you are, my lord."

Will watched Phoebe walk into the church followed by Freddy.

"Miss Olivia Langley, Miss Phoebe Langley and over there sitting down is Miss Isabella Langley, please allow me to introduce Mr. Frederick Blake to you all. He and I have traveled together these past five years."

Olivia curtsied as Freddy bowed to her and her sisters and then he said something in his booming voice that made her smile. Will's man of affairs was good at that, making people feel comfortable.

"It is lovely to meet you, Mr. Blake, are you happy to be back in England?"

Freddy nodded his head. "Very happy, although the weather takes a bit of getting used to, Miss Langley."

"Will you ever get used to it, do you think? I know I still shiver all winter and I've never left here."

Will wanted that smile on him, gentle and almost playful. Olivia let Freddy see the soft side of her but not him.

"And now you must excuse us, Mr. Blake, as we are due home," Olivia added, moving back to the flowers.

"Will you allow us to take you home?" Freddy said before Will could open his mouth. "The weather has turned and the wind has a bite to it now."

Olivia looked to where Isabella was slowly getting to her feet before answering.

"I would be grateful if you could take my sisters' home, Mr. Blake, and I will follow shortly as I still have things to do here."

"Freddy, you take Phoebe and Isabella to the carriage and I will wait for Olivia to finish and we will join you shortly," Will said, helping Isabella to her feet. He then handed her over to Freddy who, followed by Phoebe, left the church.

"I can walk home, Lord Ryder. Please join the others."

"We will wait for you, Olivia," Will said, aware of the fact that being alone in his company unsettled her. "If you keep frowning, that line will become permanent," he added. Reaching over her head as she turned to pick up the vase, he beat her to it.

"Where would you like to put it?"

He kept his face expressionless as she gave him a look that told him she would like to smash it over his head and then followed as she led him to the pedestal it was to sit on.

Quickly pulling on her, bonnet and gloves she then made for the door with Will on her heels.

"We'll have snow by morning."

She looked silently up at the gray skies above them to check the accuracy of his words and then made her way through the gate to where his carriage waited.

Bella was standing beside it talking to Luke, Freddy and Phoebe when they arrived. His friend had a polite expression on his face that showed none of the emotions he had experienced earlier and the youngest Langley had a rosy flush to her cheeks that Will guessed was not just from the cold air.

"Luke, how wonderful to see you again."

Will watched as Olivia took the hand Luke held out towards her and squeezed it.

"And you, Miss Langley."

"Olivia, please, we are old friends."

Funny how she urged Luke to call her Olivia yet he was to call her Miss Langley, Will thought, feeling the unfamiliar bite of jealousy.

"I shall help you inside now, Miss Isabella," Luke said, putting his hand beneath Bella's arm. "It's too cold out here to stand about chatting."

Will watched as Luke helped Bella inside, handling her as if she was made of the finest china, then Phoebe and Freddy followed.

"Climb into your seat, Luke, I shall see to Olivia."

"Yes, my lord."

"You'll keep, Fletcher," Will muttered, as he reached for Olivia only to have her step up into the carriage unaided. Snapping his teeth together and ignoring Luke's snort, he followed.

Seating herself, Livvy then moved as close to the window as she could, leaving a large space for Will. Seconds later, she felt him sit beside her, his solid thigh pressed against hers and even through the layers of clothing that separated them she felt the heat from his body.

"Did Thea tell you she is to have a skating party for her birthday?" Isabella told Will. "It will be excellent fun, my lord, and I shall enjoy watching you all, unless of course you cannot skate," Bella teased him.

"I can skate, thank you, Miss Isabella. It is the cold weather that I am not overly fond of."

"He is no longer a sturdy English gentleman, Bella," Phoebe added.

"I shall take that as a compliment, thank you, Phoebe, as a sturdy English gentleman sounds as if he should have a wide girth and red nose, neither of which I have yet to cultivate," Will stated. "Perhaps with the support of two healthy English gentleman you can skate a few times around the ice also, Isabella?"

"I hardly think that…"

"I would like to try, my lord," Isabella rushed to add, thereby cutting Livvy off. How dare Will raise her little sister's hopes like that?

"Her leg is painful, my lord, and she cannot support her weight for long periods of time," Livvy said in clipped tones.

"And yet she walked into the village today," he said calmly, still looking at Bella. "Therefore, a few laps on the ice, supported by myself and Luke, should not pose too much of a problem, should it Isabella?"

Livvy watched her sister smile at the prospect of skating. Could Bella skate if only for a little while? Perhaps, only time would tell, but she would not allow this man to raise her hopes too high. Bella had had more than enough disappointment in her life. This would not be another one.

"It needs to snow enough first," Livvy added, thereby putting an end to the conversation. She felt Will's eyes on her briefly before he winked at Bella.

"Did you acquire a new hat, Freddy?" he then questioned his man of affairs.

"Yes, my lord, and gloves."

"I hope you didn't invest in a pair in an unmanly color."

"A nice pale gray, my lord." Freddy lifted his gloves for the occupants of the carriage to inspect.

Livvy nodded her approval and thought she may have smiled, but in truth she didn't know. Will's close proximity was scrambling her thoughts. Desperately seeking a distraction, she looked out the window.

The weather had turned as Mr. Blake had predicted; in fact, the air felt still and cold and Livvy realized that Will was correct. Snow would follow soon.

"Well, I think it is a very manly color, Mr. Blake, and matches your lovely eyes very well indeed," Phoebe said.

Studying the darkening landscape as they traveled through the village, Livvy listened as Phoebe flattered Mr. Blake with ease as she did every man. There had been a time when she had been able to converse like that. Now, all she seemed to do was argue or censure people. In fact, Livvy was fairly certain that she was turning into a brittle-tongued harridan.

"Don't flatter him too much, Phoebe. He already has a sizable ego," Will drawled.

Livvy tried to move closer to the window just to gain even an inch of space between them, but as she moved he merely shifted his legs and trapped her skirts. Trying to be circumspect, she gave them a small tug but still she could not move.

"I seem to have my skirts trapped beneath your leg, Lord Ryder," Livvy whispered when all her attempts failed. Luckily, Mr. Blake and her sisters were having a loud discussion over the colors men now wore and didn't hear her.

"So you have."

Livvy's mouth dropped open as Will leaned closer to her with these words, thereby making any movement on her part impossible. Livvy only managed to draw a shaky breath when he once again sat up straight.

"I will state here and now that I will never be seen alive in yellow clothing or pink for that matter... possibly pale blue also," Will said.

"I don't know," Livvy said, giving her skirts another surreptitious tug which yielded her precisely nothing. "I think some men are born to wear yellow and pink." Tilting her head to one side, she then added. "I believe you could be one of those men, my lord."

"Ho! Met your match there, my lord," Freddy roared.

The rogue didn't say anything further. He just smiled and leaned closer, ignoring her little squeak of outrage as her skirts pulled tight across her thighs. Thankfully, Willow Hall came into sight minutes later; soon she would be away from his disturbing presence.

"Jenny!" Isabella waved to the woman walking out the front door as the carriage stopped. "We have eaten cinnamon and plum buns," she added as Luke helped her down.

"If you will move, my lord, I can follow my sisters," Livvy said as she attempted to rise after the others had left. He, however, did not move. Instead, his fingers cupped her chin, forcing her to look at him.

"Before I do, let me just say that I hope we can be friends, Olivia. Because being away from home for five years taught me one very valuable lesson."

"Wh—what was that," she whispered. He held her gaze intently for several seconds before he spoke.

"There are plenty who will say they are your friend but only a few who actually mean it."

"Were there many?"

"Many what?" He released her chin to pick up her hand.

"Who claimed to be your friend?"

Placing his lips on her palm, he held them there until Livvy could feel the imprint of his mouth on her skin. Only then did he look at her.

"Too many to count, Olivia." He smiled gently and Livvy felt herself returning the gesture. Releasing her hand, he moved to the door.

"Goodbye, Olivia, and I will state once more that if you ever need anything, I hope you will come to me," he said after helping her from the carriage.

Livvy opened her mouth to refuse, but before she could utter a word he had the door shut. Taking a step back, she watched as the carriage rolled away.

CHAPTER SEVEN

"Phoebe," Livvy said as she followed her sisters through the front door.

"Yes?"

"I… I think we must ride out tonight." Livvy felt her stomach sink at the thought of robbing another carriage. "My shoulder is healed and we must do it before the snow sets in." Pulling off her gloves, she began to rub her tingling palm. She could still feel the heat from Will's mouth.

"If you're sure that your shoulder is up to it."

"My shoulder is fine."

Phoebe snorted but said nothing further.

"Settle yourself in the parlor and I shall bring something to warm you," Jenny called from down the hall.

"The guilt is the hardest part, don't you think, Phoebe? Knowing we are taking from others and causing them distress?"

"I know, I feel the same. But it must be done, and perhaps after tonight we may have enough for Bella's treatment."

"I cannot think beyond what we must do now or the panic engulfs me," Livvy whispered. "What of next year or the year after? Will we have to do this again…?"

"Enough," Phoebe said, taking Livvy's hand. "You're the strong one, remember? I'm the one who gets scared."

Squeezing the hand, Livvy nodded. "Yes, you're right, and there is no going back now as we have already broken the law once.

They followed Isabella through the cold house and climbed the staircase where they entered the second door on the right into the small parlor that was for their use alone. They had furnished the room with things that were both comfortable and comforting. The four chairs were old but well-loved and the table before the fire had scratches and chips but the sisters knew who had made each mark.

"Pull the curtains, Phoebe, and the room will soon be warm."

Livvy willed herself to relax. Being trapped in the carriage with Will had made her feel fluttery inside.

"I wish I could go to the Assembly with you and Phoebe tomorrow night, Livvy." Bella perched on the arm of the chair Phoebe had fallen into. "I want to wear one of your creations, Phoebe."

"You do every time we leave the house and when you go to visit Thea," Phoebe reminded her sister.

Bella made a small noise, indicating this was not what she meant, which her elder sisters ignored.

"Just because I cannot dance does not mean I do not want to go and watch and have scintillating conversations with people."

Livvy laughed. "I've had more scintillating conversations with Boris than I get at an Assembly. And the answer is no," she added, unmoved by the look on her younger sisters face.

"I second that, Bella, so don't think I'll support you," Phoebe added.

Livvy held her hands out to the fire hoping that the heat would remove the sensation of Will's lips.

"Here's the tea," Jenny said, bustling into the room.

Jenny Bell was more than a housekeeper. She was a friend and a sympathetic ear when any of the Langley sisters needed one. Livvy watched as she placed the tea tray on the small table before the fire.

"Sit, Jenny," Livvy instructed and the housekeeper folded herself into one of the worn chairs. Bright-eyed with boundless energy, Jenny had been with the Langleys for as long as Livvy could remember, but it was after the deaths of Lord and Lady Langley that their relationship had progressed into friendship.

The room was quiet for several minutes as they tucked into thick slices of bread and jam and tea.

"I think one of you should marry Lord Ryder and then we would no longer have any worries."

Livvy, who had just taken a mouthful of tea, proceeded to spit it all over the skirts of her dress. "Bella!" she spluttered.

"Surely the idea is not that repugnant," Jenny said, getting out of her chair to mop it up with her apron. "He's a handsome man, after all, and once you cared for him a great deal."

"I… I…" Livvy couldn't find the words to refute that claim as she swatted at her damp skirts.

"I suppose I could marry him as he would be as accommodating as the next man and far more handsome," Phoebe mused as she chewed delicately on a corner of toast. "Although I feel no attraction for him, nor he for me."

Breathe, Livvy. Her lungs had seized at the thought of Phoebe and Will together, which was foolish because she had no claim upon him nor did she wish to… not at all.

Bella flopped onto the rug beside her. Livvy knew that innocent look. It usually meant she was going to say something that would be better left unsaid.

"It will have to be Livvy then."

Absolutely not!

Taking an even bigger gulp of tea, Livvy winced as it burned its way down her throat. Fighting the need to cough again, she made several loud, throat-clearing noises instead.

"I rather think Lord Ryder will take exception to you picking his bride for him, Bella. Furthermore, like Phoebe has already stated, if there is no attraction it would make for an unhappy match." Livvy felt quite proud of the fact that she managed to keep her voice even and her words calm.

"Actually, Livvy, what I said was that he and I weren't attracted to each other. You, however, are another matter entirely."

Livvy's foolish heart raced at Phoebe's words, which was ridiculous. Will was not attracted to her; he was a flirt and a cad and she would never again fall for such a man.

"Lord Ryder is not attracted to me, Phoebe. He is a man used to female adoration and is constantly seeking it from the nearest available source."

There was silence in the small room after these words. Bella was slurping her tea and Livvy was too tense to reprimand her. Jenny and Phoebe were looking at Livvy.

"What?"

"You're blushing," Phoebe said.

"I am not!"

"No, you are, Livvy," Bella said, pressing one hand to her sister's hot cheek.

"I will change our diet to gruel if you don't stop tormenting me," Livvy said, pushing the hand aside and fighting the urge to cover her face.

"Jenny doesn't know how to make gruel." Bella looked smug.

"I'm sure she can manage boiled cabbage," Livvy said darkly.

"Well, if Lord Ryder comes around here courting, I hope that Mr. Blake keeps his distance," Jenny said, sensing that a change of subject was required.

"Mr. Blake is a lovely man, Jenny!" Phoebe declared, dragging her eyes from Livvy's flushed face.

The housekeeper had regained her feet and was bustling about, gathering up the tea tray which the Langley sisters had not yet finished with.

"Far too forward, he was, and far too charming. Told me my eyes sparkled like a new penny and my smile would light up the darkest of days."

"Surely those are lovely compliments, Jenny, and nothing for you to scowl over," Bella said, noting the housekeeper's fierce expression.

"I don't have time for such foolishness, and a man of his age should know better than to behave in such a manner." With these words Jenny left the room, much to surprise of the three women she had left behind.

"I hadn't finished my toast," Phoebe said, frowning at the now closed door

"Nor I my tea," Bella added.

"I am sure neither of you will expire from lack of nourishment," Livvy said, making for the door as well. "We shall leave after our evening meal, Phoebe. Please be ready."

Bella and Livvy looked at each other and then at the door.

"Me thinks they protest too much, Phoebe," Bella giggled.

"Do you know, little sister, I believe you could be right."

***

Livvy lifted the collar of her father's old black overcoat so the blast of cold air did not traverse her spine.

"It's freezing!" Phoebe hissed, rubbing her gloved hands together. "Hopefully, Jenny will have some tea ready for us when we get home."

They had been waiting silently for a carriage to appear on

the road for at least an hour now, and the temperature had dropped, making it much colder than the night they had robbed Will.

Tea!" Livvy rasped. "I'm a bloody highwayman, woman! Give me gut-rotting gin distilled in some bawdy house in a seedy part of London."

Phoebe look startled as her sister spoke.

"What?" Livvy questioned.

"Firstly, how do you know about gut-rotting gin and bawdy houses? And secondly, I forget sometimes you have a wicked sense of humor. It has been lost of late under the weight of responsibility you shoulder, and I'm sorry for it."

"I've overheard men talking about seedy things like gin and bawdy houses," Livvy said, her words muffled behind the scarf.

"And you never told me? Shame on you, sister."

Livvy snuffled and wiped her nose on her sleeve in a very unladylike gesture. "I'm also sorry that I seem to have lost my sense of humor, Phoebe, and promise to show more levity in the future."

"See that you do." Phoebe gathered up her horse's reins as the sound of carriage wheels carried to them on the stiff breeze.

"Let's do what we came here for," Livvy said, taking a deep, bracing breath as she tried to settle her nerves.

"Pistol at the ready."

Livvy did as Phoebe ordered and then, touching her heels to Boris's flanks, she urged him out from under the cover of the trees at a gallop. Pulling alongside the slow-moving carriage, Livvy pointed her pistol at the driver.

"Halt at once!"

He hauled on the reins and the carriage shuddered to a stop.

Phoebe then trained her pistol on the driver while Livvy pointed hers at the carriage door.

"Those inside the carriage, step outside at once!" she said, using the coarse voice she had perfected after weeks of training with Phoebe.

Livvy heard a squeal of terror and felt the heavy weight of guilt that she was causing someone torment. Then a deep voice issued a terse command and seconds later the door opened and a man and a woman stepped down.

"I will have you shot for this. How dare you rob me?"

As if she had thrown off her cloak, Livvy felt the burden of guilt lift as she looked at the couple before her. She may not like doing this, but she would make an exception for these two people.

"I am Major Bruntly and am a man of great influence and power in this area!"

"I don't care if you're the King of bleedin' England, hand over all your money, which there should be plenty of if you're as important as you say," Livvy drawled. Beside her, Phoebe snorted in amusement.

"I will not!"

Pompous twit, Livvy thought. She had always loathed the man as had her mother and father.

"I'll give you a five-count, Podgy, and if you ain't done as I asked, I'll blow a hole in your carriage," Livvy said.

"Podgy!"

Livvy coughed to dislodge the bubble of laughter as Major Bruntly raged at her. She was a very bad person for getting so much enjoyment out of this, even if the Major was the most disliked man in the village of Twoaks. If only it was daylight and she could see his furious features clearly.

"A rotund middle suggests too much fine living."

"Rotund!"

Livvy winced as he roared. Major Bruntly prided himself on his appearance and took great pains to keep himself in excellent shape. Mrs. Cally, who was once a servant for the Major, said he wore a corset to ensure his trim physique.

"How dare you speak to my husband that way!"

Lady Bruntly was not Livvy's favorite person, either. Like her husband, she believed herself superior to everyone else and was often the deliverer of a caustic, spiteful comment. She had once told Bella that she was the lame ugly duckling of the Langley family and no one upset the littlest Langley and got away with it.

"Don't speak or I'll take your jewels as well!"

Livvy heard the snap of Lady Bruntly's teeth as she shut her mouth quickly.

"I'll have you swinging from a rope by the end of the week!"

"As amusing as this conversation is, Podgy, hand over your money now or I'll shoot you," Livvy stated calmly.

"We are the two most important people in this area!" The Major roared.

"I know a bit about this area meself," Livvy said. "Making it my business to fleece only the wealthy, you understand. And, unless you're a Duke or an Earl, I don't reckon you're all that important."

Both the major and his wife spluttered.

"Now hand me the money or I'll shoot you, and as the target is vast I won't miss." Her words had the desired effect and Major Bruntly pulled out a large pouch from inside his jacket pocket. Livvy heard the satisfying clink of coins as he clenched it in a fist.

"Throw it."

Livvy caught it and tucked into her jacket pocket.

"Now you, driver, get down from the seat," she added, remembering what happened last time and having no wish for either she or Phoebe to be shot or stabbed in the back.

"Oh, Bertie, what is he going to do with our driver?" Lady Bruntly cried.

"Start walking and don't stop," Livvy directed the driver. "That way," she added, looking in the direction the carriage had just come from.

"You would not be so cruel as to leave us stranded!"

"Get in your carriage," Livvy ordered the couple and then watched as Major and Lady Bruntly climbed inside and closed the door behind them. Signaling to Phoebe, she then turned Boris and galloped back into the trees behind them.

***

"I hate these affairs."

"I love them," Phoebe said as they gingerly made their way down the icy path to the Twoaks Assembly rooms the following evening. "It's not so bad, Livvy. After all, we have known most of these people for years and some since childhood. We get to dance and flirt and then there is the food and drink. Plus, let us not forget the fact that they will have all seen us arrive in style with Lord and Lady Erdington."

"Yes." Olivia looked over her shoulder at the elderly couple behind them. "I'm not sure how you managed that, but excellent work. I'm pleased we did not have to go to the expense of hiring a carriage."

"I sent a note around to Lady Erdington this morning, telling her our carriage was off the road and would it be too much of an imposition for them to pick us up."

Clapping her hands over her ears, Livvy said. "Tell me no more. I have no wish to know that you lied to that lovely old lady."

"I did not lie; our carriage *is* off the road. I merely omitted the fact that it will never again be on the road due to four broken wheels and the mice currently nesting in the upholstery.

Rolling her eyes, Livvy stepped over a patch of ice. It had snowed as Will had predicted, and as reluctant as she was to attend this evening's Assembly in the village, she knew that doing so was important for Phoebe. Especially if some gentleman caught her eye—a wealthy gentleman, who might love Phoebe in spite of the fact she had no dowry.

"Perhaps I'll walk through the door and fall in love and then we won't have to find the money for a season."

Guilt sliced through Livvy as her sister's words mirrored her thoughts. Grabbing Phoebe's hand, she squeezed it.

"Phoebe, you must promise me not to rush this. If you do not find a husband this season then we will get the money for another one the following year. It would destroy me to see you unhappy."

"Relax, sister. I will find someone who I can tolerate and if he is very wealthy, I will not be displeased."

There was no time to say anything further as they were now walking through the entranceway of the old stone building. Handing over their cloaks, they then followed the other guests along the hallway toward the hum of voices and music.

"I hope Lord Ryder is here. That will stir things up nicely," Phoebe said as she straightened the seams of her long evening gloves.

I don't.

Livvy had thought about him constantly. Helping Jenny knead dough, she had thought about the blissful expression on his face while eating the cinnamon bun. Brushing Isabella's hair, she remembered the dark hair at his nape curling over the brim of his hat, and when she had lain awake, unable to sleep, she had imagined his thigh pressed to hers and the touch of his lips on her mouth.

"The women will all preen and push out their breasts while making silly simpering noises; and the men will huff and try to impress him and some will remember the atrociously-behaved young man he was before."

"I'm not sure you should say the word 'breasts' in polite company, Phoebe," Livvy said, checking behind them to see if anyone was near.

"Heaving bosoms?"

Livvy giggled. "Now who's been reading Bella's books?"

"One thing is for sure. Lord Ryder will stir things up this evening, Livvy, that I can guarantee."

Livvy had come to the realization, while she lay wide awake in the early hours of the morning, that she needed to try to act as if they were acquaintances just as she had told him they were. Be polite and emotionless, surely then he would leave her alone.

"You look lovely by the way."

"Thank you, Phoebe, so do you," Livvy said, meaning every word.

They had spent ages getting ready, with both Jenny and Isabella fussing around them. Phoebe's dress was in pale blonde silk with darker satin stripes. A ruffle of matching lace stood around the bodice and above that seemed to be vast amounts of her chest. Her hair was pinned high with several long curls trailing down her spine. She looked like a goddess and would surely put several women in a very bad mood and several men in a very good one. Livvy was dressed in rose satin with matching, small darker silk roses decorating the hem. It was a lovely dress, although looking down at her chest, she too, seemed to be exposed.

"Stop scowling Livvy. You will have a permanent frown line soon!"

"I'm just wondering why we need to show so much… ah…"

"Heaving bosom?" Phoebe suggested.

"Quite."

"I'm rather proud of mine," Phoebe said, looking down. "As you should be of yours."

"Phoebe!" Livvy said as they stepped through the door.

"That is enough on that topic, thank you."

"Miss Phoebe, how wonderful of you to grace us with your presence."

Olivia watched as three men moved to intercept Phoebe as soon as they entered the room.

"The room has just grown brighter with your arrival."

"My sister is also here, Mr. Robertson," Phoebe chided, looking at Livvy, who forced a smile onto her face.

"Forgive me, Miss Langley. I could see nothing past your sister's beauty… of course that doesn't mean that I don't think—"

"Think nothing of it, Mr. Robertson, it happens all the time," Livvy said, feeling sorry for the young fool as he proceeded to force his foot deeper into his mouth. Livvy hoped her sister never settled for someone so young and silly.

"I am going to dance, Livvy."

Nodding, Livvy then moved to find a comfortable place to watch the dancers. The hall was long and wide and allowed people to dance down the middle. Chairs and tables were set aside in several alcoves and servants bustled around providing refreshments. There was plenty of noise as everyone spoke loudly over the top of each other to be heard above the music.

"Got a nice rub for young Miss Isabella's leg, Miss Olivia."

"I shall call on you tomorrow, Mrs. Melnock," Livvy said to the elderly lady hunched in a chair. She was the town healer and had been for many years. This would be the fifth potion she had concocted for Bella, but Livvy would get it if only to please the old woman.

She nodded and smiled when required, as she knew most of the people present. The problem for Livvy was that she was no longer the carefree woman she had once been, the woman who had longed for just such an occasion to flirt and chat as her sister was. For her, these nights were a form of torture. The fear of someone questioning her over her family's circumstances or asking when she would go to London for the season always loomed. Livvy had believed that someone would see right through the Langley façade if they just took the time to look close enough. However, no one had and for that she was grateful.

Finding a chair behind a gathering of women and beside two others deep in conversation, Livvy knew it looked like she was part of one or other of the groups, which was her intention. Tapping her foot to the lively music, she watched Phoebe move around the floor. Of course, there were plenty of people she could talk to, yet she was more than happy with her own company this evening.

"Miss Langley, I was telling Lady Bruntly about your foolish intention to ride in the Derby again this year!"

Livvy swallowed her smile, as she remembered last night's robbery, before standing to face the Major and his wife.

"Major Bruntly, Lady Bruntly." Livvy sank into a curtsy.

"Well, girl, is it true that you are to break with tradition once more? A tradition, I hasten to add, that has been in place for over fifty years."

"I fear you have forgotten that Miss Bottsworth rode in the Derby, Major, for five years," Livvy said.

On the latter side of fifty, the major still had a full head of dark hair and a body that did not show any signs of turning to the fat she had accused him of last night. Phoebe called him Major Braggart as he spent his days telling people how wonderful he was.

"That was many years ago and she was a brutish female with little to recommend herself," he said, dismissing Miss Bottsworth's feats with the flick of a wrist.

"I am appreciative of the compliment you just paid me, Major, and am happy not to be termed 'brutish.' However, I will be once again riding in the Derby this year.

"I offered you no compliment!"

Livvy went for a look of surprise. "Oh dear, silly me, I had thought your words suggested you found me lacking in brutish qualities and that, in fact, I have plenty of commendable ones."

Color washed into his face as she continued to needle him.

"A woman of commendable qualities would not be riding astride in a horse race!"

Livvy withstood his glare and even managed to keep a smile on her face as the Major roared at her.

"Disgraceful conduct for a lady," Lady Bruntly said, sniffing into her French lace handkerchief.

"Absolutely disgraceful," Major Bruntly agreed. "Your father would be displeased with you, young lady, as would your grandfather, God rest their souls. At least they are not here to see the disgrace you have brought to the Langley name."

Looking around her, Livvy realized no one appeared to be coming to her aid; in fact, most had moved a safe distance away. Major Bruntly was a wealthy landowner and no one liked to cross him. *Patience, Livvy*, she counseled herself; he is a fool whose opinion you care nothing for.

"Your father should have done a better job of educating you on a woman's place in the world," Major Bruntly added as he warmed to the task of censuring her. "Were you my daughter, I would have kept a firm hand on the reins and never given you your head."

For the most part Livvy was fairly good at holding her temper in check, but sometimes someone touched something inside her that was still raw, and unfortunately for Major Bruntly, her father was one of those somethings that made her unreasonable. Suddenly, all the noise around her faded, she was no longer aware of the people laughing and chatting; instead, she was consumed by anger that this man had dared to use her father's name to strengthen his argument, the man she and her sisters had worshipped from the day they were old enough to understand just how wonderful he was.

"My father and grandfather would be very proud that I have stood up for what I believe in, Major," Livvy said slowly as she tried to rein in her temper. "And I would be grateful if you did not insult me or them by suggesting they would believe otherwise. Furthermore, I will in future ensure to take a small measure of time each day to thank the Lord that I was not born with you as my father."

Perhaps the last she could have kept to herself, Olivia realized, as both the Bruntlys looked like they were about to have a seizure.

"How dare you speak to me in such an insolent manner, Olivia Langley! As you are without the firm hand of a man, it is my Christian duty to guide you in your sire's absence."

"I have neither asked nor wanted your hand, firm or otherwise, anywhere near myself or my sisters, Major, and I would pray that you remember that in the future."

CHAPTER EIGHT

Will arrived at the Assembly with Joseph and Penny. They were greeted effusively by Squire Patrick, the man who was responsible for most of the entertainment in Twoaks.

"Lord Ryder," he boomed from the depths of his barreled chest. "'Tis glad we are to have you back home."

"Thank you, Squire Patrick, as you can imagine I, too, am pleased to have returned to my family."

"Like you to meet my daughter, my lord. Blossomed into a taking thing, as you'll see."

Beside Will, Joseph snorted softly as the squire took his daughter's arm and urged her forward.

"And so it begins, brother."

Shooting Joseph a foul look, Will bowed to the short, plump girl now standing before him. Perhaps in a few years she would be termed homely, but at the moment even that tag would be flattering. She resembled her raw-boned father in every way, with brown hair pulled back in a severe knot on top of her head, which only served to enhance her round face. Her dress was yellow velvet which did little for her pale complexion or dumpy figure.

"Lord Ryder, how pleased I am to meet you."

"The pleasure is all mine, Miss Patrick."

Over her shoulder he saw Phoebe dance past, flicking him a quick wave which he acknowledged with a nod. He wanted to tell Miss Patrick to keep as far away from Phoebe Langley as possible. The comparisons would do the woman no favors, he thought, eyeing the stunning figure clad in pale, striped satin.

"I have a space free on my dance card, Lord Ryder," Miss Patrick said, fluttering her lashes at him.

"I should be honored if you will place my name on it, Miss Patrick."

Giggling she did just that, and then he offered her another bow and set off after his brother who had wandered away.

"You cannot spend the entire evening scowling, brother. You had to know that there is a shortage of eligible men in the area, and as your pedigree would suggest, you will be the most sought after," Joseph said as he reached his side.

"I'm not a stallion, Joe." Will scowled at him. "I'd forgotten that although the women are to appear meek and mild, they are in fact anything but."

"I shall try not to let it slip that your wealth outstrips mine or you will be besieged."

"I'll thrash you if you do," Will hissed as two young ladies walked past giggling and sending him flirtatious glances.

"You forget, Will, we are reared and tutored to find a suitable match nearly from the cradle." Penny slipped her arm through his as she spoke. "Most will end with men old enough to be their fathers with only a select few finding love or even a comfortable match.

Will patted her hand. He had never given much thought to the plight of young, unwed women.

"It was merely a stroke of luck that I found someone I could tolerate," she added, which made her husband roll his eyes.

"She threw herself at me, of course," the Duke drawled. "Relentless in pursuit. No one else but I would do."

Blinded by animosity towards his brother, Will had never taken the time to notice the love Joseph and Penny felt for each other. The looks they shared, the tiny, knowing smiles. He was glad that in his absence Joe had had this woman at his side.

"And now I wish to dance," Penny said, removing her hand from Will's arm and placing it on her husband's.

"If I must," the Duke said, smiling down at his wife. "Try to stay out of trouble brother," Joe added with a wink before leading his Duchess onto the floor.

Shaking his head, Will was amazed that in the space of a few days the relationship he now had with his brother was stronger and more comfortable than it had ever been.

Nodding to a man who seemed vaguely familiar, Will began to make his way to where he hoped the food was. It was usually the only thing worth investigating at these events. He wondered where Olivia was. Phoebe was still dancing, but he had yet to see the elder Langley sister.

"My lord, let me introduce you to my daughters."

It took twenty minutes to extract himself from the elderly lady whose name was double barreled and had sounded like a small village in Yorkshire. She had told him that her three daughters, all of whom were delighted to make his acquaintance, had talked of nothing else but meeting him since they had arrived at the Assembly. The blonde daughters had simpered and fluttered their eyelashes at him until he was ready to place his hands around their necks and squeeze. How the hell had he stomached this before leaving England, and enjoyed it?

Standing on his toes, he looked over the people towards the back of the room in the hopes of seeing a table groaning with delicious and tempting treats, and it was then he saw Olivia. Her back was to him, yet he knew it was her because suddenly he was happy to be here, when seconds before he would rather have faced a firing squad.

Dressed in pale rose, her gown caressed and clung to her lovely figure and her red-gold curls were piled high, exposing the vulnerable curve of her neck. But what drew his eye, and held it, were the gloved hands fisted at her sides. He made his way quickly through the people and as he drew closer he heard a few words and realized that she was under attack from the Major and his wife.

"Lord Ryder!" Lady Bruntly trilled, and her scowl was immediately replaced by a smile. "How wonderful of you to join our little gathering."

Bowing to Lady Bruntly and her husband, Will then placed his hand beneath Olivia's elbow. She was rigid, every muscle clenched so tight he was left in no doubt that she was in the grip of strong emotions. He wasn't sure yet if it was anger or fear.

"Thank you, Lady Bruntly. As you can imagine, I am very happy to be home with my family."

"Sorry state our village has come to, Lord Ryder, since your departure," the major stated loudly as he offered Will the barest of bows, his eyes still firmly fixed and glaring on Olivia. "I was robbed just miles from home last night and Miss Langley here…"

"By two highwaymen?"

Major Bruntly frowned at his interruption but answered the question.

"Yes, two highwaymen who robbed us of all our jewels and money and then bound us hand and foot while our driver was shot."

"Doesn't sound like the two who robbed me. In fact, I'm sure that one of them was a woman," Will mused.

"Don't be ridiculous, Lord Ryder. No woman could hold up a carriage or outmaneuver a man," the major stated loudly, making sure everyone around them heard.

Will had neither liked nor disliked the major; in fact, before today he had not given the man a thought. But he now had all of Will's attention.

"My statement was based on my beliefs, Major, ridiculous or not," Will spoke the words softly. For years, he had controlled sailors and disreputable men who would slit a throat for a few coins, and he had realized that to control them he had to gain their respect. Yelling or using his fists had not worked every time; therefore, he had learned to get what he wanted through talking.

The major, however, failed to heed the warning in Will's tone and simply changed tact by re-launching his attack on Olivia. Not a very smart move to Will's way of thinking. Flushed with self-importance and the fact that he had the Duke's younger brother as his audience, the major glared at Olivia, who glared right back. She had a backbone, did little Miss Langley, but she would not beat a bully like Bruntly alone.

"She dares to compete in the Derby, Lord Ryder. A woman!" Major Bruntly spat the last word out, as if she were a species of rodent. "She has brought disgrace on her family and the village."

Will felt a swift flood of rage and beside him Olivia fared little better. He felt her brace herself as she prepared to launch a verbal attack on the major. Squeezing her elbow, Will was surprised when she obeyed his silent command and remained quiet.

Looking steadily at the older man for several seconds, Will made sure he had the major's complete attention before he spoke.

"I take exception to your insulting words, Major. The Langley family are respected members of this village and friends to the Duke and I." Will watched the man's mouth drop open as he spoke. "She has as much right as any of us to ride in the Derby. If she wishes to do so then it will be with the full support of my family and I will not tolerate your slurs on her character."

"Now, listen here..."

Cutting him off, Will finished what needed to be said.

"If I hear one whisper about this matter in the future, you will have me to answer to. I hope you understand me, Major Bruntly. I do not tolerate men who threaten women, especially not a woman whom I count as my friend."

Steering Olivia around the Bruntlys, who were now gasping like landed fish, Will urged her onto the dance floor. Placing her in the line, he then stood opposite. He saw she was stunned into silence and thought that was possibly a good thing; however, he was not foolish enough to believe this condition would last much longer.

She didn't know what to say or how to thank him, yet thank him she must, Livvy realized, looking to where Will stood across from her. He had just defended her to Major Bruntly and Livvy had not had anyone stand up for her in years. Lord, it should not feel so good. He smiled at her and then turned to chat with Squire Patrick on his left, as if he had not just torn strips of Major Bruntly's tough hide.

"What were you and the Braggerlys' talking about and why did Lord Ryder appear so suddenly at your side?"

These words were hissed at Livvy as the dance began by Phoebe, who took her hand to form a circle.

"The major was expressing his opinion on my participation in the Derby," Livvy said quickly before they parted. Mr. Oglivy, Phoebe's partner, then appeared beside her.

"I wonder, Miss Langley, if you could persuade your sister to allow me to be the one to procure her some refreshment after this dance."

"I don't think... oh dear, are you all right Mr. Ogilvy?" Livvy bit her bottom lip as the man tripped over his feet and landed at hers. Bending, she was just about to help him rise when two large hands beat her to it.

"Up you get, Ogilvy. We must ask someone to look at that loose floorboard," Will said as he brushed the dust from the other man's jacket and tweaked his now hopelessly ruffled neck tie before nudging him back into place with the other dancers.

"Th—thank you, Lord Ryder. Yes, it would be terrible if a lady were to trip." Mr. Ogilvy's cheeks resembled rosy apples.

Noting the wicked look in Will's eyes, Livvy quickly dropped her own to the floor before she laughed. Handsome in his navy blue coat and buff breeches, the other men seemed pale and insipid beside him and yet his dress was not dissimilar to theirs. It was his presence, the vitality of the man that seemed to eclipse all the others around him. As he turned once again to face her, she noted a flash of emerald. His waistcoat was striped with blue and emerald and should have made him look like a preening peacock yet the effect was quite the opposite.

"You're frowning, Olivia."

"I fear it is instinctive, Lord Ryder," Phoebe said loudly before once again turning away.

Laughing, he took Livvy's hand as they navigated a turn.

"I'm sorry you were subjected to that fool."

"Tis not your fault, my lord. I am used to Major Bruntly's ways. Please do not give it another thought."

"She always frowns," Phoebe interrupted, crossing in front of them.

Livvy rolled her eyes as her sister and partner swept by, Phoebe in a series of elegant movements, her partner stumbling over the steps.

"And why do you think that is, Phoebe?"

As if Livvy wasn't within hearing distance, Will and Phoebe proceeded to discuss her.

"She tends to worry, my lord. Grabs hold of a problem and

gnaws on it. In my opinion, she needs to have more fun."

"Shut up, Phoebe!"

"Fun you say?" Lord Ryder murmured, and then to Livvy's relief the dance pulled him away.

"If you say one more word, sister, your room will be let and I will have your bed set up in the stables!" Livvy whispered as Phoebe took her hand again.

"Boris and Harvey would be extremely put out, Livvy. You know how they like to sleep late." Phoebe gave her a cheeky grin.

"Who and what are Boris and Harvey?"

"Horses, Lord Ryder," Phoebe said.

"As to my earlier request, Miss Langley," Mr. Ogilvy said, appearing at her side once again. This time he managed to remain upright. "Do you think you could ask Miss Phoebe if she will let me procure her some refreshment?"

She couldn't help it. Mr. Ogilvy's request tipped her over the edge and suddenly Livvy was giggling. It was all so ridiculous. They were dancing, for pity's sake, surrounded by people, and she was having three conversations at once and one was about the sleeping habits of her horse. Pressing a hand to her lips she tried to stop but the laughter kept coming.

"Are you hysterical?" Phoebe questioned, bending at the waist to peer into her sister's eyes, which only made Livvy worse. Waving her free hand about for no reason other than to indicate she was all right, Livvy tried to stop, yet couldn't.

"Fresh air is the only cure for hysteria," Lord Ryder declared.

With those words, Livvy found herself propelled towards the back of the room.

"Excuse me. Yes, I fear Miss Langley is not feeling quite the thing. Vapors, I think. Most distressing," Will said as they moved through the crowds to the door that led to a balcony.

"She should be fine in a few moments; you know how delicate women can be."

If Livvy wasn't giggling she would take exception to his words, but she was still overcome with laughter. She tried to nod to people as they looked at her but more laughter kept spilling from her lips. Perhaps she was hysterical after all?

"Through you go," Will said, opening the door and ushering Olivia outside. He then closed it behind them.

A blast of cold air greeted them, but she did not seem to mind. Her pretty face was alight, eyes sparkling, and small snuffling noises told him she was still seeing the funny side to something. He saw the carefree girl she had once been in the smiling woman before him.

Will watched as she walked to the railings and looked out at the night sky. She drew in several deep breaths and, to his regret, the laughter in her died.

"I can't remember the last time I did that in company. I should imagine everyone in there will think I am now a trifle queer in the attic. Still,"—she sighed—"I suppose that has its merits, at least then I could wear odd gloves and sing loudly while walking through the village."

"Not something my heart has ever desired, yet we are all cut from separate cloth, luckily," Will said, enjoying the fact that she appeared to have dropped all her barriers and was just Olivia; sweet, funny and achingly beautiful. He watched as she lifted one hand and pointed it skywards. He followed the gesture with his eyes and found a bright twinkling star.

"After my parents died I would stand outside late at night after my sisters had gone to bed and look at that star and wish."

"What did you wish for?"

Will didn't think she was going to answer him as she fell silent, and when she finally spoke he knew that her barriers were once again firmly in place.

"The usual things a lady asks for, my lord. The latest style of bonnet and gown."

"I used to wish to see my parents again when I looked up at the sky. Just one more time," he said. "I would have told them I loved them."

Her shoulders slumped; telling him her wishes had mirrored his own.

"I would like to say I'm sorry and thank you, Lord Ryder."

"For what?"

Will studied her delicate silhouette as she continued to look up at the sky.

"The apology is for my behavior towards you since your return to Twoaks. I have been churlish and rude and that is not acceptable and for that, I apologize."

"Why did you feel the need to be churlish and rude, Olivia?"

He moved to stand beside her, his hands next to hers on the rail, shoulders nearly touching.

"And thank you for speaking to Major Bruntly in my defense," she added, ignoring his question as he noticed she did when he asked her something uncomfortable. "Normally, I would not accept another speaking on my behalf, but the major will never listen to the word of a woman, and as I was about to become—"

"Enraged?"

"As good a word as any, my lord," she acknowledged. "That man is a fool, but not someone I wish to make an enemy of. Well, at least any more of an enemy," she amended.

"Men do not like to be challenged by women, especially not in something like the Derby."

She made a little huffing sound.

"Men have all the appearance of strength, my lord, yet the male ego is a fragile thing, I fear."

He laughed at her despondent tone.

"Cheer up, Livvy. Not all of us mind a woman dominating them."

She turned to face him then, and he was subjected to a thorough inspection while he did the same. Her cinnamon eyes seemed almost black out here and her face pale in the moonlight. He wondered if she was cold with so much of her lush bosom exposed. His hands itched to stroke the creamy flesh.

"I feel your words have a deeper meaning, my lord, yet I have no wish to delve into what that is; therefore, I shall ask you to escort me back inside."

"Wise as well as beautiful, Olivia."

She had been about to turn away yet stopped, once again looking up at him.

"There is no need for empty flattery between us, Lord Ryder. Therefore, save your compliments for the women who seek them."

Interesting, Will thought. She didn't like his compliments and he wondered why. "My words to you are never empty flattery, Olivia. I hope you will always remember that fact," Will said. Giving in to his need to touch her, he ran a finger down the line between her eyes. "You're frowning again."

She stilled as his finger touched her mouth and then traced her bottom lip.

"The book of beauty, Miss Olivia Langley, should have been written about you. The curve of your cheek and softness of your lips tempt a man to forget he is a gentleman." Her eyes fixed on him as Will lowered his head and brushed her lips with his. "The color of your hair resembles my favorite time of day and the depths of your cinnamon eyes urge a man to delve into the secrets you hide deep inside."

"Please, Lord Ryder, you must stop this."

"Never forget that you are beautiful, Olivia." Will cupped her face between his hands. "Now, tell me why you felt the need to be churlish and rude to me."

"Please don't ask me any more questions, my lord."

"Will." He lowered his head. "You once called me Will," he said against her lips.

"Will," she whispered.

"Why must I ask you no more questions, Olivia?"

She blinked, her long lashes resting briefly on her cheeks before once again looking at him.

"Because I have no wish to tell you lies."

"Is the truth so hard to speak?" Will tilted her face up as he spoke.

"Yes."

Unable to resist the lure of her lips, he kissed her. Olivia Langley had always made his head reel and even though only their mouths touched, his body was a furnace in seconds. Sliding one hand down her back, he pulled her in close and the feel of her lush curves pressed against him was sweet torture. The sensual pull tugged him deeper and Will knew that he should stop, aware that at any moment someone could walk through the door and see them. But the need inside him drove him on. She was his, always had been, and now he wanted her to know it, too.

"No!"

"Livvy." He reached for her as she wrenched from his arms.

"I must go, my lord," she whispered, staggering backwards. "Th—thank you once again, Lord Ryder, for coming to the aid of a… an acquaintance."

She bobbed a quick curtsy and Will then watched her hasten back through the doors. She was using the term acquaintance to put some distance between them, but it would not work. He wanted Olivia Langley, and she wanted him. The insipid term acquaintance had never been further from his mind.

Livvy managed to slip back inside unnoticed. Searching the room, she found Phoebe at the supper table surrounded by admirers. Joining her, she offered the group a tight smile and then squeezed into the only seat left. Chivalry, it seemed, was long dead, as not one man had bothered to move to accommodate her.

"Try these almond things, Livvy, they're rather good," Phoebe said, waving a small square of cake in her face.

"Thank you," Livvy said, taking it and nibbling on one corner. At least if she was eating she wouldn't have to converse and she could think about the fact that Will thought the curve of her cheek and softness of her lips could tempt a man to forget he is a gentleman.

"Mr. Rutledge has just been telling me he intends to write an ode to my hands, Livvy."

"Wonderful," Livvy said, wondering what game Will was playing, if any. Was he really interested in her or just sharpening his skills before going to London to attend the season. After all, he had been in India for five years, and while Livvy understood they did have civilized company, she didn't think it was quite at the standard that he would find in London.

"Apparently, my hands are like silken doves that flutter gracefully when I speak in melodious tones."

"Melodious tones… you?" Livvy looked at her sister. "You don't have a melodious bone in your body."

"Oh, I must protest to that, Miss Langley!" Mr. Rutledge declared, turning his whole body to look at her because his ridiculously high shirt points would not let him turn his neck. "Her every word sounds like the twinkling of a thousand melodious bells."

Livvy looked at the man. His eyes certainly seemed clear enough so he wasn't inebriated. Perhaps he was mad?

"A bullfrog is melodious compared to my sister," Livvy

muttered and then crammed the rest of the cake in her mouth because this conversation was ridiculous and she no longer wished to be part of it.

"I'm wounded to the depths of my soul, Mr. Rutledge, that my sister should say such unjust things about me!" Phoebe cried. Livvy, however, merely chewed her food and turned to look at the dancers and there he was.

She sighed. Well, really, who wouldn't when faced with such a man. He was as beautiful to her as he had declared she was to him. He moved with elegance that was solely his, an unconscious grace that drew the eye of every woman. He was partnering the giggling Miss Chillervy, who was doing her best to show him everything she had on offer and Livvy had to admit they looked good together.

"As pale as a dove's wings, her fingers flutter as though made of silk."

Pinching the bridge of her nose, Livvy tried to shut out Mr. Rutledge's exuberant prose. Miss Chillervy laughed, showing two perfectly-placed dimples as she twirled around Will. Livvy told herself that jealousy was beneath her and just because he had kissed her, that did not mean anything other than a mild flirtation.

"Skin like dew drops and voice as sweet as… a…"

"A babbling brook?" Livvy offered, her eyes still on Miss Chillervy.

"See, gentlemen, she does love me!" Phoebe declared.

Stealing another cake off her sister's plate, Livvy went back to her thoughts. Had Will ever promised her anything? Thinking back, she realized that he had not; in fact, before that kiss they had shared, they had been friends who had enjoyed the occasional light-hearted flirtation. The infatuation had been all on her side. She had fallen in love with him, not he with her. Everything seemed awfully clear to Livvy suddenly. She had thought the sun rose and set with Lord William Ryder and the fault for that had been hers alone.

"May I have this dance, Miss Langley?"

"Thank you, Mr. Oakley," Livvy said, brushing the crumbs from her hands as she reluctantly climbed to her feet. She would have to think some more about William Ryder, but she would leave that until she climbed into bed later.

Blowing out the candle at midnight, Livvy pulled back the covers and fell onto the mattress, exhausted. She had danced the remainder of the evening away and laughed and chatted with the people of Twoaks. Closing her eyes, her last thoughts were for Will. He had danced with her once more. They had not uttered a word between them, yet his eyes had been on her constantly and left her even more confused as to his intentions. Yawning, she pulled the blankets up to her chin. She really needed to stay away from him, yet how was that possible when everywhere she went, he seemed to be there also? She couldn't allow herself to be lured close to him again, especially considering that she was a highwaywoman and her family were living a lie, because one thing Livvy knew was that if anyone was to see through her, it would be William Ryder. Closing her eyes, she began to drift off to sleep with the memory of their kiss still lingering on her lips.

CHAPTER NINE

"I would venture out if I did not fear that I would be found frozen in an undignified position by a handsome stranger passing by," Phoebe said, scowling at the windows.

"Yes, because that happens frequently." Livvy looked up from the letter she was writing.

"Have you no romance or adventure in your sturdy soul, Olivia Langley."

"One wonders how it would be romantic, being found in an undignified position by the man of your dreams."

"It's called extending your mind." Phoebe snapped. "It's what forward-thinking people do."

"Oh, that's where I'm going wrong then," Livvy muttered. "My mind is already extended to its fullest."

Phoebe flounced out of the chair she was currently lounging in, huffing loudly. She then came to look over Bella's shoulder to see what she was reading.

"I'm forward thinking. Why, just this morning I discussed having boiled mutton or mutton pie with Jenny." Livvy was subjected to a glower from Phoebe as she finished speaking.

"The real problem is, Phoebe, that you have not been showered in compliments and badly-worded prose for days, and you are missing the adulation."

"I suspect you're right." Phoebe sighed, not the least put out that her sister had called her, in a roundabout way, shallow.

It had snowed for five days since the Twoaks Assembly when Will had told Livvy that her hair reminded him of his favorite time of the day, and she had thought of him endlessly. In fact, she was sick of him popping into her head when nothing else was occupying it.

"I would even find Mrs. Popplehinge's company stimulating at the moment," Phoebe added.

The Langley sisters had been inside for most of those five days and nights and were heartily sick of each other's company. This morning, Livvy had thrown her hairbrush at Phoebe who had come into her room with the sole purpose of irritating her, simply because she was bored.

"I have linens that need mending."

Snorting, Phoebe said something vile beneath her breath. "At least it will keep me busy, I suppose."

The sound of the front door opening had the sisters rushing out to the hall in time to see Jenny stomping inside followed by a flurry of snow and blast of cold air.

"I wish you hadn't insisted on going outside in this weather, Jenny." Livvy hurried forward to take the bag Jenny handed her.

"My boy took me up on his horse and it's only a short trip to the village."

"But now you're frozen to your toes," Bella said, coming forward to take Jenny's cloak.

"Nevermind about that. A letter has arrived for you from London."

The three sisters watched as Jenny pulled it from her bodice and handed it to Livvy.

"Now you go along into the warm and read it and I'll get the tea going."

"It must be from our cousin," Phoebe said, following Livvy

up the stairs and back in to the parlor.

Tearing it open, Livvy quickly read the words. "Dear God!" Stumbling to a chair, she fell into it seconds later.

"What is it?" Phoebe appeared before her.

Livvy handed her sister the letter. "Read it out loud so Bella can hear."

Shooting Livvy a worried glance, Phoebe lifted the missive.

"Dear Cousin," she began. "Please forgive my tardiness in replying to your request for monetary assistance and the possibility of lodging with me during the season. It is with regret that I must decline both of your requests and also inform you that your free tenure at Willow Hall will cease at the end of January as I have need of the lodgings for my own use. I shall visit with you for Christmas to discuss the little secret you are holding and check on the progress of your departure. Your devoted cousin, Lord Timothy Loftus Langley."

The sisters sat in silence for several seconds. Somewhere in the house, Jenny banged a door and the clock in the hall chimed the hour.

"What secret does he think we hold, Livvy?" Phoebe questioned.

Livvy had only two secrets of any value; the first that the Langleys were poor and taking great pains to hide it, and the second only she and a dead man shared. Surely, her cousin could not mean that one?

"I don't know," she whispered.

"What are we to do, Livvy?"

It was Bella's desperate words that finally broke through the shock of her cousin's letter. Livvy quickly stood and hugged her sisters as her mind searched frantically for the reassuring words she needed to say.

"This must be an error on his part. Surely, he does not mean to throw us out," Livvy said. "He cannot be that cruel."

"He is a horrid beast of a man to treat his cousins this way." Bella sniffed, close to tears. "How can he be the same man who attended father's funeral? He talked to me many times and told me that everything would be all right and I was not to worry."

"I loathed him," Phoebe declared. "He was a braggart and a fool and I gave him no time when he sought me out."

"None of that matters now," Livvy said. "I must go to London on the next stage and talk with him. All shall be resolved by the time I return."

"I shall accompany you."

"No, Phoebe, you must stay here with Bella. Besides, we do not want to waste money on two fares to London when I can go alone."

"No, Livvy, you can't go alone. It is too dangerous. And besides, where would you stay?"

"I shall seek lodgings in a small inn when I arrive. Don't fret. It shall be the adventure I have always wanted," Livvy said, feeling sick inside. Lord, she was going to London on her own; it was a terrifying prospect.

"No, I will not allow it, Livvy. We shall both go or not at all and I'm afraid in this I am standing firm," Phoebe declared.

"But what about Bella? She will need someone to care for her." Livvy was torn between wanting Phoebe with her and worry for her little sister.

"Jenny can care for me."

"Two women alone at Willow Hall? What if something went wrong and Jenny had to visit the village?"

"Go and find Jenny at once, Bella. Bring her here and we shall sort this out now."

"Yes, Phoebe."

Livvy took the note back and sat again as the door closed behind Bella. Reading the words, she could not fathom why he had sent them this letter. Surely, he was not so cruel that he would throw them out of their home if they had no other place to go? It was all a misunderstanding, it had to be. *Did he really know her secret?*

"I don't like our cousin, Livvy, and I don't trust this note. I never said anything when he was here, but he tried to comfort me when I was crying once and his hand grabbed my breast."

"Phoebe! Why didn't you tell me?" Livvy cried.

There was nothing sweet about Phoebe's smile.

"I made him see the error of his ways."

Livvy's laugh turned into a sob as she took her sisters hand. "Dear lord, what do you think this letter is about?"

"I don't know, but we shall face whatever it is together."

Livvy wiped her eyes as the door opened again and Bella appeared.

"Mr. Blake has arrived, Livvy, and is asking for you. He is in the kitchen."

"Now?" Livvy didn't want to speak to anyone, not when her family was in turmoil.

"Yes, now."

"Tell him we will be there shortly, Bella," Phoebe said, urging her sister from the room again.

"We must see him, Livvy. If we do not, he will wonder why and then he will tell Lord Ryder and the Duke that we refused and then they will wonder why, too."

"I know." Wiping her eyes on the sleeve of her dress, Livvy drew in a deep breath and then left the room with Phoebe on her heels.

"Mr. Blake, how lovely to see you again," Phoebe said, moving forward to greet him as the sisters entered the room. "

"And it is wonderful to see you also, Miss Langely."

"What has brought you out in this weather? Surely you should be tucked safely inside Rossetter." Livvy forced a smile onto her face, which she was sure looked as stiff as it felt.

"I have brought you a gift from Lord Ryder, Miss Langley," Mr. Blake said, bowing deeply.

"A gift, Mr. Blake?"

"Is something wrong, Miss Langley?" he said, his face now concerned as he looked at Olivia's red eyes and pale cheeks.

"These are tears of laughter, Mr. Blake, I assure you," Livvy said quickly. "We have just been telling each other funny stories, and Phoebe has been making me laugh."

"I see. Well, that is a relief." Livvy knew he did not believe her but was too polite to push for the truth.

"Firewood, Livvy. Lord Ryder has sent us a pile of chopped wood and Luke and another footman from Rossetter are stacking it for us now," Bella said. "So we will not need to cut any more for a while."

Aware that she was being studied thoroughly, Livvy kept smiling. Firewood, Will had sent her firewood, and she wanted desperately to cry and not just because her nefarious cousin may know her secret. No, because Will had sent her a gift that really meant something to her. How had he known? And then she remembered that day at the church. He had asked how she got the callous on her finger and she had told him that she received it chopping firewood.

"Please offer Luke and the other man some refreshment for their efforts when they finish, Jenny," Livvy said quickly. "Mr. Blake, will you stay and take tea with us?" She hoped he didn't take up her offer yet manners demanded she ask him.

"I would be delighted. Thank you, Miss Langley, and would offer my services to Mrs. Bell if she will let me assist her with the preparations."

"Don't need a man's help in my kitchen, Mr. Blake. Never have and don't plan on starting anytime soon."

The three Langleys stared at their housekeeper. Jenny was usually sunny natured and quick with a smile, yet she was scowling at Mr. Blake and her cheeks were flooded with color.

Well, then," Phoebe said to break the awkward silence. "If you'll come with me please, Mr. Blake, we shall find a place to have our tea."

Mr. Blake didn't look offended by Jenny's words; in fact, he gave her a gentle smile that reached his eyes and made the corners crinkle just like Livvy's father's had when he was smiling, and then followed Phoebe and Bella from the room.

Livvy stayed in the kitchen because she needed to talk about Lord Langley's letter with Jenny. Taking down some clean cups, she set them on a tray as she began to talk.

"Did Bella tell you about the letter, Jenny?"

"Yes, and you have no need to fear for Miss Bella, I will send word to my sister who is recently widowed. She can join me while you are gone."

"Thank you, that is one weight off my shoulders." Livvy gripped the edge of the bench hard. "I'm so scared, Jenny. How will we cope if we have to leave here?" Her words sounded desperate as she struggled to keep the fear inside her at bay.

"There now, my love," Jenny soothed as she pried Livvy's fingers off the wood and turned her. "T'will work out in the end," she added, pulling her into an embrace. "Between us, we will always have a home and all we need. The rest will come. You'll see," she clucked, patting Livvy's rigid back.

Livvy inhaled the scents of Jenny, this wonderful woman who had given her life to the Langley sisters. She was humbled and strengthened by the sacrifice. With a last sniff, she reluctantly eased out of the welcoming bosom.

"I can never thank you enough for all you have done for us." Her voice was choked as she struggled to hold back more tears. "But when we come about, you can be sure that I will try."

"I'll hold you to that, my love. You just see that I don't. But now we better make that horrid Mr. Blake some tea."

Livvy frowned as she watched Jenny get the hot water to pour into the teapot. It was not like her to be so critical, especially when Mr. Blake was far from horrid.

"It is true I'm not a great judge of character, Jenny, and that I have met Mr. Blake only once before today, but I must own to liking him very much and am surprised that you do not. He has a kind face and even kinder heart, as is evidenced by him coming out in this weather just to make sure we have firewood."

The housekeeper slapped the pot onto the tray and added milk and sugar.

"To be sure it was nice of him, but he didn't have to say that seeing me had brightened his day. He's a smooth-tongued rogue, is what he is."

She had nothing to smile about. In fact, Livvy would gladly lie on the floor and cry her eyes dry right here in the kitchen. Yet the notion that her housekeeper was unsettled by one Mr. Frederick Blake made her smile; of course, she hastily swallowed it as Jenny turned to look at her, but it stayed on the inside, a little warm glow that gave her hope.

"Will you take tea with us, Jenny?" Livvy said as she took the tray from the housekeeper.

"Wouldn't look right, Miss Olivia, as you very well know."

"I don't care if it looks right or wrong. I'm asking you to take tea with us," Livvy said, keeping her face expressionless.

Jenny huffed for several seconds and then said, "Well, I suppose someone needs to chaperone you girls from that man."

"To be sure, he is a scoundrel." Livvy laughed as Jenny swatted her shoulder as she left the room. They then headed for the good parlor where she knew Phoebe and Bella would have taken Mr. Blake.

"Well, the trick was to sleep in shifts on the boats so no one stole anything from you."

Livvy opened the door to Mr. Blake's words.

"Did you have things stolen, Mr. Blake?"

Bella's eyes gleamed as she questioned their visitor. She had such a passion for information about foreign countries.

"Please have my seat, Mrs. Bell." Mr. Blake leapt to his feet as Jenny entered the room. She, in turn, appeared flustered and shooed him back into it as she took over serving the tea from Livvy.

The hour that passed with Mr. Blake, Livvy knew, was only a respite from what awaited them when he left, but she could not begrudge them this time. Freddy, as he urged them all to call him, was a wonderful storyteller and genuinely nice man. He made them laugh and encouraged Bella's questions. He was clearly smitten with Jenny and even coaxed a laugh from her, and for those sixty minutes the Langleys were able to push aside their worries and enjoy the company of a man who expected nothing from them other than to listen to his stories.

"And what of Lord Ryder, Freddy? Surely he did not climb the masts as Luke did?"

"Oh, indeed he did, Miss Isabella. In fact, whatever his men did, he did too."

Livvy could imagine the man Will was today doing the things Freddy said, but not the spoiled nobleman who had left here many years ago. She did not ask the questions burning inside her; instead, sitting quietly, she listened to every word, eager for information about the man who had owned her heart. She knew Freddy skimmed over many things and told them only the stories which would make them smile and gasp, yet she was grateful for the respite from her thoughts. When the time came for him to leave, Livvy was genuinely sorry to see Mr. Blake go.

"Thank you for the tea, ladies; however, as the sky is darkening I must make the journey home."

"And we shall hope you will visit us again soon, Mr. Blake, with more of your adventures," Bella said as they escorted him to the door.

"I should be delighted," he said with a final wave and smile that was mostly for Jenny, who offered a tentative one back before she hurried back into the parlor.

"I think Mr. Blake is sweet on our Jenny," Bella whispered. "And I think Jenny likes him back but is reluctant to show it."

"However, we shall let things run their course and not interfere," Livvy added.

"Interfere, us?" Phoebe tried to look wide-eyed and innocent, a look she had never quite perfected. "I'm wounded that you believe us capable of such a deed, sister."

Livvy didn't say any more about the matter as they were once again at the parlor door and Jenny was inside. Instead, she began to discuss the preparations for their journey to London.

"We shall have to hire a carriage to take us to Damply, Phoebe. I will not been seen getting on the stage to London in Twoaks."

"My boy can do that," Jenny said as she tidied the room. "He'll be here in the morning. I'll send him to Damply to book two tickets for the stage to London leaving tomorrow afternoon and he can hire a carriage while he's there. Then he can go and collect my sister afterwards."

"Thank you, Jenny, and please thank Jaccob for us."

"For the sake of appearances, it will cost us more, Livvy," Phoebe cautioned.

"I'll hold onto my pride for as long as I can," Livvy said. "But now we must pack and prepare ourselves for the journey."

They talked over every detail, discussed emergency plans for both Livvy and Phoebe and Jenny and Bella, and only when Livvy was absolutely certain they had missed no detail did they all retire for the night.

"We're sleeping with you tonight, Livvy," Phoebe said, appearing with Bella in the doorway of her room in their nightdresses.

Livvy didn't argue. She knew the night would not bring her much sleep and was more than happy to have company. Moving over, she lifted the covers and her sisters climbed beneath. They talked for a while, keeping the conversation light until finally Bella fell asleep.

"It will be all right, Phoebe, I promise." Livvy reached over her little sister's slumbering form and gripped the hand Phoebe held out to her.

"Promise?" Livvy heard the uncertainty that Phoebe usually hid deep inside.

"With all my heart."

Their hands remained linked and resting on their little sister as they lay still in the darkness until the gray fingers of light told Livvy dawn was here. Only then did she slip quietly out of bed to prepare for the journey to London.

***

"You could always just sit inside in the warmth with us, Luke, and let one of our men drive us."

"Don't you ever stop?" Luke's frustration was obvious as he pulled himself up onto the driver's seat and turned to glare down at Will. "I'm driving you to London, so just get used to the idea. Someone needs to see you there safely in these conditions."

"And, of course, none of the other men are capable," Will drawled.

Luke simply clamped his lips together and stared at the horses before him, signaling an end to the conversation.

"Problems?"

Will turned to face Joe as he joined him beside the carriage.

"You know when we were younger and you had that pony that wouldn't let you lead him anywhere?"

"Bramble," the Duke said, looking from Will to Luke.

"Well, Luke is my Bramble, Joseph. A more stubborn creature I have yet to meet."

Behind him, Luke stayed silent but Will could almost feel him vibrating with anger.

"Give him time, Will, he'll come about," Joe said softly. "England is full of prejudices and not all of them are from titled people."

Nodding, Will looked up at the gray skies and wondered if they were in for rain or more snow. Whatever came, he knew it would be bloody cold.

"If the weather worsens, make sure you stop and stay put until it eases."

"Yes, Joe, you have said that already," Will said, preparing to climb into his carriage. "London is a two day trip on good roads. There really is no need for this hand-wringing and fretting, brother."

"Dukes neither wring hands nor do they fret and I should give you a sound beating for suggesting otherwise," the Duke muttered. "However, you left us once and returned five years later. I have no wish for an accident to befall you now."

Will sighed, the sound coming from the soles of his highly polished boots. Would the guilt he felt about abandoning his family never ease?

"I'm sorry, Joe. Sorry that I caused both you and Thea pain, but I'm back now and have no plans to leave again, in any form."

Joseph looked at the carriage and then back at Will.

It still amazed him that the brother he had left behind was such a changed man. He loved his wife and son to distraction and, surprisingly, Will seemed part of that love now, too.

"No, it is I who am sorry, Will. I just don't want to lose you again," Joseph's voice was gruff as he grabbed him and hugged him hard. Surprised at first, Will took seconds to respond, but soon he was hugging his brother back.

"All will go well, Joe, I promise. Freddy will make me stop if it snows. He's a shocking traveler at the best of times"

"'Tis true, your grace," a voice called from inside the carriage.

"Christmas is two weeks away; I shall expect your return before then." Joseph released him and stepped back.

"Yes, your grace." Will gave his brother a final nod before climbing into the carriage.

"The Duke is a good man, my lord, and cares for you deeply," Freddy said as the carriage started to move.

"Aye, I had not realized how much he mattered to me until I returned; Thea and Penny, also." Will kept his eyes on his home until it left his sight. "And let us not forget that little rascal, Billy."

"He's a bonny wee boy, that one," Freddy added, pulling the rug out from beneath the seat he was on.

"You're cold already? Surely that heated brick at your feet is offering some warmth?"

"Not near enough," Freddy huffed, tucking the rug around his legs.

"Well, spare a thought for our stubborn friend driving us."

Freddy tsked and snuggled deeper into his blanket. "That boy is a fool, but I'm sure if we keep at him he will come to his senses in time."

I hope you're right," Will said.

Freddy had informed Will yesterday that he needed to head to London to attend to some business matters and Will had decided to accompany him. He wanted to purchase a town house and have some more clothes made, plus see to several other things he had put on hold since his return.

"I accompanied Luke to drop the firewood to the Langley sisters yesterday, my lord, as you instructed."

Will looked at Freddy, sensing there was more to the story.

"I arrived at the back door and Mrs. Bell reluctantly let me in."

"Don't tell me there is a woman on this earth who is capable of withstanding your charms, Freddy?" Will laughed at the disgruntled look on the man's face.

"She's a tough one, that Jenny Bell, but there was a thawing as the afternoon progressed, I'm sure of it."

"And the Langley sisters, how did they take the gift?"

"They were pleased, although Miss Langley did say she should not be accepting gifts from you."

"I bet she did, the little baggage." Will had thought of Olivia constantly since the night of the Assembly.

"If you don't mind me asking, my lord, is there trouble in the Langley family at all?"

Freddy's face was solemn as he met Will's eyes.

"I had wondered if things were not right, but as yet have no evidence. Why do you ask?"

"When Miss Phoebe and Miss Olivia came into the kitchens to greet me, it was obvious that Miss Olivia had been crying and Miss Phoebe's smile did not reach her eyes. In fact, all the ladies, Mrs. Bell included, looked distressed."

The thought of Livvy in distress did not sit well with Will.

"I asked if anything was wrong but she brushed it aside by saying they were tears of laughter."

"And you believe they weren't?" Will questioned.

"No, and they could have been upset over something minor, yet I don't believe so because all of the woman in that house were tense and worried."

Leaning back in his seat, Will thought about what Freddy had said. Thea had told him she believed everything was not as it should be within the Langley household, and when he questioned Luke his friend told him that his mother believed they did not have a lot of money as she had heard they had been behind with payment on their bills in the village. Will didn't think Livvy would have blisters from chopping wood if she had servants to do the job, so did that mean the only servant they had was Mrs. Bell?

"Did you question Phoebe or Bella?"

"No, we talked of my travels for the remainder of my visit."

"Did you see any other servants in the Langley house while you were there, Freddy?"

"No, my lord, I did not. Only Jenny Bell."

Looking out the window as they passed through Twoaks, Will wondered if the Langleys were living a lie.

"Perhaps we will dig a little deeper upon our return from London, Freddy."

"I can manage that, my lord, as you know there is not much I cannot unearth when I set my mind to it. But now, as we have a long journey ahead of us, I shall discuss the business matters we are to attend in London."

"Discuss away." Will waved his hand around, indicating that Freddy had the floor, and for the next hour they talked about ships, investments and warehouses. While he listened and contributed, Will still thought about Livvy and what had made her cry.

"What village is this, my lord?" Freddy looked out the window as houses and shops started to appear.

"Damply, I believe." Will looked out the other window. It was gray and miserable and he was glad to be inside the carriage rather than out there.

"Good lord, I wonder what they're doing here?"

"Who?"

"Miss Phoebe and Miss Olivia."

CHAPTER TEN

Looking out Freddy's window, he saw Olivia and Phoebe standing in the cold beside several other people. As they had bags at their feet, he guessed they were waiting for the stage. Opening the hatch above his head, Will roared at Luke to stop at once. He had the carriage door open before it stopped and was out and striding across the street in seconds. She saw him coming, and her cinnamon eyes were wide and wary as he reached her.

"Hello, my lord." Phoebe gave him a nervous smile which instantly put him on alert. Nothing made Phoebe nervous.

"Phoebe, Olivia," he acknowledged, keeping his eyes on the latter.

"L—Lord Ryder, how nice to see you again. Please let me thank you for the firewood. It was wrong of you to send those men to us on such a cold day but—"

"Where are you going on the stage, Olivia?" Will cut her off.

She hadn't looked at him yet. Her eyes were on the buttons of his waistcoat.

"Where are you going on the stage?" he asked again while he fought the urge to shake her.

Seeing her standing there with only her sister to protect her, looking small and vulnerable with her coat buttoned to the neck and her bonnet tied in a neat precise bow, made him want to strike at something. It was freezing and could snow again soon. They were about to get into a coach with several other people whom neither he nor they knew. The thought of what could happen to them made him go cold all over. The carriage could have overturned or someone could have harmed the Langley sisters and he would have never known.

"On a trip, my lord."

"And where is this trip taking you, Olivia?" His words were clipped and a long way from the gentleman she had once known.

Will noticed that, for once, Phoebe was happy to keep her mouth shut and let her sister do the talking.

"To London, to see our cousin."

"Yet you never felt it necessary to mention this trip when I saw you at the Assembly, or when Freddy visited you yesterday, Olivia?"

"I… I did not think our travel plans would interest you, Lord Ryder."

She was stuttering and anxious, but Will felt no sympathy for her. He was too angry.

"You thought your travel plans would not interest me?" He questioned softly. "Especially if those plans included a trip to London, a city I believe that you have never visited?"

She looked at him then. Raising her chin several inches, she attempted to glare at him which was spoiled by the fact that she was shaking.

"And where is Bella? Don't tell me you dragged her out in these conditions, too?" Will looked around but could see no sign of the youngest Langley.

"Bella is at home, safe and warm," Phoebe said quickly. She obviously thought this would reassure him. She was wrong.

"And who is to accompany you both to London if your

sister is at home, presumably with your servants? Surely you had not intended to journey there unchaperoned?" Will knew that was exactly what Olivia had intended, but he wanted to hear the words from her.

Her fists clenched and he wondered if she intended to hit him or if it was to stop her fingers from trembling.

"I do not need a chaperone at my age, Lord Ryder, nor are our travel plans any of your business."

"Olivia," Phoebe cautioned, but her sister was past listening.

"D—do you have a full itinerary of all the traveling plans of your acquaintances, my lord? Perhaps I should just send a note every morning as to my daily activities!"

"That's enough, Olivia," Will warned.

"Yes, I believe it is enough," she said, looking over his shoulder now. "Because here c—comes our stage, so please step aside at once so we can board."

Will didn't turn as the jangle of harnesses and thunder of hooves reached his ears. "You can travel with Mr. Blake and I. We are also journeying to London."

"Thank you, but that will not be necessary," she said in a curt tone. "We have booked seats. Therefore, you need not trouble yourself any further on our behalf."

"It is no trouble," he said, picking up both hers and Phoebe's bags before they could stop him and walking back towards his carriage without waiting to see if they were following.

"Freddy, you and Luke load these bags. Olivia and Phoebe will be accompanying us to London."

"At once, my lord," they said in unison, no doubt after one look at the savage expression on his face.

"Give us our bags back!"

Handing one to Luke, he passed the other to Freddy and then turned to face the furious woman who now stood before him.

Pointing to the carriage, he said, "In you get," with remarkable calm, considering his insides were boiling.

"I certainly will not. Now give me my bag," Olivia said through clenched teeth. It seemed she was no longer anxious; now she was furious. "My sister and I cannot travel alone with two men."

"Yet you can travel alone with several men whom you do not know and lodge at some dirty carriage house for the night?" Will said, although this time his voice was louder.

"Give us our bags, Lord Ryder. I have no wish to miss the stage!"

"You can either walk into my carriage or I will throw you in there," Will stated. "It is going to rain shortly and I, for one, have no wish to be standing here when it does."

Her mouth opened and a screeching sound came out so she snapped it shut again. She then sucked in a large breath through her nose and tried again.

"We cannot travel with you to London. We have paid for our fares and lodgings for one night and we are traveling that way. Now, I must insist you give us our bags," she said, her voice several octaves louder this time.

"No," he said. "Get in the carriage, Phoebe," he added, knowing she would see reason even if her sister didn't.

"Come, Miss Phoebe, I shall help you," Freddy said, taking her arm and urging her forward.

"Why are you doing this?" Olivia hissed at him. "I am an adult and, as such, I can take care of both my sister and myself."

"You are a young woman who has never even left her village, Olivia. Now, I don't know why you're doing this but am aware that if I return you to Willow Hall you will simply take another stage; therefore, I shall escort you to London to ensure your safety."

"You didn't care about me five years ago, so why now?"

Will wasn't about to answer that question, and seeing the desperation in Olivia's eyes knew that she was past reasoning with so he took the choice away from her and simply picked her up and walked into the carriage, setting her down on the seat. Freddy quickly closed the door behind him.

"Go, Luke!" he then roared and the carriage was soon traveling out of Damply.

The journey to where they would stop for the night was probably the longest of Will's life. Freddy and Phoebe talked of everything and nothing to break the strained silence and, beside him, Olivia looked out the window, her back stiff and her gloved hands clenched tightly in her lap. Every inch of her was rigid and he could only imagine the furious thoughts that were tumbling around and around inside her head.

"Will… will we stop soon, my lord?"

"Yes, Phoebe, not long now," he said, knowing that the strain was getting to her as well. She kept looking at Olivia and then back to him and her eyes were clouded with worry.

"It will be all right," he mouthed. She nodded once but said nothing further.

Finally, as the sky began to darken and the snow fell, they pulled into the inn they were scheduled to stop at.

"Freddy, take Phoebe inside and organize rooms for her and her sister. Olivia and I will be along shortly," Will said as the carriage stopped.

"Yes, my lord."

Squeezing Phoebe's hand as she reached for her sister, he signaled for her to leave. She gave him a long look and then followed Freddy from the carriage.

"I'm sorry that you're angry with me, Olivia, but I'm not sorry that you are not, at present, on an uncomfortable stage with people you do not know, staying at an inn with no one to protect you."

She didn't move, just looked out the window as she had for the entire journey. He could see her face now as it was dark outside, saw the strain and fatigue etched in every line.

"When I saw you and Phoebe standing there in Damply, alone with your bags at your feet, I thought of Thea," he lied, because his sister would never be in that position. He and Joe would make sure of it. "I knew that if she was ever in that situation, I would hope someone came to her rescue."

"It was a stage, Lord Ryder. Hundreds of people travel on them every year."

It was a start that, at least she was talking to him.

"And hundreds of people get robbed and abused. Do you want your sister to be one of those people, Olivia?"

"You had no right to do what you did. Perhaps if you had reasoned with me or at the very least asked us to join you, but you didn't, you—"

"I asked but you refused," Will interrupted her. "Furthermore, the stage was arriving and if I had not taken decisive action you would have gotten in it somehow."

"It was my decision, not yours. You had no reason to interfere. My sister and I are nothing to you."

"That is not true. You have always meant a great deal to me, Olivia," Will said softly. "Will you tell me why you were catching the stage from Damply to London?"

"That is none of your concern and you should not have intervened."

"I will not apologize for protecting you and your sister."

"Why do you care? If we choose to walk all the way to London it should be of no matter to you, Lord Ryder."

She still faced the window, and for that Will was glad, because he did care but had no intentions of telling her that yet.

"Any person would care if they saw a friend waiting for a stage when they could journey to London in the comfort and security of a carriage."

Her shoulders slumped and then slowly she turned to face him.

"I would never put my sister in danger, Lord Ryder, and I do not like being manipulated and handled by you."

"Me or anyone?"

She stifled a yawn behind one hand.

"Come, you are tired and in need of a good meal and sleep. Tomorrow you will be invigorated and ready to launch another attack on me, but for now we shall call a truce."

Her hand touched his arm as he turned to step from the carriage.

"I still do not believe what you did was right, but there is little I can do now but accept your assistance in getting to London. I shall insist on paying my share of tonight's lodgings."

She gave him a fierce look that was spoiled by another yawn.

"Come." He wasn't going to let her pay, of course, but tomorrow was soon enough for her to learn that. "I'm hungry and cold and have yet to adjust to this bloody English climate."

Inside they were quickly led to a small room that had a roaring fire where Phoebe and Freddy were warming themselves.

"Livvy?"

"It's all right, Phoebe. I can do nothing but yield so you will ride to London in comfort tomorrow," she said hugging her sister.

"Excellent, then come and join us before the fire. A maid will shortly bring us tea," Mr. Blake declared.

"Tea." Will shuddered as he removed his outer clothing while Livvy did the same.

"I read somewhere that drinking tea is a sign of intelligence," Livvy said as she walked to the chair before the fire. Will swallowed his smile. She may be tired but her sharp tongue was still working.

The dark paneled room was not overly big. Blue rugs appeared swept and clean at their feet and the couch and chairs had plumped pillows at their backs.

"Have you stayed here before, my lord?" Phoebe questioned.

"No, my brother recommended it to me. Of course, he's a Duke, so we shall see if the service matches his expectations."

The tea and, thankfully, ale arrived and was quickly dispensed, and the thick slices of orange cake were eaten with relish.

Will watched Livvy hand her cup to Phoebe and then rest her head on the back of the chair. In minutes she was asleep. Moving closer, he warmed his backside and looked down at her. Her hands were folded one on top of the other in her lap, knees pressed together. Even in slumber she was contained, making sure to keep up appearances. He wanted to lean closer and kiss one satin smooth cheek and whisper in her ear to let go and that he would keep her safe, make her a million promises just to see the pain and worry leave her eyes.

It had to be longing that he felt looking at her, but he wasn't sure he felt comfortable with the emotion given he had little experience with it. Will had been a loner for years, but returning home he suddenly had a family who stirred up his feelings, and now this fierce little hellion, who was determined to keep him as far away as possible, which only made him want her more.

"Pardon me, Lord Ryder, but a gentleman and his wife are seeking shelter from the snow. Would it be acceptable to you if they shared this parlor while their room is being arranged?"

Will looked at Freddy and Phoebe, who nodded, and then down at Olivia, who had woken as the man entered. He saw the confusion in her eyes as she looked up at him.

"What?" he questioned as the proprietor went to get the guests.

"How will you explain this… us?" she added, pointing to Phoebe and then herself.

"Don't worry, Olivia, I shall make the introductions. Just follow my lead."

Why didn't she trust that smile? Livvy wondered. She felt rumpled and dirty and thoroughly out of sorts, having woken from a short and unfulfilling nap, yet she was too tired to question him further. Let him win this round. Tomorrow would be another day and she would tell him exactly how she felt about his high-handed methods again. Smothering another yawn, she tucked a loose curl into the bun at her nape and smoothed down her skirts.

Livvy tried to regain her feet as the parlor door opened but Will simply moved to the back of her chair and placed a hand on her shoulder, holding her in place.

"Don't get up, Olivia, you're exhausted."

"Let me go," she whispered furiously.

She felt both his hands brace her shoulders and then suddenly his face was beside hers as he bent over the back of the chair.

"Be a good girl for once and do as I say."

I'll show him good girl, Livvy fumed. How dare he speak to her as if she were a badly behaved child?

"My name is Mr. Munford, Lord Ryder," the man said, walking forward to take Will's hand, which was thankfully no longer resting on her shoulder. "Please let me thank you for allowing us to share the parlor. As you can imagine, my wife is quite set down by the long journey and now that the snow has begun in earnest, we thought it best to stop for the night and seek shelter and nourishment."

Mrs. Munford may need recuperation but by the size of both her and her husband's girths, they did not need nourishment.

Seated as she was, Livvy was able to study the couple undetected as they greeted Lord Ryder. Small and round, both spoke in a thick Scottish brogue.

"Allow me to introduce my wife to you."

Livvy blinked. Had she just misheard Will? Surely he had not said the word wife?

"Please excuse her from rising. She is exhausted after our journey and in her condition, I think we will forgive her if she does not."

Livvy didn't look at Phoebe as she coughed loudly; she was too busy glaring at Will.

"Your first?" Mrs. Munford said, rushing forward to take Livvy's hand. "I was quite fatigued when I carried my wee little Fraser."

Livvy wasn't sure, but she thought she smiled at Mrs. Munford and said 'thank you.' Climbing to her feet, she then sank into a curtsy.

"How do you do, Mr. Munford, Mrs. Munford."

"You really should stay seated, darling."

Livvy wondered if the proprietor could lay his hands on boiling oil as only that would satisfy her thirst for revenge at this point. Will had moved to her side and was rubbing circles in the small of her back. She tried to ease herself away yet his large, warm hand just followed.

"This is my wife's sister, Miss Phoebe Langley, and the gentleman is Mr. Frederick Blake."

Perhaps she could simply shoot him; it was not as if she wasn't an accurate shot and she could slip into his room while he slept. No one need know until morning.

"Your rooms are ready, Lord Ryder," the proprietor appeared once more at the door.

"Excellent, my wife and her sister are ready for a rest. Mr. Munford, Mrs. Munford, if you will excuse me I will escort them upstairs," he said, bowing before he guided Olivia and Phoebe from the room.

Livvy didn't speak as he urged her up the stairs before him. In fact, had anyone addressed her she would probably just have snarled a response. She remained silent as a maid opened the door to the room she would share with Phoebe. In fact, only when Will had followed the maid to his room did she exhale… loudly.

"Well, that was entertaining," Phoebe said, throwing their belongings onto the only chair in the small room. She then took off her shoes and fell onto the bed. When Livvy didn't immediately speak, she lifted her head and looked at her.

"Speak, sister. I know you want to vent your spleen."

Livvy walked to the basin of water left for them on the dressing table. Lowering her face she plunged it straight into the icy water.

"Livvy!" Phoebe giggled as she raised her head, water running in rivulets down the front of her dress. Reaching for the cloth she briskly rubbed it up and down her face and then she made a decision.

"Excuse me, Phoebe. I shall return shortly."

Leaving the room, Livvy didn't take the time to change her damp dress. She just closed the door with a decisive click and then walked to the first door she came to and knocked.

"Are you in there, Lord Ryder?" No one answered so she moved on to the next and did the same. Livvy didn't stop to think how it would look if a strange man opened the door and found her outside. She was too angry to care. She wanted to find him and tell him exactly what she thought of him having fun at her expense.

"Did you want something, Olivia?"

His handsome head appeared further down the hallway after she had knocked on a further two doors with no success. Taking the few paces it took to reach him, she slapped her hand on the wood beside his head and pushed the door wider, making him stumble back several paces. Entering, she then slammed it shut with her heel and advanced on him.

"How dare you!"

Will kept his features expressionless as Olivia approached. She was fuming; her eyes were narrowed, her feathered brows almost meeting in the middle as she scowled at him. For some reason the front of her dress appeared damp, and on closer inspection the hair that framed her face also looked wet.

"Is there a problem, Olivia? Something I can help you with?"

He shouldn't antagonize her further but couldn't seem to help himself. In fact, he wanted her to lose that tight rein she had on herself. He wanted to unleash the girl he once knew that flirted and giggled and punched him in the nose when he deserved it.

"You—you… of course there is a bloody problem!"

To his credit he didn't wince as she screeched, nor did he mention that fact that she had just cursed."

"Then tell me and I shall do my best to fix it for you." He tried to sound reasonable. Olivia didn't seem to think so and made a growling sound. Christ, it was hard to hold his laughter in the face of her wonderful fury. She couldn't speak, only make small animal noises as her mouth opened and closed several times. Flashing eyes, flushed cheeks, she breathed deeply and finally got herself under control.

"You are my problem!"

Placing a hand on his chest, Will said, "I? How is that possible when I have done everything I can to help you?"

"Help me! How is telling Mr. and Mrs. Munford that I am your wife and expecting our first child helping me? You…you cad."

She was quivering with emotion and Will had never wanted a woman in his arms more than Olivia, right here, right now. However, he was also aware that if he did so in her current state he would probably lose an eye or sustain some form of injury to his manhood.

"Livvy, be reasonable, I was trying to protect your reputation and saying you were my wife was the only thing I could think of on short notice."

"Could we not have been your sisters or cousins?"

She had him there.

"But that is not what I'm angry about, Lord Ryder. No, your sins this day are vast and give me many reasons to want to… to hit you with a large, heavy and sharp-edged object. Yet it is the fact that you made a game of me that incurs my wrath. It was cruel to say I was with child."

Hell, she just sniffed. He'd never meant hurt her; it was only to tease her into a reaction, nothing more. Cursing himself as she turned to leave, Will reached the door as she did. Placing his hands on the wood above her head, he stopped it from opening.

"Let me leave."

"I never meant to hurt you, Livvy, please believe me."

His front was pressed to her back, his hands and body caging her.

"It was cruel," she whispered.

"Why was it cruel?"

She shuddered as his breath touched the skin of her neck. Will could smell the sweet essence of her, the scent more tantalizing than the most expensive French perfume.

"I—I may never have a child."

"Why will you never have a child?" he whispered, the soft skin at the base of her neck drawing him. He wanted to stroke it and feel her tremble against his lips.

"I do not intend to wed."

Lowering his head, he brushed his lips just above the neckline of her dress. She gasped but made no effort to pull away. "You will wed, Olivia Langley. No man could resist you."

"It matters not," she said, her voice ragged. "Wh—what matters is that in saying what you did today, you were making a game of me."

Will kissed his way along the neckline of her demure dress and felt his head start to reel. The taste and scent of her was pure sin.

"Forgive me. I would sooner cut off my arm than hurt you, yet I seem to make a habit of hurting the people closest to me."

Livvy knew she shouldn't turn and face him. Her neck tingled from his lips and what she should do is open the door and leave like her mother would have expected. He would let her go if she forced the issue, yet something made her turn. Something in his tone when he had just spoken made her want to see his face. Turning, she pressed her back into the doors.

Now that she wasn't blinded by anger, Livvy could see him clearly. He'd removed his jacket and his necktie was loosened and she could see the smooth skin of his throat. Livvy had the ridiculous urge to lean forward and kiss it as he had her neck. She was caged within his big body, alone in his room just the two of them, his hands braced on either side of her head.

"Your family are no longer hurting, Will."

"But how long before I hurt them again, Livvy? You know I will. It's what I'm good at."

Livvy heard the pain in those words and could see the shadowed depths in his gray eyes. As if of their own violation, her fingers moved to touch his face, trailing the slopes and angles.

"You did what you believed you needed to do, Will, and came back a better man for it. You're not capable to deliberately hurting anyone."

Closing his eyes he leaned into her fingers.

"I am a self-serving bastard, Livvy, and I apologize for the use of that word, yet it best fits the man I am."

"Was," she amended. "Best fits the man you were," Livvy added, trailing her fingers over his chin and down his neck.

He caught them raising them to his lips, slowly kissing each knuckle. "How do you know I am no longer that man? Look how I treated you today. Can you have forgiven me so soon? Do you not remember just minutes ago stalking into my room ready to deliver me to Lucifer himself."

The sudden intensity in his eyes told her the answer to that question was important to him. She felt each kiss on her hand, each brush of his lips made the fire within her burn brighter.

"Y—your humor needs adjusting, my lord, as surely what you find funny I do not. Yet now my anger has fled. I know you meant no malice, although at the time I had wondered if boiling oil would suit my purpose."

His laugh held little humor. "I hurt you without thought and that is the man I am."

"No, my lord," Livvy flattened the palm he now held pressed to his chest and felt the steady beat of his heart beneath. "That man would never have brought me firewood because I hurt my hand, nor tried to avoid the beautiful young ladies of Twoaks. That man would not have taken the time to tell Bella of his travels and taken Major Bruntly to task on my account."

"Will, Livvy. I like to hear my name on your lips."

"Did you hear my words, Will?" Livvy slapped her palm against his chest for emphasis.

"I heard them."

"But do you believe them?" she said as he lowered his head. Livvy wanted his answer, but when his lips touched hers she forgot to think and began to feel. His lips devoured and captured, urging a response that she could not fight.

She felt his hand move to her hips and then he pulled her off the door so he could wrap his arms around her body and press her closer. His chest was hard against hers and made her breasts feel full and sensitive; an ache had taken up residence deep in her stomach and between her thighs. Never had she felt anything so wonderful. Each brush of his lips and touch of his hands was exquisite pleasure. She moaned as his hot breath reached the tops of her breasts. She felt cool air on her skin and realized he had loosened her bodice.

"I knew what you had laced and buttoned beneath your clothes would take my breath away," he rasped.

With a final tug Livvy felt her chemise give and then she was exposed to him, his eyes studying every inch of her.

"You're beautiful, Olivia Langley."

"Will…" Livvy could not continue with that thought as his tongue licked the length of one breast. Shuddering, she arched into his mouth and was rewarded with more. He licked until she moaned and begged and only then did he place his mouth over her aching nipple. She cried out long and low as his tongue swirled around the peak.

"Will…" Her sigh hitched as he bit down gently and then sucked on the sensitive bud, a slave to the sensations he was creating deep inside her.

Lifting his head Will looked at her, watched her eyes open and the cinnamon depths held so much sultry promise he wanted to lift Olivia and wrap her legs around his waist; his body could almost feel her slick heat as he plunged inside her. She shivered as he ran his fingers around a ruched nipple. Will knew that if he took her now it would change the course of their lives forever; in fact, what they had already done would do so. She was an innocent and a lady, and as such this would determine their futures. Was he ready for that? Looking at her lovely face flushed with pleasure he knew he was more than ready.

"Touch me, Livvy."

Her fingers shook as she unbuttoned his shirt and pulled it from his breeches. It humbled him that she looked at him with such longing and then she surprised him by placing a hot, open-mouthed kiss in the middle of his chest, the sensation branding his skin. Her smile was alluring in its innocence.

"I knew that what you had buttoned beneath your shirt would take my breath away, William Ryder," Livvy said, repeating his words.

Wrapping a hand around her neck, he pulled her forward for another kiss. They both moaned as his chest touched hers, the friction delicious as she stood on her toes and wound her arms around his neck, pressing her breasts closer.

They dueled as he took the lead and then she wrested it from him. It was a sensual battle they both willingly entered into.

Will bunched her skirts up in his hands until he could slide his palm beneath and up the outside of her thigh. Reaching the top of her stockings, he moved to cup the curve of one buttock through the material of her drawers. She murmured her encouragement, so he caressed every delectable inch in slow circles until they were both burning for more.

"Lord Ryder, may I have a word?"

Will stilled as Freddy's words reached them through the door. Lowering her skirts he placed his hands on her shoulders and held her away from him. Shaking his head, he indicated that she remain silent.

"Lord Ryder, are you in there?"

He watched as the horror of exposure dawned on her, trapping her lip between her teeth she held herself still. Pulling her into his arms, Will could feel the thud of her heartbeat against his chest. He had never really felt the need to protect and cherish. He'd been too self-absorbed to understand the meaning behind the words, yet at that moment they became utterly clear to him and he knew he would do whatever it took to keep her safe.

"He's gone, Livvy."

He reluctantly released her as she pushed against his chest and then quickly moved to fix her clothing. The fire still burning inside him urged him to stop her, but knew that would be a mistake. The moment had passed and she would not yield to his touch again tonight.

"What's between us has only just begun, Livvy. Tell me you understand that."

"Yes, I understand, Will."

Did she really or was she just saying what he needed to hear before running back to her room.

"We will talk soon, Livvy, when we have more time." He stopped her movements by trapping her hands and then he kissed her again, just a brief brush of his lips, but the contact was enough to reassure him she felt everything he did.

"Come, we must get you back to your room because Freddy is nothing if not tenacious and he will keep searching for me until he finds me. Therefore, I will check the hallway and then when it's clear, I'll signal you."

"Thank you."

He cupped her cheeks and simply looked at her for several seconds.

"Remember my words, Livvy. We have only just begun to explore what lies between us."

"Yes, Will."

He buttoned his shirt and then opened the door and slipped out to check if it was clear for her to leave. Seconds later he watched as she hurried towards her room, stopping with one hand on the door to give him a final look before slipping inside. Closing his door, Will went to his bed. Sitting on the edge, he willed the fire inside him to cool. His head was still full of the taste and smell of Olivia and he knew that had Freddy not interrupted them, he would have taken her innocence and then she would have been his.

I do not intend to wed. Why had she said that? Again he wondered what secrets she was hiding.

If Olivia thought he would drop her in London tomorrow without a backward glance, she was mistaken. Something had happened to send her there and he was sure it involved her cousin, so he would be keeping her close until he knew where the threat came from and why.

CHAPTER ELEVEN

Will found Olivia and Phoebe already in the breakfast parlor, seated with Mr. and Mrs. Munford, when he entered the following morning. She shot him a quick look and then lowered her eyes.

"Good morning, everyone," he said, moving around the table to bend and plant a loud kiss on her cheek. "How are you feeling now, darling?"

"Well, thank you, my lord." She kept her eyes down.

"She had a fretful night," he added, looking at Mrs. Munford.

"Tsk, poor wee lassie, nothing worse than missing out on your sleep when you really need it."

Will sat beside Olivia, and began to load his plate with food from the dishes before him.

"I'll pour your tea, my lord."

He reached out a hand to stop her.

"I am happy to do this wifely duty for you, my lord, as I know just how you like it," she added, pouring the vile liquid into his cup. He watched in horror as she added three spoonfuls of sugar and too much milk. Stirring it thoroughly, she then placed it directly in front of him with a sweet smile that did not reach her eyes; she then waited expectantly for him to take a sip.

"My sister remembers every little thing her husband tells her, you know?" Phoebe said chattily across from him. "Why, just the other day we were indulging in one of Olivia's weaknesses, cinnamon buns, and Lord Ryder told us how a lovely hot cup of tea would complement them superbly."

The look Phoebe gave him matched her sister's. He narrowed his eyes but lifted the cup. Trying not to smell the hideous brew, he then took a large gulp and forced himself not to shudder.

"I shall have the maid replenish it, my lord."

Lowering his hand under the table cloth, Will clamped it onto Olivia's thigh and squeezed.

"That won't be necessary, my darling, as we must continue our journey if we are to reach London before nightfall. I have no wish to travel after dark in these conditions."

Olivia's mew of disappointment was blatantly insincere, yet Mr. and Mrs. Munford seemed to believe it, their faces wreathed in benevolent smiles. She tried to remove his hand by prying his fingers from her leg but Will simply grabbed it and slipped her fingers through his. He kept them captive for the remainder of the meal and he could never remember a breakfast he had enjoyed more.

They left the inn shortly after their morning repast.

"There is more snow this morning, don't you think?" Phoebe said, looking at the fields and trees topped with white.

"Yes, but it is safe to travel or I would not have let us," Will added.

She flashed him a smile that he was sure would drop many men to their knees and returned to looking out the window, so he sat back beside Freddy and looked at Olivia.

She had not yet told him why she was traveling to London or what had happened to make her rush there in haste.

"Are you proposing to stay with your cousin in London, Olivia?"

She had been staring out the window like her sister; however, this pulled her eyes back to him. Dressed in her smart blue coat and matching hat she looked again the proper young lady; however, he knew what lay beneath that prim exterior and that when he licked her beautiful breasts, she was anything but a proper young lady.

"I think not, my lord, as he lives alone and is not aware that we are coming to visit him. Phoebe and I had thought to find a small lodging house."

He seemed to either want to shake or kiss this woman. Right now it was the latter. The image of Olivia and Phoebe walking around London seeking lodgings close to dark was not a pleasant one and he struggled to subdue the resurgence of his temper.

"Excellent. Mr. Blake and I are staying at the Grillion Hotel. I'm sure they will also have room for you both."

"We shall see to our own accommodations, my lord. I have been reliably informed that there are many small lodging houses that will suit our needs."

Will knew how to win this battle and it was not by dictating to Olivia. She was stronger now having looked after her family and not easy to intimidate, so he needed to coerce her into his way of thinking.

"I would be honored if you would allow me to secure rooms for both you and your sister, Olivia. I could not, in all conscience, rest easy if I did not."

She studied him for several seconds, trying to see what was behind his words yet he kept his face calm.

"I fear Grillion's Hotel will be fully booked."

"Not many families will be in London, Olivia. Most are still in their country homes. And as it is close to Christmas, I'm sure there will be plenty of vacancies."

The line appeared between her brows as she thought about

how to get around him. *Not this time, my sweet. This time I'm going to win without a fight.* Will knew one of her concerns was the cost, so he addressed it because he knew her pride would not allow her to do so.

"The price, I believe, is not overly grand is that right, Freddy?" Will looked at Freddy to support his lies. In fact, the Grillion Hotel was very expensive, but Olivia did not need to know that.

"No, indeed," Freddy rushed to add, realizing at once what Will was about. "Most inexpensive, Miss Langley."

"Thank you then, my lord, I shall think about your suggestion."

Will knew by the set of her shoulders that this was something that had been bothering her. The shadows in her eyes when she thought he wasn't looking told him there was much she held back from him, but he would find out her secrets soon. Reaching beneath the seats of his carriage, Will then pulled out two warm rugs.

"Those hot bricks at your feet will cool soon; perhaps these will also help keep you warm."

They thanked him and tucked them around their legs. Will had to fight the urge to lift Olivia onto his lap and wrap the blanket around them both.

Freddy gave him a foul look as he usually had one on his knees, but now he would have to behave like a man and brave the cold weather.

"I will share with Olivia, Mr. Blake," Phoebe said handing her blanket to him. "Then we shall be quite snug for the remainder of our journey."

Will snorted as Freddy said something complimentary to Phoebe.

"I shall make a man of you yet, Frederick Blake."

"Wanting to be warm does not mean a man is not ah… well,

a man, surely?" Olivia said.

Will wished they were alone in his carriage because he would take that smart mouth beneath his and put it to better use.

"Freddy is soft, Olivia. If he is to survive the rigors of English life once again then he needs to be toughened up, and I am just the man for the job."

The heated debate that followed flowed from one topic to another and finally, as the carriage rolled into London, he was relieved to see that Livvy had lost some of the tension in her shoulders. Both Olivia and Phoebe had a lively wit and Freddy was always ready with a dry quip or two. Will had laughed and scowled and Olivia had never backed down. With each minute he spent in her company he wanted her more. It was as the carriage began to wind through the London streets that she finally said the words he had been waiting to hear.

"We will only be in London for a few nights, Lord Ryder; therefore, I have decided to take you up on your offer of seeking lodgings at the Grillion Hotel, if it is still acceptable to you?"

She didn't want to. Will could see that by the way her chin tilted and the clipped tone of her words; however, she knew that to find a place to stay in London, a city that until today she had never entered, would be an unpleasant task for two women alone. He would have to watch her closely now, because whatever reason brought her here would have her leaving the hotel to deal with it and Will would make sure that when she did he would be at her side.

Livvy looked at the dark, dreary skies. She shuddered to think how horrendous their journey to London would have been had Will not forced them to accompany him. She couldn't see much, just buildings jammed closed to each other and streets lined along the edges with snow that would turn into slush.

"What is that building, Lord Ryder?"

Livvy listened to the deep rumble of Will's voice as he answered Phoebe. Had she made a mistake accompanying him and Mr. Blake to London? If anyone found out, surely they would be ruined, and yet as none of the Langley sisters had had a season, surely no one would know. Was it wrong for two young women to stay at the Grillion Hotel un-chaperoned? Probably, but again, who would know and how could it be helped? Lord, it was taxing, making these decisions with no one to guide her.

She would send a note to Lord Langley as soon as she had a chance, requesting a meeting with him. Hopefully, he would change his mind about evicting them from their home when Livvy explained her family's situation in full to him. Her pride was not pleased about throwing herself at his mercy, yet until one of the Langley sisters found a match, they would need his support. She did not want to think of where they would live if he forced them from Willow Hall.

"You're frowning, Olivia."

Ignoring Will, Livvy looked first at Phoebe and then Mr. Blake. Both were looking out the windows so she turned back to Will and crossed her eyes as she had often when they were younger. It was a foolish, infantile gesture that made his gray eyes fill with silent laughter and one that made her heart feel lighter if only for a few precious seconds.

Minutes later the carriage pulled to halt.

"Freddy will go in and organize our rooms and we shall remain here in the warmth."

"Oh, but surely I should assist in some way?" Olivia said, preparing to follow Mr. Blake from the carriage." A hand snaked out and grabbed a handful of her skirt to stop her reaching the door.

"A young, single woman does not go into a hotel and request a room, Olivia. Freddy will do it and we will enter when he returns."

"Of course," Livvy mumbled, realizing how foolish she had been. Twitching her skirts free from his grasp, she then reseated herself and sat silently until Mr. Blake returned.

Thirty minutes later they were out of the carriage and walking up the grand front steps into the brick building where a uniformed man awaited them. He then led them up several flights of carpeted stairs to the floor their room was on. Opening a white door, Will then motioned them inside.

"Oh, my," Phoebe said, walking into the sitting area. Silk curtains in lemon and silver stripes were closed against the gray sky and a fire blazed in the hearth. Thick carpets muffled their feet as they moved deeper into the room. The walls were lemon, the two chairs the color of the drapes and the rest of the furniture was polished to a high sheen.

"This cannot be our room!" Livvy dragged her eyes from the glimpse of two big beds placed side by side in a room off this one. "It is too grand and… and t—too expensive," she stammered, looking at Will who lounged in the doorway.

"I'm in heaven!" Phoebe cried as she ran into the other room and threw herself face first onto one of the beds.

"No, we cannot stay here." Livvy was mortified. She could never afford this and surely neither could Will. "I won't let you pay for this… us," she added, waving her hand around the room.

Will grabbed her fingers and hauled her into his arms.

"Will!" Shooting Phoebe a look, she was relieved to see her sister was not in sight.

"I can afford it, Livvy, so be a good girl and shut up and just enjoy the luxury."

"I will not."

He robbed her thoughts and breath with a hot, seeking kiss.

"A meal and bath will arrive shortly along with your luggage, my sweet, and I shall see you in the morning."

"Will!"

Livvy's words met a closed door.

"Come and see the view, Livvy, although you can't see much. But still, we're actually in London!" Phoebe cried.

Giving the door a final look, Livvy went to join her sister. Tomorrow would be soon enough to tackle the arrogant Lord Ryder.

***

The Langley sisters slept deeply and woke refreshed after their long journey. Last night's meal had been delicious and the beds more comfortable than any they had slept in and now they were enjoying an equally delicious breakfast when a note was pushed under their door.

Opening the missive, Livvy scanned the page.

"Well, what does it say?" Phoebe said, lounging in a chair before the fire.

Her sister wasn't going to like the reply to the note she'd sent their cousin last night, but Livvy would have to do as Lord Langley had requested.

"He wants me to call upon him this afternoon, to discuss our situation."

"You're not going to see him alone, Livvy. I forbid it!" Phoebe declared.

"I will go alone and you will stay here."

"I don't like it, Livvy. He's not a good man and I worry he will upset you in some way."

The genuine concern in her sister's eyes made Livvy's stomach flutter with nerves, but she had to do as Lord Langley wished. It would not pay to upset him when she was asking for his help.

"I promise to leave if he says or does something that upsets me, Phoebe. However, this must be done and the sooner it is, the sooner we can return to Bella."

"I just don't trust him, Livvy."

"It will go well, Phoebe. Trust me."

"All right, but I'm not happy about any of this."

Fortunately, a knock on the door stopped any further discussion, Livvy hurried to open it.

"Good morning, Luke."

"Good morning, Miss Langley. Lord Ryder and Mr. Blake left early for an appointment, but Lord Ryder has asked if you would like to visit his warehouses."

Phoebe appeared beside Livvy to look at Luke.

"What does he hold in these warehouses, Luke?"

"All kinds of things, Miss Phoebe."

"Yes," Livvy said, making the decision for both her and Phoebe. She did not want to sit around in their room getting nervous over her upcoming interview with Lord Langley, and if she was honest she wanted to know more about William Ryder. "We want to see them, thank you, Luke. If you will give us a few minutes to gather our things, we shall be with you shortly."

"Lord Ryder in trade! Scandalous." Phoebe laughed as she rushed to retrieve her bonnet.

"And we are highwaywomen, sister. I would not go casting aspersions on another's character were I you," Livvy said, doing the same.

Twenty minutes later they were in the carriage and traveling through London. The weather was cold and gray, but perhaps a little warmer here than out of the city. The streets were narrow and the horses and carriages were turning the snow to a nasty gray sludge.

"It's quite drab, don't you think, Livvy? The people seem to be hurrying everywhere and the buildings are so close together. It seems a dreary place out there."

"People tend to hurry around when it's cold, sister, and yes it does not look very appealing. However, I'm sure it is a very different city during the season. Besides, we are probably not in the areas most frequented by society."

They traveled through the narrow streets, passing buildings which she tried to peer into. In some people worked, in others they lived. All were wrapped up warm against the elements.

"I would love to explore the shops, wouldn't you, Livvy? I would find lots of wonderful styles to create for us to wear."

"I was wondering if we could get some kind of women's fashion periodical while we're here so we don't have to rely on village gossip to keep up with the latest styles. It would be worth spending a few of our precious pennies for that, don't you think?"

"La Belle Assemblee!" Phoebe cried. "I would love a copy of that!"

"Perhaps Luke will know where we can get one, and if not him then definitely Mr. Blake?"

Before Livvy could stop her Phoebe had opened the hatch and stuck her head through, letting in a blast of freezing air. She then told Luke to stop at a store that sold La Belle Assemblee, to which he replied that he had no idea what that was or where to get it from.

"It is hardly likely to be something he reads, Phoebe. Be fair." Livvy laughed at the frustrated look on her sister's face as she flounced back onto her seat.

"I am determined to have a copy before we leave London, Livvy, now that you have planted the seed in my head."

"I'm sure Mr. Blake will be the man for the job."

"I hope so. Oh, look," Phoebe said, pointing at the tall masts of several ships. Livvy watched as they passed the last building and soon they were able to see the ships in all their glory.

"They're so big, and look at all those people and carriages," Livvy said as Luke pulled to a halt in front of a large, long building.

Stepping down, Livvy sniffed at the sea air as around her masts and rigging clanked and creaked. There seemed to be a mass of movement and noise everywhere she looked, buildings with signs advertising ropes and ship rigging, plus taverns that seemed to have many patrons even at such an early hour.

"That lady nearly has her breasts exposed!"

Turning at Phoebe's hissed words, Livvy felt her jaw drop at the sight. The woman had gold hair and painted lips and the bodice of her dress was straining against the fabric above which her breasts were spilling from.

"Come along," Luke said, seeing the direction Livvy and Phoebe were looking. "Lord Ryder will be waiting."

"I would like to look at the water, Luke, if I may?"

He looked startled at Livvy's request.

"We have never seen or touched the sea, Luke, and we may never get another chance."

"Lord Ryder said I was to take you straight into the warehouse, Miss Langley, as there are many undesirable people in this area."

"All right, Luke," Livvy soothed. Seeing his concern, she allowed him to herd them into the warehouse.

Windows above offered light and Livvy was able to see rows and rows of tables and shelves filled with goods as they entered the long room. The scents permeating the air were wonderful.

"Spices and tobacco." Phoebe sniffed loudly.

"Look at the fabric," Livvy added. "It's amazing!" Wide-eyed, she hurried to the nearest table and looked at the rainbow of colors.

Phoebe touched a piece. "This is expensive silk. Look at the texture."

The Langley sisters walked slowly down the row with Phoebe examining everything they saw.

"See anything you like?"

He was directly behind her and Livvy had to fight the urge to turn with a ridiculously wide smile on her face. Instead, she faced him saying calmly, "Lord Ryder, thank you so much for inviting us here today."

"My pleasure, Olivia."

He looked vital and handsome and there was something different about William Ryder from other men, Livvy realized, a carefully leashed strength that he had not carried before. He was a man now and one who was not to be trifled with. Livvy had the ridiculous urge to touch him and absorb some of that strength for herself.

"Do you own all this, my lord?"

"Freddy, I and one other," he said, shooting Luke a dark look which puzzled Livvy. "We also own two of those ships you saw out there."

Ships! Livvy thought, *he owns ships.*

Will had watched Livvy enter his warehouse and look around in surprise at the variety of goods on display. Phoebe had touched the fabrics reverently, but not Livvy. She had kept her gloved hands tightly clasped behind her.

"Come, I will give you a tour." Taking Livvy's arm, he guided her down the rows. She didn't resist, her eyes going from him to the goods before her.

"So you bring all these things to London from India, or wherever they come from, and then sell them?"

"Exactly, Phoebe." Will nodded. "I have two more warehouses with other merchandise, but this is the biggest."

"Some of these fabrics are exquisite." Will heard the longing in her voice.

"I would like to give you both something. Whatever you wish, you can have."

Phoebe did a little leap in the air clapping her hands. Her

sister however, shook her head and took a step away from him.

"Thank you!" Phoebe cried.

"No, thank you," Livvy added firmly.

Ignoring Olivia, Will said, "I'll show you around, Phoebe, and then you can decide what you want. Your sister, of course, can't see her way clear to accepting the offer in the manner it was issued, that of one friend to another."

She looked disgruntled at his words and he wanted to lift her up on to one of the benches then step between her legs and kiss her until she could form no other thought but those that included him.

"You have done so much for us already, brought us to London, helped us secure lodgings, and now want to offer us more. I'm sorry, Lord Ryder, it would not be right to accept."

"She's right, as usual," Phoebe said, deflating.

"Would you excuse us, Phoebe?" Will took Livvy's arm and urged her down the row and into a small office at the end. Closing the door, he kept hold of her arm as she tried to free herself.

"What are you doing? I cannot be alone in here with you. What will Phoebe be thinking?"

Nudging her back a few feet until she reached the bench, he then caged her in with his arms. "I have lots of money, Livvy, lots and lots, and if I choose to spend some of it on you and your sister, then so be it."

Her mouth formed a perfect circle as she stared at him. The big, floppy cream bow of her bonnet was tied to one side and the ends trailed onto her breasts. Will's fingers itched to stroke them.

"A few bolts of material or spices will not ruin me, Livvy. Now be a good girl and stop fighting me at every turn."

"You're rich? I… I mean you were always wealthy as the Duke's son but… oh, dear, that didn't sound right."

He didn't make it easy on her; in fact, Will enjoyed seeing her flustered because Livvy was usually in complete control. She was either taking charge of her sisters or a situation. In fact, it seemed only when he got too close that she became flustered.

"What I meant to say, my lord, is that it is not right for you to give us so much."

She recovered quickly; he'd give her that, although she was looking at his necktie rather than his eyes and her pulse was still fluttering.

"This," he said, touching the curve of her upper lip. "Is the greatest temptation."

"Don't kiss me," she whispered, trying to back up, but she had nowhere to go.

"Take my gifts and I won't kiss you, Livvy."

She tried to push him but he didn't move.

"You can't kiss me here! Not with Phoebe and Luke so close."

"Say you'll take my gifts, Livvy."

"I will not!" she declared defiantly as she pushed harder. "And you are no gentleman to behave in such a manner."

"Your words will not deter me as they once would have, Livvy, I am no longer the boy who left you and it would pay you to remember that fact." She squeaked as he picked her up and sat her on the bench. "Take my gifts, Livvy."

"Let me down!"

"No." Will leaned forward. She tried to evade him by dropping her chin but he simply lifted it and kissed her. It was right and good and everything else that he knew it would be. She was perfect in his arms, her lips beneath his, even if she was putting up the pretense of struggling.

"Say you'll take my gifts, sweet Olivia." His words brushed her cheek as she tried to turn her head.

Sealing her lips so he couldn't kiss her, he kissed her chin instead and then her cheeks, moving to the curve of her jaw. He then caught the whisper of breath as she spoke. Taking her mouth again for a slow, thorough exploration, he then lifted his head. This time, they were both breathing heavily.

"Say it again, Livvy." His words were ragged.

"Yes."

"Good girl."

Before Will could react, she had pushed him back a step and slipped off the bench. Will tried to catch her as she ran for the door.

"However, you will not manipulate me in such a manner again, my lord, or I will be forced to take action." Chin raised, she looked defiant; however, he could see the sensual heat lingering in her eyes.

"I shall look forward to your action, my sweet," he drawled, following her from the room.

They toured the warehouse and then Phoebe collected two bolts of fabric—one for herself and one for Bella, while Livvy got some spices for Jenny.

"Select something for yourself, Olivia," Will urged.

"We have enough, my lord."

She gave him a prim look which told him she thought she had won.

"You spent a long time lingering over the large satin pillows, so I shall gift you one of them." Pushing aside visions of her glorious hair spread over the emerald satin, he picked it up and lifted it high as Livvy tried to snatch it from his hands.

"Don't be churlish, Livvy. You know you want it," Phoebe said.

Will swallowed his smile as Livvy reluctantly thanked him and then, twitching her skirts, she followed Luke back outside towards the carriage.

The temperature seemed to have dropped again and the

wind was whipping along the dock.

"Will you show us the water before we go, Lord Ryder?"

Opening the carriage Will placed their gifts inside before he spoke. "It's dangerous for most people to linger here too long, Livvy, but for beautiful women even more so."

"You'll keep us safe," she said, looking longingly to where the boats were moored.

Something moved in Will's chest at the conviction in her words. She trusted him to keep them safe. He suddenly felt as if he could fell a tree with his bare hands.

"We have never been to the coast, my lord, nor touched the sea." Phoebe added her voice for encouragement.

There was a space to the left of the ships that was free. Will could take them there briefly, they could dip their fingers and then he would get them back to the carriage before anyone noticed two beautiful women wandering around the docks.

"Luke, walk at the rear!" Will called as he held his arms out for the Langley sisters to take one each.

They made it there safely and he and Luke stood behind them as they pulled off their gloves then bent to touch the water. He even smiled as they gasped at the temperature and then discussed the feel of it against their skin.

"Let's go," he then said as they straightened.

"Will! Egad, you have returned to us!"

"Viscount Marshall." Will bowed to the man who approached.

"Excellent! It shall be like old times, the five of us together again."

Will allowed the man to slap him on the back. They had been friends, after all, before he realized the man he once was was someone he could no longer be. He held out little hope that the Viscount had undergone any changes in his absence. In fact, the red veins in his face and plump figure told him he had not.

"What has you in this disgusting place? For my part, I'm charged with a commission for my father. Silly old fool, I keep him happy, thus the money keeps coming," Viscount Marshall declared loudly.

Of average height, he looked as if he had stepped out of a fashionable men's club, dressed in a great coat left open to reveal a pale blue satin, embroidered waistcoat and darker blue jacket with lemon breeches. Viscount Marshall was a man whose sole focus was himself and he never left home looking anything but the dandy he was. Will felt another wave of shame at the group he had been a part of and the drunken, idle pursuits they had undertaken in the name of boredom.

He realized the moment the man saw the Langley sisters, because he straightened and his eyes started moving, running over them from the top of their heads to the soles of their feet, just like he would have done had the opportunity arisen many years ago.

"Will you introduce me to your friends, Lord Ryder?"

He made to move past Will, but he and Luke simply stepped together, thus blocking the Viscount's path.

"Come now, Will, such beauty and form," he said, the last in a manner that left Will very aware what part of their form the Viscount was discussing. Anger flooded him as he watched the man's eyes trailing over Phoebe and Livvy. He had once been like that, but no longer.

"They are friends from the country here to visit a relative, Marshall. They have not yet entered society, therefore no introductions will be made."

"But we never gave a fig for the rules, and surely I can get a jump on the others, especially with the beauty, Will. That bodice is filled to perfection."

"If you wish to keep breathing, I suggest you lift your eyes."

"What!"

"Luke, take the ladies back to the carriage, please."

Will's words were not spoken loudly, but his friend heard them clearly, as well as the anger beneath. In seconds, Livvy and Phoebe were being escorted back to the carriage. Neither, he was relieved to see, were questioning his orders, although Livvy sent him a look that he was sure meant she wanted a full explanation later.

"I find your manner insulting, Marshall, and were the ladies not watching us as we speak, you would be flat on your back with a very sore jaw." Will kept his tone pleasant and his fists unclenched, aware that he had an audience. "But remember this warning, my lord. If I ever see you within two feet of those women, I shall be a very unhappy man, and you more so." He then offered a quick, insultingly short, bow. "Good day to you. I shall spend no further time in your company now or in the future."

The man's lips curled in a snarl as he looked Will over.

"It's hardly surprising you now have the manners of a savage, considering you have spent five years in their company, Lord Ryder. Believe me, it shall be no hardship to exclude you from the ranks of my friends."

"I'm desolate, of course," Will drawled.

Viscount Marshall's eyes widened as he noted the hostile gaze directed on him. He then spat out something vulgar and turned on his heel and fled.

One down, Will thought, knowing this was the first in a long list of encounters he was not looking forward to.

"You are traveling back to the hotel with us, my lord?" Phoebe asked when he entered the carriage and closed the door behind him minutes later.

"Yes, I have another appointment not far from the Grillion," he said, taking the seat next to Olivia.

"And all is well, my lord, with you and that man?"

He smiled at the concern in Livvy's eyes. "My past is rearing its ugly head, I'm afraid, and that encounter was something I knew was coming, Olivia. I'm just sorry you had to witness it."

"We will not be overset by a few heated words, my lord." Livvy twitched her skirts out of his way as he moved closer to her. "Indeed, our household has a conversation like that most days before breakfast."

Phoebe nodded. "'Tis true, my lord. We are not an even-tempered family; Livvy, of course, is the worst of us."

"Oh, like anyone would fall for that obvious falsehood, sister."

Will felt his mood lighten as the sisters started bickering. Laughing, he raised both hands. "All right, you have made your point, ladies; you can cease arguing as I am now going to be your tour guide."

"Wonderful." Livvy smiled at him which made the last of his anger disappear.

He pointed out buildings and places of interest as they traveled and he endeavored to answer their questions; although he had been absent from London for years, not much appeared to have changed.

"Why are we stopping, my lord?"

"You shall see," Will said as he got out of the carriage after Luke had pulled to a halt in front of a small building with a curved white front door and mullioned windows.

Livvy watched as Will disappeared into the shop.

"What do you suppose he is getting?" Phoebe said looking out the window.

"I'm not sure."

Minutes later, he returned carrying two large cups, a man followed carrying a plate loaded with cake and another two cups clasped in a beefy hand.

"How strange," Phoebe said, opening the door for Will as his hands were full.

He handed one cup to Phoebe and one to Livvy and then, taking the third cup and plate, he thanked the man who closed the door behind him as he once again seated himself.

"Who was the fourth cup for?" Phoebe questioned, sniffing the contents of hers.

"Luke," he said. "Had I not given him a cup he would have moaned for days."

"You and he have become friends since your absence, my lord?" Livvy questioned gently. He gave her a short nod and she believed that was to be his answer but then he surprised her by saying, "He is my best friend, and one I could not have survived the past five years without."

For some reason, the sincerity in his voice made Olivia want to cry so she quickly lifted her mug and inhaled the fragrant beverage. "It certainly smells nice," she said and then took a small sip. Her mouth was instantly filled with the smooth, tart, chocolate drink that was sweetened with honey. It was blissful and she felt the warmth travel slowly through her body.

"This was the best chocolate drink in London before I left and this," he said, holding out the plate, "was the best cake and I have great hopes that has not changed."

"I smell cinnamon and currants," Livvy said, looking eagerly at the treat Will was now waving under her nose. Clutching her cup in one hand, she pulled one of her gloves off with her teeth and reached for a piece of the cake.

"She loses all propriety when there is anything with cinnamon or fruit around. It's quite cute, actually," Phoebe said, showing more restraint as she took the plate Lord Ryder offered and placed it beside her while she took off her gloves.

"Very cute."

Livvy could not interpret the look Will gave her as she bit

into the cake. For a few seconds, he was her sole focus. Then he looked away and she drew an unsteady breath.

Silence filled the carriage while the occupants ate and drank, and then Will took the empty cups and plate back into the shop.

"Thank you, that was delicious," Livvy said upon his return.

"Believe me, the pleasure was all mine," he said, watching her pull on her gloves once more. "I had no idea that all it took was food and drink to subdue you."

"Hardly subdued, my lord; however, I am partial to cake with cinnamon or currants in it."

"I shall secure the recipe at once in that case, Olivia, as I may need to manipulate you in the future."

CHAPTER TWELVE

Livvy pressed a hand on her stomach. Nerves churned at the prospect of seeing her cousin again. One of the hotel staff had hailed her a hackney and now she was traveling to his address. It was cold inside, unlike the warmth and luxury of Will's carriage, and smelled of disgusting odors she had no wish to analyze.

Will had told both her and Phoebe not to leave the hotel without Mr. Blake, Luke or himself for company after returning them to their room; however, Livvy did not want anyone to know where she was going, or why, so she'd slipped out when no one was looking. Phoebe had, of course, tried once again to accompany her but Livvy had refused. She had no wish for her sister to start arguing with Lord Langley if he said something she took offense to.

The carriage halted minutes later outside Lord Langley's town house. Climbing down, she looked fleetingly at the stone façade before turning to pay the driver.

"Will it be difficult for me to hail another hackney from here, driver? I am not sure how long I will be at my appointment," Livvy questioned as he prepared to leave.

"Just walk up the street to the corner, miss, and you'll get one. I'll drive by again in a while to see if you're waiting."

"Thank you."

Why did she feel suddenly alone as the carriage rolled up the street? Forcing back her shoulders, she took a deep bracing breath and walked up the steps to knock on Lord Langley's front door. Her father and mother had once spent time in this house, as would she and her sisters if her father still lived.

"May I help you?"

The door was opened by a footman. Livvy explained why she was here and the man ushered her inside.

"Lord Langley is expecting you, Miss Langley. If you will hand me your coat and hat, I will take you to him."

Livvy did as he asked and then tugged up the neckline of her white dress. Why did Phoebe insist on making them so low?

Looking around her as she followed the butler, Livvy knew that the house had been redecorated since her parents' deaths. The colors were loud and garish and her mother would never have lived in such a place. Every wall was painted a different color and was bordered in gold. Small alcoves held naked statues of people in strange positions. It was decorated to excess and to show those who walked here that the owner was wealthy. Livvy felt her anger begin to simmer at the extravagance. What kind of man will not support his family but lives like a king?

"Miss Langley has arrived, my lord."

Livvy pulled her eyes from a couple formed in marble, doing unmentionable things that she had never imagined two people could do, and quickly walked into the room. The curtains were still drawn, even though it was daytime, and the fire roared in the grate as she moved towards the couch her cousin sat on. In here there were more signs of his lavish taste and the walls were filled with paintings of nude people. After a brief survey, Livvy did not look back as one glance had been enough to tell her every one depicted a crude scene.

"My dear cousin, come and take a seat beside me as surely

you must be exhausted from your journey."

Lord Langley did not stand as she entered the room. Ignoring the slight, Livvy took the seat he indicated.

"I had forgotten how beautiful you are, Olivia."

"Thank you, cousin." Livvy tried not to shudder as he stroked her arm.

"Most unusual hair, red and gold. It shines, cousin."

He touched her head, his fingers stroking a curl that had come free behind her ear. She shouldn't feel ill at his touch; after all, he was her cousin, but suddenly Livvy had an urge to run from the room. Clenching her fists, she stopped herself from slapping his hand aside.

"How are you, cousin?" Livvy said quickly.

"Very well as you can see, Olivia," he said, giving the curl a sharp tug, which left her scalp stinging before he released it. "But tell me, how is it that you are staying at the Grillion when you have no money?"

"Lord Ryder procured the rooms for us, cousin."

"And what payment is he asking for such a generous offering?"

"Offering, cousin?" Olivia kept smiling as she looked at his sweaty, blotted face. He was a vile-looking man, even more so now he had put on weight and his teeth, she noted, were stained yellow as he smiled back at her.

"Come, Olivia, why would Lord Ryder put you up in an expensive hotel if he did not want something from you?'

She knew then what he eluded, too.

"We are friends of longstanding, Lord Langley. Lord Ryder is merely doing Phoebe and I a favor, nothing more." Livvy held her breath as his eyes swept over her chest.

"How kind of him," he said, as the door once again opened and a maid brought the tea tray and placed it on the table.

"Thank you, Hester. We shall look after ourselves."

Livvy wanted to tell Hester to stay, yet knew she had no right to do so. The sound of the door shutting behind the maid did nothing to ease her tension.

"Do you like what I have done with the room, cousin?"

No, it's vile, Livvy wanted to say. Instead she said, "It is lovely, cousin."

"It took me quite some time to get it exactly how I wanted it but I think the effect is quite something, don't you? The pictures, of course, are what make it so special. Have a good look at them, cousin; I'm sure you will get pleasure from them as many of my guests do.

"I fear they are not to my taste," Livvy said, reaching for the teapot. "Shall I pour, cousin?" she then asked, eager to change the subject before she told him what she really thought of him and his paintings.

His chuckle was unpleasant.

"Forgive me, Olivia. My artwork must frighten you. After all, you are just a naïve, young innocent."

"Do you take milk and sugar, cousin?"

"Both," he said, and chuckled again.

Livvy handed him his tea but did not take hers because her hands were shaking and she did not want him to see that. He was a loathsome, hideous man and she wanted to leave the room, but would not until she had said what she'd come to say. He was also a pig, Livvy thought, as he took a large mouthful and made a gulping sound as he swallowed. She tried to shift along the seat but he was so fat and seemed to take up most of the space, and she would fall off the edge if she moved any further.

"Now, cousin, tell me all your problems and I shall endeavor to find a solution for them."

Did he mean that? Livvy wondered as he finished speaking.

"I fear we have no money, and if you force us to leave

Willow Hall then we will have nowhere to live, either. I have tried not to burden you, cousin, but now, however, our plight is desperate."

"You are to be commended, Olivia, for looking after your family for so long. However, now it is time to lean on me."

"Really?" Olivia hardly dared to believe what he said. Was it really going to be all right? She watched him lower his cup to the table and then accepted the heavy arm he draped around her waist as surely it was a comforting gesture. Perhaps Phoebe had misjudged him and he was a good man after all? Livvy pushed aside the niggling fears inside her and forced herself to smile

"Of course, my financial support will come at a price that I'm sure will be acceptable to all the lovely Langley ladies."

"A price?" Livvy felt an icy chill of fear.

"You are really quite beautiful, aren't you, little cousin. My friends are going to be most happy with you."

"I don't understand, my lord. What have your friends to do with your support of us?"

"Here are my demands, Olivia, and if you do not accept them then I will be forced to tell your naughty little secret to the world."

The arm around her waist tightened and Livvy felt his other hand touch her thigh as he moved her closer.

"Please unhand me, cousin."

"Don't you want to know what secret, Olivia?"

She began to struggle against him as the hand slowly moved higher.

"I know that your father killed himself, Olivia, and that you hid the evidence."

"No!"

"Stop fighting and I will tell you how I found it," he whispered into her ear.

Nausea clawed at her as his hand stroked her stomach. Biting her lip, she tried to keep still as he spoke.

"When I came for the funeral I found myself in your room, Olivia, and under your bed there was a small box. I took it and kept it because I knew one day that what was inside would be useful to use against you."

"No!"

She had wanted to destroy the note her father had left behind, begging his daughters' forgiveness for ending his life, but had never found the strength to do so.

Fool!

"Those words brought a tear to my eye, sweet cousin. 'I'm sorry, daughters, for leaving you, but I can no longer endure the pain in my heart'."

"H—he was not himself," Olivia cried, trying to push his hands off her body. "Pain from his injury had twisted his mind."

"But the shame that will be brought down on you, cousin…how will you and your sisters ever hold your heads up? And what of your parents? Their reputations will be in tatters at your feet.

"You're a monster!" Livvy's anger drove her on. "An unfeeling beast to treat your family like this." Panting now, she was pushing against his chest as he pulled her closer, his arms holding her prisoner.

"And for my silence, my sweet, innocent cousin, I will have these things. Firstly I shall announce my engagement to your sister in the New Year and then we shall wed next spring."

"Phoebe will never marry you!" Renewing her struggles, she scratched him. His laughter made her skin crawl.

"Phoebe! I would never take that she-devil to my bed. I shall get her off my hands by marrying her to one of my friends. It is your lame little sister Isabella who I will take as my wife. I will take her because no one else will and she'll be treated as other

English wives are, with gifts and pretty things and once a week I will rut her until she produces my heir."

"I will never let you wed my little sister as long as I draw breath!" Livvy hissed as his hand moved upwards and grabbed her breast. She bit her lip to stop from crying out as he pinched her hard.

"I will treat her with respect, Olivia, and do you know why?" he said, reaching for her bodice.

"Let me go!" He was so close and his hands were now squeezing her breasts hard and pulling at her bodice. His foul breath made her gag as he pushed his face into hers.

"You are too old to wed so you are going to be my whore, little cousin. Your sister will stay safe as long as you do whatever I wish you to do, whenever I wish you to do it. I will teach you to pleasure me, Olivia, and others. In fact, I think we can start your education now as you have me quite excited. I enjoy a fight, especially if I can take a virgin at the end of it."

Livvy heard her bodice rip and then felt his mouth and hands on her skin.

"I'm going to be the first man to take you, Olivia Langley."

Livvy realized his intent was to rape her. She renewed her efforts and fought with everything she had at her disposal. Rage gave her strength, and she screamed as he bit the tender flesh of her breast.

"You will never have me!" Livvy yelled. He made the mistake then of placing one of his hands over her mouth to stop her screams and she bit down hard on the soft skin of his palm, not letting go until she felt him release her.

"Bitch!" he roared. "If you defy me, Olivia, I will tell everyone what a slut you are, dirty your name and that of your sisters and then I will tell them all that your father was a coward! Society will shun you all and there will be nowhere to hide."

Livvy swung her fist as hard as she could and it connected

with his jaw. He grunted and fell backwards and she was off the couch and running to the door in seconds. Her punch had not slowed him for long, however; he was soon behind her, spewing foul, furious words and speaking of retribution as she raced down the hall to the front door. Searching the entrance she found her coat and bonnet. Grabbing them, she pulled the front door open and ran down the steps and along the street, uncaring of the icy surface under her feet.

Aware that her bodice was torn, Livvy quickly forced her arms into the sleeves of her coat and buttoned it. Pulling on her bonnet, it took several attempts to tie the satin ribbons because her fingers were trembling, but finally she was covered and looking respectable once more. Reaching the corner, she looked up and down the street but saw no sign of a hackney. Knowing she could not wait as her cousin would catch her, Livvy turned left and ran down the street. Looking around her, she tried to find anything that was familiar. Why had she not taken note of the direction the hackney had taken on the way here? *Because you had not thought for one moment that your cousin's intentions were to rape you.*

"Faster, Olivia," she urged herself as her steps began to lag and her sides began to heave. He would catch her if she stopped, and this time he would not let her go. She needed to return to the Grillion Hotel. She would be safe there with Phoebe.

Where are all the people? Livvy wondered as she ran on, past houses and then shops until the pain in her sides grew so bad she had to stop. Hiding in a doorway, she drew in deep, shuddering breaths, forcing the tears to stay away. Was he still looking for her? Dear God, he knew where she was staying. She had to get to the hotel before him and gather up Phoebe and run.

Running onto the street once more, Livvy nearly cried as a

hackney game into sight. She did cry when she recognized the driver as the one that had taken her to Lord Langley's town house earlier. Waving frantically she keep looking down the road as he pulled to a stop beside her. There was no other carriage in sight.

"You all right, Miss?" The driver said noting her tears.

"Yes, please just get me back to the Grillion Hotel as fast as you can."

Livvy climbed inside and seated herself in the corner so no one could see her if they looked in the window. She breathed deep and slow for several seconds until her heart began to stop thumping.

Lord Langley may have hurt her, but she was strong and would recover and, more importantly, she had thwarted his attempts to take her innocence. She hoped his head hurt and his hand needed stitches. Now, however, what mattered most was what would the Langley sisters do? She would have to tell Phoebe what had taken place in their cousin's town house, as there was no way she could hide it, or how their father had died any longer, especially if their cousin used it against them.

Thoughts tumbled round and round inside her head as nausea churned in her stomach. She prayed that Will was not in the hotel foyer as she did not want to see him until she had herself under control, because one look or soft word from him and she would throw herself into his arms and beg him never to release her.

Will could not help her now. She would die of shame if he found out about what had just taken place and furthermore, he would confront their cousin and Lord Langley would tell them about her father and she did not want that, could never allow that to happen. Her parents had been well-respected and loved; she would do everything she could to ensure their reputation stayed intact. Nearly everything, Livvy thought, remembering what her cousin wanted from the Langley sisters. Dear God, how were they to stop him?

Hopeless tears rolled down her cheeks. She realized that deep inside she had found hope in Will, hope that he would love her as she now knew she loved him. Not the sweet love she had once felt. This wasn't comfortable, this was a fierce pain in her chest, a deep churning heat that she knew would be inside her forever. A small kernel of hope had unfurled in Livvy even though she had denied it, hope that in Will she had found both lover and savior and now that was gone.

Livvy blotted the tears with her gloves as the carriage stopped. Paying the driver, she entered the hotel and slipped quietly up the stairs. Keeping her head down, she hurried to her room. Phoebe opened the door after she knocked.

"What did that man do to you?"

Livvy stumbled forward and fell into her sister's open arms. "He won't help us, Phoebe."

Phoebe closed the door and then helped her sister to sofa.

"Tell me what he did, Livvy."

"It doesn't matter what he did, Phoebe." Livvy sniffed loudly as she struggled to regain control. "I—it matters that he will not help us," she added, gripping her sister's hands tight.

"Damn you, Livvy. I know he hurt you, now tell me how."

Livvy didn't speak, just let her sister wrap her in her arms. She held on as tight as she could. The tears came again and she let them fall, until eventually her cries eased to sniffles and finally she stopped with a tired sigh.

"I don't want to cry anymore. It makes me weary."

"Fine, be angry, then. But for pity's sake, speak, Livvy, and only the truth as I shall know if you lie."

Livvy began with her visit to their cousin and the things he had said he would do to Bella and herself and how he had tried to violate her.

"I will go around there and shoot him," Phoebe declared, fury glinting in her eyes. "I shall shoot him between the legs," she added.

"Had I a knife, I would have stabbed him, Phoebe, I was so enraged. But I did leave him hurting."

"You must have been terrified." Phoebe's voice wobbled as she battled tears of her own.

"There is more that I must tell you, sister," Livvy said, knowing this next part would be the hardest to say but that it must be done.

"Our father took his life."

"How could you?" Phoebe cried when Livvy finished telling her what had happened that day. How she had found the poison and note at his side and hidden them from her sisters. Pushing Livvy from her arms, Phoebe glared at her; fury making her brown eyes appear almost black.

"How dare you keep the details of father's death from me? To shoulder that burden on your own because you believed I was to be protected is inexcusable."

"I'm sorry, Phoebe, please forgive me." Livvy felt terrible at her sister's distress. "I realize now it was wrong, but at the time you and Bella were struggling with father's death and her injury. I had no wish to give you more pain."

"Yet you felt comfortable with the entire burden. So big and brave, you were able to shoulder everything while we, your pathetic, weak-willed sisters, could grieve knowing their father was a good man instead of a bloody coward who left his daughters with not a penny to their names!"

"He wasn't a coward, Phoebe, he wasn't in his right mind."

"He must have had a moment of clarity when he wrote that suicide note!" Phoebe hissed furiously.

"Never forget that he was the best of fathers to us, Phoebe," Livvy said, determined that her sister listen to her words. "We loved him and he us, and I won't let any of us lose sight of that. Remember the good years, Phoebe, the love he and mother lavished on us."

Phoebe left her side to walk to the window and stare out at the London streets below.

"I'm sorry, sister, you're right. I should not have kept it from you." Lowering her head into her hands, she wondered if Phoebe would ever forgive her arrogance. She had believed that, as the eldest, it was her responsibility to protect her younger sisters, yet Phoebe was stronger than that and had deserved to know the truth.

"I know I have no right to ask for your forgiveness, Phoebe, but if you give it I shall promise never to behave in such an arrogant manner again. I… I had no right not to tell you. My only defense is that I wished to protect you, yet I see now I was wrong."

Phoebe didn't look at Livvy, her shoulders rigid as she continued to look out the window.

"I understand your anger, sister. Lord knows I've battled my own for long enough," Livvy said. "But Lord Langley threatened to ruin us if we did not do as he asked, Phoebe, and I cannot deal with this alone. Please, I need your help," she said, climbing to her feet.

Phoebe turned as Livvy made her way towards her. She must have seen the desperation in her older sister's face because in seconds she was at her side.

"Livvy, are you hurt? Tell me please."

"I must wash the feel of his hands off me," Livvy begged as they walked into the bedroom. "Please order a bath."

"He didn't? Dear God, tell me he didn't?"

"No!" Livvy shuddered. "No, I stopped him before that…" She couldn't finish the sentence. "I punched him after biting his hand."

"Thank you, Lord," Phoebe rasped, briefly staring at the ceiling. "And I hope you drew blood and his injury gets so infected he loses the hand."

Livvy snuffled but remained silent.

"Now, you sit here," she said, pushing Livvy to the bed and wrapping a blanket around her. "And I will call for a bath and hot tea."

Livvy sat and stared at her knees while the maids came and went with the bath and pails of hot water and then, finally, it was just she and Phoebe again.

"Stand up now and I will undress you. You still have your bonnet on, for goodness sake."

"I can undress myself," Livvy protested.

"Your hands are shaking."

Were they? Livvy lifted them in front of her and saw her sister was right.

"Oh, Livvy," Phoebe said as she removed the coat and saw her sister's torn bodice. She started to cry as she saw the red welts on her breasts and the bite mark close to her nipple.

"Phoebe, I hate to see you cry."

"Too bad, I will bloody well cry if I want to. Someone has hurt one of the two people I love most in the world and the rage inside me demands retribution."

"I'm not the only one hurting, sister. Our cousin will be sporting a few bruises himself."

"Good, he'll be sporting a few more if I ever see him again."

"I love you too, Phoebe, so much. Please say you'll forgive me."

"I forgive you. How can I not when your every thought since father died has been to protect Bella and me? I was just angry that you shouldered so much alone."

The relief at Phoebe's words took the last of her strength and Livvy sagged against her sister.

"Come, let's get you washed before you faint and I'm left holding you," Phoebe said, guiding her into the water.

"Langleys do not faint!"

The water felt blissful on her aching body. Closing her eyes, Livvy laid her head back on the rim.

"Promise me you will remember what we once had as a family, Phoebe. You must, because for so long we had so much love in our lives and it's my hope that one day soon we will again. Because of our mother and father, we will know how it should be, because they taught us to love, sister."

"I do, Livvy, and I promise to always remember," Phoebe vowed solemnly.

Nodding, Livvy then began to make plans for tomorrow. "We shall return home as soon as it can be arranged. I shall inform Lord Ryder of our plans and if he cannot take us, we will take the stage," Livvy said.

"Do you fear Lord Langley will come here, Livvy? Seek us out and demand retribution for what you did to him?

"It's possible, but I think he will wait until tomorrow, believing me terrified and cowed."

"And what will we do when we return to Twoaks?" Phoebe said quietly.

"What can we do but gather up everything we can find and leave as soon as it can be arranged." The words hung in the air between the sisters as Phoebe helped Livvy wash. Her sister was thinking; Livvy could see the thoughts coming and going over her pretty face.

"We need to buy ourselves some time, Livvy, so you can win the Derby, which is only a few days before Christmas. With that and the money we took from the Bruntlys and Lord Ryder, we will have enough to flee."

"Yes, but how?"

"We shall send a note to Lord Langley before we leave

London and tell him you are sorry that you reacted the way you did…"

"I am not sorry!"

Ignoring her, Phoebe continued, "And that you will do as he has requested, and could he postpone his visit to Willow Hall until January to give us more time to prepare Bella for the announcement of their betrothal."

"To give us more time," Livvy said, realizing what her sister was aiming for.

"Exactly."

Livvy shivered thinking about her cousin. "Do you think it will work, that he will keep our secret, Phoebe? I—I punched him hard and bit his hand before I left."

"Of course he will believe the letter, Livvy. Pompous bastard, he'll think he has you cowed and us trapped, but what we will actually be doing is gathering more money so that wherever we run to, we can secure some kind of future."

Livvy knew Phoebe had a point and that their cousin was arrogant enough to believe she would follow his orders.

"You know what we risk if he does not believe your letter and decides to tell everyone now that I am a loose woman and our father took his own life, Phoebe, don't you? If we are still in Twoaks, then we will be ridiculed and censured and there will be nowhere we can hide. Our parents' reputations will be tarnished alongside our own."

"He won't tell, Livvy, because he thinks he has won as we are merely three silly, brainless women. He won't believe we have ulterior motives. By the time he begins to spread his tales, we will be far away and somewhere he'll never find us."

They were silent while Phoebe poured her a cup of tea heavily laced with sugar. Taking the cup, she sipped the hot brew and began to feel her strength returning.

"The other option is to tell Lord Ryder, Livvy. He cares for you and is not a man who will worry about what our cousin says."

"No!" Livvy spluttered, spitting a mouthful of tea into the bathwater. "He, of all people, must never know. I will neither have his pity, nor will I have his name linked to mine if the scandal breaks before we can leave. His brother is a Duke, Phoebe. I could not do that to him."

Once again, Phoebe was silent, although this time her eyes were intent as she looked at Livvy.

"You love him, don't you?"

Livvy didn't look at her sister as she spoke, instead keeping her eyes on the wall before her. "It matters not anymore; all that matters is that I win the Twoaks Derby and then we shall flee."

"I'm so sorry, Livvy."

"So am I," she whispered, dropping her head to her knees.

CHAPTER THIRTEEN

Will had spent the afternoon inspecting houses that were for sale in London. The first two had not held his interest; the third, however, had been perfect. Honey-colored stone with white-trimmed windows and doors had welcomed him as he walked up a path heaped on either side with shoveled snow.

"This is a smart home, my lord," Freddy had said and Will agreed.

He had wandered through the empty rooms, studying each with an eye to what he would change and what he would keep and it was when he placed his bed in his chosen bedroom he knew this was the house he would buy. Will had wondered what colors Olivia would chose to decorate the rooms, and when he had walked through the gardens with Freddy grumbling about his frozen appendages, he realized that he wanted her by his side as he made plans for the future, their future.

Knocking on Olivia's door later that day, Will felt anticipation surge through him at seeing her. He would ask them if they needed anything and then suggest that they dine with him in his suite and to hell with how it looked.

"Hello, Phoebe, this is for you from Freddy," he said, handing her a copy of 'La Belle Assemblee' as she opened the door. "May I come in?"

"Hello, my lord. Please thank Mr. Blake for me."

Alerted by Phoebe's subdued tone that something was not right, he dragged his eyes from the opening behind her and looked at her face. She was pale and he could tell by her eyes that she had been crying.

"What has happened?"

"Nothing," she said too quickly.

"Where is Olivia?" Will reached for the edge of the door above her head and gently pushed it.

"Olivia is not feeling well, Lord Ryder. I must insist you leave!"

"No." Will eased her aside and walked into the room. He found her on the sofa, staring into the fire that was roaring in the grate. Her face was pale and she, too, had been crying. Reaching her side, he dropped to his haunches before her, taking her chilled hands in his.

"Tell me," he ordered, his words sounding gruff. "What has happened to upset you?" She didn't speak, just looked at him. "Tell me, Livvy, please. When I left you a few hours ago you were laughing and happy."

"I… I… there is nothing wrong, my lord, merely a headache," she said, looking over his shoulder.

"Liar. There is something you're not telling me and I want to know what it is," he demanded, taking her chin in one hand and making her look at him. "Your eyes are filled with pain. Let me help you."

"My head is very sore, my lord, nothing more. I wish only for solitude and sleep."

"Your eyes tell a different story, Olivia." Will watched as Phoebe took the seat beside her sister in a show of solidarity.

"Livvy and I wish to return home as we are worried for our sister, Lord Ryder, nothing more than that. We should not have left her and come to London. It was irresponsible," Phoebe said looking at him, her eyes filled with the identical anguish that clouded her sister's. "We need to go home tomorrow, my lord, and if you are unable to take us, then we shall organize to catch the stage."

Will released Livvy's chin and took the handkerchief out his pocket. Leaning forward he wiped the tears from her face and she made no effort to stop him. Something had happened to these women since he had seen them last and he would find out what.

"Shall I call for a doctor?"

"No, please, Lord Ryder. I have need of nothing but what my sister can provide and I urge you to leave us so I can rest."

Her eyes were now on the hands she held clenched in her lap.

"Why won't you trust me enough to help you, Livvy? I am now a rich man and my brother is a Duke. Surely between us we can be of some use to you."

She looked at him then, and he saw the emotions she was trying to hide.

"Livvy, I cannot stand to see you hurting," Will begged her.

"Please, Will, say nothing more," she whispered, placing her fingers over his lips. "Phoebe and I must go home tomorrow and you have already helped us so much."

They looked at each other for several seconds, both uncaring that Phoebe sat only inches away and then she closed her eyes and Will knew she would say nothing further.

"I will find out your secrets, Olivia Langley." He gave her fingers a last squeeze before he regained his feet.

"We hide no secrets, my lord. We are merely missing our sister and Livvy has a headache," Phoebe said.

"Have you ordered your evening meal?" he added, deciding to do some investigating to see if he could find out what had put the Langley sisters into a spin, seeing as neither Phoebe or

Olivia was going to tell him anything.

The sisters both shook their heads but remained silent.

"I shall do so and I'll organize the carriage to take us home in the morning. We shall leave at ten," he said, pocketing the damp handkerchief.

"We have no wish to inconvenience you further, my lord. Therefore, we can take the stage home to Twoaks."

He stood looking down at Olivia when she finished speaking. All the fight had gone out of her. She sat huddled against her sister, seeking Phoebe's comfort and strength and that frightened him the most. Before today he had never seen her cowed. He had seen her feisty and funny, even sad, but never beaten.

"I would never allow you and your sister to return home unescorted, Olivia, especially in your current condition."

"I will be better tomorrow, my lord. My head is very painful."

"I'm not a fool, Olivia. Don't insult me by repeating that lie. However, I will leave you for now as I have no wish to distress you further, but I'll have the answer to my questions soon. Someone has hurt you and I want to know who that someone is." He bent and kissed the top of her head and then, brushing a reassuring hand over Phoebe's, he walked towards the door.

"I must leave the hotel briefly but both Freddy and Luke will be near. Should you need me, ask one of them and they will send for me immediately."

Phoebe nodded; Olivia looked silently at her hands. Walking away was almost as hard as what he had done five years ago; however, this time he was not leaving. This time he was retreating to think and regroup and gather information. He would be back because Olivia Langley was his now whether she believed it or not.

An hour later, Will walked into his old club. His mood was

dark with worry for Olivia. He knew she was safe because Luke would discreetly watch the door to her room until he returned; however, that did not stop him from worrying or wondering. Many scenarios had played through his head since he had seen her and after talking to the porter who had seen Olivia into a carriage that afternoon, his mind was a riot with speculation.

Someone had hurt her and the only person that someone could be was her cousin. Will's first instincts had been to simply confront the man and beat the truth out of him, but something had stopped him. He needed to know what he was dealing with so he had to get Freddy to start investigating and when he was armed with all the facts, then Will would deal with Lord Langley as he saw fit. For now, it would be enough to get the Langley sisters out of his reach and safely home.

Taking a deep breath, he inhaled scents of brandy and cigars as memories of the last time he was here washed over him. Some were good, others made his toes curl inside his shoes as he remembered his callous behavior. The hum of voices was not overly loud as most of the members were still from town; however, the gentle rumble was not unpleasant.

"May I help you, my lord?"

"I have arranged to meet Lord Levermarch here," Will said to the footman, and was then led to a wood-paneled room where his friend was seated before the fire. The carpets had been replaced but not much else had changed. Various pictures and plaques hung on the walls of the male bastion and newspapers and ashtrays were sitting on the surfaces.

"Will, take a seat. I have taken the liberty of ordering you a brandy. Bloody chilly out there."

He and the Marques of Levermarch had disliked each other intensely before Will left England. An unsmiling, serious man known to be ruthless in business and boring in play, Finn was the opposite of what Will had once been.

"My thanks, Finn." He took the seat beside him. "I'd forgotten how this cold seeps into your bones and stays there," he added, picking up the glass of amber liquid on the table before him and taking a sip.

"Did you find a town house that was to your liking?"

"I did, actually—Freddy will negotiate the price tomorrow while I return to Twoaks."

"So soon?" the Marques said, raising one black eyebrow.

As big as he, Finn had hair black as midnight, liberally laced with silver, and eyes so blue they were piercing in their intensity.

"I am to escort two old friends who need to return home immediately."

"Old friends? Why do I sense there are women involved?"

The Marques had come across Will in India when he was attempting to educate a thief not to steal from him. The thief had had friends and Will had only Luke so they were outnumbered. Finn had evened the odds. They had then shared a drink to nurse their bruises and talked, and when Finn realized that Will was no longer the spoiled nobleman that had left England, he had stayed with him and they had become friends.

"Sisters who grew up not far from my home," Will added, staring hard at the fire. *How was she?* He should be there watching over her.

"I sense there is more to this story, my friend."

"What do you know of Lord Langley?" Will asked

Finn snorted. "More than I want to. He's a man with licentious hobbies and very little sense. I have heard rumors of late that he is rapidly running through his inheritance and incurring debts all over town."

"I am friends with his cousins and they are the ladies I am to escort home," Will said. "It was their father who was the previous Lord Langley."

Finn gave him a steady look before he spoke; however, he

did not ask the questions Will saw in his eyes and for that he was grateful.

"Supposedly he has redecorated his house with lewd paintings and statues and throws wild parties for his friends when they are in town. Apparently, these parties are orgies with many of the women in attendance being young enough to be his daughter."

"Does he live in London all year?" Will questioned.

"Yes, they say life in the country does not suit his carnal appetites; however, he has been known to attend a house party or two, especially when the entertainments suit his needs."

The thought of Olivia under the same roof as the man Finn described made Will feel ill. Is this why she was upset: had Langley done something to her?

"I've heard rumors that he is marrying soon; however, no one seems to know the bride's identity," Finn mused.

Marry! Will would kill the man before he reached the church if he attempted to marry one of the Langley sisters.

"So, why the interest in Lord Langley? Don't tell me a woman has finally captured your interest."

Will's instinctive response was to deny it but instead he said, "Perhaps."

"About time you returned to us, William!"

A bell clanged in Will's head as two men appeared before him and Finn. *Round two*, he thought. Of course, he had known that he would eventually run into the men he had befriended in his rebellious years; he had just thought it would be during the season.

"Lord Rathbourne, Sir Humphrey," Will said, gaining his feet and bowing to the men. Rathbourne slapped him on the back and then pumped his hand.

"Rathbourne, Sir Humphrey, you know Lord Levermarch," Will said, making the introductions.

Frowning, Rathbourne gave Finn a short bow to which Finn nodded but did not reciprocate. Sensing the animosity, Will said, "What are you two doing in town?"

Neither had changed. Both were dressed as Viscount Marshall had been at the docks earlier that day.

"Got bored in the country so we came to town for a spot of gambling and a visit with Madam Genevie, and now you are here you can join us. It will be like old times," Sir Humphrey said. "Plenty of whores looking for excitement at this time of the year, Will."

Confronting one's past, especially his, was never going to be easy but Will hadn't thought his shame would cut quite as deep as this when he did. He had been a wastrel, intent only on indulging himself, just like the men before him.

"Thank you, but no, I am to dine with my friend here and then in the morning I'm returning home to my family."

Silence followed Will's statement and then Rathbourne glared down at Finn.

"He is no friend of ours. Now come, enough of this nonsense," Rathbourne said. "We need to get you back in shape. All this extra weight will scare off the ladies. You need a reminder on how things were and then all shall once again be as it was."

"I believe you just insulted my friend, Rathbourne, and I do not take kindly to such a slight."

Will's words had not been loud yet their intent was very clear—apologize, or there would be retribution.

"You have changed!"

"For the better, I believe," Will said softly. "Now apologize and then leave the club."

"Think you're better than us now, Lord Ryder? All that time spent with savages has obviously made you forget how to be a gentleman!" Sir Humphrey sneered.

"You believe you are better than I when the only way you know how to live is off other people?" Will questioned softly. "Neither of you have experienced a day that wasn't self-indulgent in your life and simply live like leeches off your family. I no longer wish to drink and gamble my days away and whore through the nights. If that makes me better than you, then so be it."

"You'll be sorry for those words!"

"I'm sorry I ever thought of either of you as a friend," Will said, meaning every word. "Now apologize and leave the club. I have no wish to look upon either of you again this evening."

"I will never apologize to him!" Rathbourne stated, glaring down at Finn.

Sighing, Will began to take of his coat. Behind him, the Marques was laughing softly.

"Wh—what are you doing?"

"I have no wish to get your blood on my new coat."

Apologies were muttered hastily before he could even pull out an arm, and then the two men fled from the room. Taking his chair again, Will downed the last of his brandy.

"Thank you. However, it was unnecessary, I assure you. I have been insulted by far worse than those two," Finn drawled.

Will looked at his friend and then the glass in his hand.

"Do you know, Finn, it is never pleasant to be faced with one's failings. Yet today, I have been faced with mine twice. I cannot believe what a self-indulgent boy I was. It is a wonder my brother didn't beat me frequently to knock some sense into my thick skull."

"Had you been mine, I would have."

Will snorted.

"Now tell me what troubles you, my friend. I can see it is a woman, because I have never seen that particular look in your eyes before."

"No, I think not, Finn. I'm not sure what the hell is going on yet. However, if I need your assistance then you may be sure I'll ask for it."

"Fair enough," Finn said. "And as my brothers are away and I have business your way I shall take up your invitation to stay with your family for Christmas, if it is still open? I'm looking forward to this Derby you have told me so much about."

"Of course it's still open, and you are welcome anytime."

Will started going over business and soon Finn was as immersed as he and the remainder of the evening was spent discussing this while he tried to keep Olivia's pale face out of his head.

Arriving at the Grillion two hours later, Will summoned both Freddy and Luke to his rooms.

"No one has come in or out of the Langley sisters' room," Luke stated after Will questioned him.

"Pay one of the hotel staff to watch the door 'til morning, then both of you get some sleep as Luke will be driving us home tomorrow while you stay in London, Freddy. Organize the purchase of the town house and then find out everything you can about Lord Langley, his associates and the previous Lord Langley, Olivia's father," Will said. "In fact, I want to know everything about the Langley family even if it appears unimportant."

"Is something wrong?" Luke questioned, looking worried. "I've known the Langleys my entire life and would not wish them any harm."

Will loosened his necktie and motioned for his friends to seat themselves on the sofa across from him. They were all comfortable with each other, having spent the last five years together.

"The truth is I don't know, Luke. But it is my belief that all is not as it should be with them, plus I think something has happened here in London and that it has something to do with the current Lord Langley." Will went on to explain what he had seen when he visited Phoebe and Olivia and found them in tears.

"Well, I'd say something is definitely amiss then, my lord." Freddy looked worried, his usually happy face solemn. "As those two were not in that a state when I saw them earlier."

"And that is why you will dig deep, Freddy, and when you are done in London come back to Twoaks and start there."

"As shall I, Will," Luke said, regaining his feet. "I'll just go and make sure everything is in readiness for the morning now."

Freddy followed Luke out the door and Will was left alone. Stripping off his clothes, he climbed into bed. He was tired, but his head was filled with Olivia. What the hell was going on with that woman? Whatever it was he would fix it because one thing was for certain, he would not lose her now, not when he finally understood what she truly meant to him.

***

They left early the following morning and the first part of the journey was carried out in silence. The sisters had seated themselves opposite Will and proceeded to stare out the window, rarely looking his way. Every time he tried to engage them in conversation, they answered briefly and then resumed their contemplation of the winter landscape. Livvy was pale and drawn. She gnawed her lip and picked at the end of her gloves and occasionally sighed, and he knew she was totally unaware of doing so. Will was not one to speak without something to say and enjoyed silence as much as the next man, but the weight of this was heavy and oppressive and steadily driving his frustration and anger to a head. Seeing Olivia like this was making him feel helpless and he had no idea how to get her to tell him what worried her. Perhaps he should make her forget her problems for a while.

"Perhaps Major Buntley has the right of it, Olivia. If a little head ache can lay you low, surely you will never be able to manage to ride in the Derby with all those strong healthy men to compete against."

"I beg your pardon!" She looked at him in stunned surprise.

"The Twoaks Derby. Remember, it is not far away and you had mentioned riding in it. I'm not sure now that you are capable."

Now that was better, Will thought. The fear had gone from her eyes.

"B—but you defended me against, the major!" Olivia spluttered.

Will flicked something invisible from his sleeve before he answered. "That was before I realized how delicate your constitution was."

Livvy looked at her sister who seemed just as surprised as she, although Will thought he saw the hint of a smile in Phoebe's eyes.

"I do not have a delicate constitution. I had a headache!"

"If a mere headache can lay you low then surely a stray whip or kick from another rider will put you in bed for weeks."

Will wondered if he got her angry enough whether she would tell him what had happened yesterday.

"I wish I had a whip now!"

"Livvy!" Phoebe gasped. "That's not very nice when Lord Ryder has cut his trip to London short to accompany us home."

"Well, he's not being very nice," she muttered, folding her arms in a defiant gesture that made Will want to lift her into his arms and kiss her senseless.

"Forgive me. I had thought my words showed concern, Olivia. I did not mean to offend you."

She sat on the edge of her seat scowling at him.

"Yes, you did, and I do not appreciate your words at all. I will ride in that bloody Derby and do you know what, Lord Ryder?"

What was it about this woman that made him feel so much? Just looking at her made something stir inside his chest.

"No, but I'm sure you're going to tell me, Miss Langley."

"I'm going to beat every one of those so-called strong men and then we shall see what you and the major have to say."

"And I hope that you do, Olivia," he said, holding her eyes steady.

That deflated her; she sank back on the seat and looked at him. "You provoked me deliberately, didn't you?"

"Of course not."

The sisters snorted their disbelief at his innocent expression but said nothing further. Will was relieved that, for the remainder of the journey at least, the conversation was livelier, even if occasionally Livvy's eyes clouded with worry when she thought he wasn't looking.

Darkness had fallen as had more snow as the carriage pulled into the small inn they had stopped at on their way to London.

"Come," Will said stepping from the carriage and indicating the sisters should follow. The proprietor was pleased to see them again and Will ordered food to be served in their rooms, then escorted the sisters up the stairs.

"We shall head for home after our morning meal," he then said, stopping outside their door. He smiled at Livvy and she offered him a tentative one back, and then as Phoebe went inside he ran a finger down one of her cheeks.

"Leave your worries at the door tonight, Olivia. Rest and know I am only a few minutes away should you need me."

"I shall try," she said before following her sister inside and shutting the door softly behind her.

***

Livvy woke up shivering. Phoebe was snoring softly beside her and every time she moved she took the blankets with her, exposing Livvy to a blast of chilly air. Slipping from the bed, she pulled on her coat and boots. She needed more blankets or a hot brick, anything to chase away this chill that seemed to have taken up residence inside her. Opening the door, she closed it quietly behind her and then winced as a board creaked under her foot.

"Olivia, where are you going?"

Livvy saw Will's head first and then his bare torso followed.

"I had thought to get another blanket, my lord, as the room is cold and I cannot sleep." She couldn't look away from his chest. Were all men as muscled as he?

"Come, I will give you one of my blankets to keep you warm while I see about getting you what you need," he urged.

Livvy shook her head and made her way towards the stairs. "I shall just get some more from the proprietor. It will take but a minute."

"You are not walking around here alone at this hour, Olivia."

Livvy suddenly felt herself lifted in the air.

"Put me down," she whispered loudly. "I can look after myself, Lord Ryder."

He placed her back on her feet inside his room and shut the door behind them.

"Do you have to fight me every step of the way?"

"Yes," Olivia said as memories of when she had last been in this room filled her head. She had opened his shirt and lay against that heated skin and it was foolish to want the same again. Dragging her eyes from him, she looked at the candle she still held.

"I'm not your enemy, Olivia," he said, taking it from her and setting it down on the table, walking back to where she stood he then wrapped his arms around her and held her close.

"What are you doing?"

"Warming you up."

The blissful heat from his body felt so good.

"I need to go back to my room. Please, Will, let me leave."

"Soon," he whispered, pressing her head onto his chest.

Laying one hand on the solid-muscled plains of his chest, she felt the steady beat of his heart beneath, and the last of her resistance fled. How could anything this right be wrong, Livvy wondered. She couldn't fight him anymore, not tonight.

"Thank you, Will."

"For what?" he said, taking her fingers in his and kissing them softly, leaving each one alive with sensation as he moved on to the next.

Olivia knew she had no rights to this man and that they could have no future together, yet as she lay there, pressed against his big warm body, she came to a decision. If she had only one night with him then she would take it and store it in her memories for the times when she missed him most. She wanted him to be the first and only man to know her body intimately, because Livvy knew that after tonight there would be no other for her. In truth, there never had been.

"The buns, the firewood, taking us to London—in fact, everything." Olivia sighed, lifting her head from his chest to look up at him. Running her fingers along his jaw, she then trailed them down the column of his throat. He swallowed and she knew he felt her touch as deeply as she did his.

"I want to give you so much more, Olivia." His hand cupped her face. "Share your worries with me, let me help you."

Livvy placed her fingers over his mouth. "We can have this night, Will, but no talk of tomorrows, please," Olivia added. "Tomorrows are too uncertain."

"This will not be the only night we share, Livvy, I'll make sure of it." His words were a vow and it broke her heart to know that she could never allow them to happen.

He kissed her softly, drawing a response from her and soon Livvy arched into him, wrapping her arms around his neck. Only then did he deepen the kiss.

"Over the years, my memories of you remained clear yet they didn't do you justice," he whispered against her lips. Picking up several of her curls, he wrapped them gently around his fist and urged her closer. "You're so beautiful, Olivia. Everything about you touches something inside."

"I missed you so much." Livvy needed to tell him that.

"I know, sweetheart, but had I stayed then the man I was, would not have been good enough for you. It was not just my family who deserved more from me."

"Make me yours, Will, please," Livvy said. She did not want to hear any more of his words when one day she would have to walk away from him as he had her. Livvy knew the pain of their last separation would be nothing compared to this time.

"You've always been mine, Olivia Langley, just as I have always been yours."

Stepping out of his arms, she reached for the buttons on her coat.

"Are you sure, Livvy?"

"I have never wanted anything more."

CHAPTER FOURTEEN

Will's throat went dry as Livvy slowly opened her coat. Each movement of her hands told him of her nerves, her fingers fumbling with the task. Her innocence made him want her more, the sensual sweetness in her eyes as she shot him nervous glances turning his body hard with need.

"I want you so much," he rasped, looking at the white nightdress she wore beneath. Her small candle offered little light, yet he could see the outline of her body through the soft, worn fabric, as she wore nothing beneath. Full and unbound, her breasts were partially covered by long coils of silken hair, the dark circles of her nipples peaking under the fabric, urging him to touch them. She looked up at him, her eyes holding the promise he had wanted since their first kiss.

"Touch me, Will."

Slipping an arm around her waist, he gathered her back into his arms.

"I will, my sweet, everywhere." Will placed his lips on her neck, tasting the smooth skin.

"Pl—please blow out the candle."

She was an innocent and this one time he would do as she asked him, but when next they made love it would be in his bed and he would have branches of candles lighting the entire room so he could see her beautiful body.

Picking her up, Will walked to the bed and, sweeping the covers aside, he then laid her on the sheets beneath. He felt her eyes following his every move as quickly he pulled off his boots. Then, clad only in his breeches, he joined her.

"This," Will whispered, stroking her hair, "was what first drew me to you. It has so many colors, both sunrise and sunset, the blaze of fire and golden hue of the brightest day." Lifting a lock to his lips, he then stroked it down her cheek.

She gently laid the palm of her hand on his chest, and that single gesture made an ache start deep in Will's belly. Need consumed him. She was fire in his blood. Easing her onto her back, he unbuttoned her nightdress and then with her help, removed it.

"I want to kiss you, Livvy, every inch of your soft skin, every dip and hollow, every lush curve is mine to explore."

"Can I touch you?" she whispered, her voice thick with need.

"Yes." He shuddered at the thought of her hands on his body. "I long for your touch."

Climbing from the bed, he quickly removed the rest of his clothing and then lay beside her again. The room was dark, with only the faintest shaft of moonlight now filtering through the window, but it was enough to see the dark bruises on her breast.

"These marks," Will said, tracing each raised welt. "Tell me how you got them." She heard the threat in his words, because she went still.

"'Tis nothing, Will, just a few scratches from the brambles at home. I fell into them while picking blackberries."

"Those marks are not from blackberries, Olivia, especially as they are not ripe at this time of the year." He rose over her and braced his hands beside her head. "Who did this to you?"

"No one did this. I fell, there is no more to it than that," she whispered.

"Stop lying to me," he growled, trapping her legs beneath his as she tried to move. "Tell me now, Olivia, and I will see they are punished."

She arched up into him, wrapping her arms around him.

"Livvy," he warned, trying to ignore the feel of her breasts against his chest. "Tell me who did this."

She moved against him again, the friction causing them both to moan. Tracing her tongue along his lips, she then kissed him deeply.

Will lost every rational thought as one of her hands began to stroke him. She kissed his jaw and cheeks and then her fingers brushed along the base of his spine, making him shudder.

He took her mouth beneath his, deepening the kiss. Where one stopped another started. He kissed her neck and shoulders, making his way to the full slopes beneath.

"My luscious Livvy," he breathed against her silken skin. He licked the top of her breasts and she moaned as he began to travel down one creamy curve reaching the taunt nipple, eager and waiting for him. He bit softly into the crest and she made a small sound that hiked up his passions another notch. Lust consumed him; later, he would find out who had dared to hurt her and make them pay, but right now he would make love to her until she realized she belonged to him now, body and soul.

Livvy tried to breathe as Will lathed kisses over her breasts. Driving her fingers into his hair, she raked her nails over his scalp. Her body was taut and need was pooling between her thighs. Sensation was building inside urging for release. He moved to her ribs, where he brushed soft kisses over them and then down to her belly. Each sweep of his tongue made her writhe, and when she felt his breath on her curls, she gasped. He placed one hand on her stomach, anchoring her in place and then he moved lower. Dear God, he was kissing her there, between her legs and it was… magnificent! She cried out as he touched his tongue to the plump folds and then moaned when he found the taut little bud which he tugged gently between his teeth until she arched off the bed. He pushed a finger inside her and Livvy felt her body give and then she was spiraling over the edge as pleasure washed through her. Still reeling, Livvy felt Will's large body climb up hers and then his lips were on hers again, seeking a response which she willingly gave.

"Open your legs, sweetheart, and wrap them around my hips."

She did as he asked and felt him begin to enter her body.

"There will be pain, love."

"I know. Please, Will, make me yours," Livvy begged as he stretched her further.

"I don't want to hurt you, Livvy." She heard the strain in his voice as he held back.

"You could never hurt me," Livvy whispered. Running her fingers over his sides she felt the tension in him. Arching upwards, she took the rest of him inside her.

"Livvy!"

"Yes, Will, now I am yours."

He placed his forehead on hers and remained still for several seconds, letting her adjust to him.

"The pain has eased," Livvy whispered.

He pulled out and thrust back in; she didn't wince or tense so he did it again and soon her cries were matching his moans. Livvy felt the delicious tension build inside her once more. Wrapping her arms around his neck, she held him tight.

"Yes, love, let go for me."

"Will!" Livvy cried as again she felt the sensations swamp her. Seconds later, he stiffened inside her and called out her name, following her into oblivion.

"Are you all right, Livvy?"

He lay slumped beside her. Both of them were breathing hard.

"Yes." Was all Livvy could manage.

Wrapping an arm around her, he pulled her head onto his shoulder and then, reaching for the blankets, he tugged them up. Livvy settled against him, her nose pressed into his chest, one hand resting over the steady beat of his heart, and in seconds they were both asleep.

Livvy opened her eyes as gray streaks of dawn filtered slowly into the room. Looking at the broad chest beneath her cheek, she could not remember a night when she had slept so deeply. She felt warm with him holding her close to his body.

Moving slowly, she sat up and his hand fell to the bed beside her. His face was relaxed in sleep and she saw the boy he had once been. Livvy studied him; she would never see him like this again, never wake in his arms or feel his lips on hers.

Making herself move before he woke, she slowly climbed from the bed. The floor was cold and she was soon shivering as she searched the room for her nightdress and coat. Hurriedly pulling her clothing on, she tiptoed to the door and opened it and then with one last look at the large handsome male she loved slumbering peacefully, she slipped into the hall and closed it behind her.

Phoebe still slept the sleep of the undisturbed as she entered their room, so Livvy climbed into the chair and wrapped her hands around her knees and waited. Memories of last night washed over her, of the gentleness and words Will had used. She shivered as she remembered the delicious sensations he had made her feel with his hands and lips. She would have to hold those memories close. Tuck them inside and only bring them out when she was desperate to remember him.

"Livvy?"

"It's all right, Phoebe. I rose early and decided not to wake you so I have been watching the new day arrive."

"Oh," was all her sister said as she huddled beneath the covers. "Perhaps as you are awake you could see about getting us some tea."

Climbing to her feet, Livvy ignored the new twinges in her muscles last night's activities had left her with.

"As you wish, Madam."

"And toast!" Phoebe called as she left the room once more.

Will opened his eyes and reached for Livvy, only to find the space beside him cold and empty. Looking around the room, he searched for any sign of her but she had gone. He understood she had left because of Phoebe but he did not like it. He wanted her in his arms and beneath him.

She was his now, his to cherish for the rest of their lives. Eager to see her, he hurried out of bed to wash and dress.

Two hours later, his fingers itched to lunge across the carriage and grab Olivia and shake her until her teeth rattled. She had greeted him at breakfast politely, as though they were strangers, her smile false and overly bright like any silly, young debutante. If Phoebe hadn't been seated next to her he would have hauled her back up the stairs and ravished her. What the hell was she playing at? She had said last night that they could have one night together as tomorrows were uncertain, but he hadn't believed her.

"I am glad we have just passed through Damply, my lord. I must admit to feeling heartily sick of the inside of your carriage," Phoebe said.

"Yes, I imagine you had greater plans for your first foray into London, Phoebe. One hopes that your next visit will be of a longer duration."

Livvy was looking out the window but Will noticed her flinch as he mentioned

London.

"You never did tell me if you managed to see your cousin, Olivia. It would have been a shame to go all that way and not catch up with him."

"H—he was otherwise engaged and unable to find time to see us, my lord."

Livvy reluctantly turned to face him as she spoke, and he knew she was lying because it was something she had never done well.

"I have not met your cousin; I hope as your only remaining relative he is doing his duty by you all."

Both Phoebe and Livvy stiffened at his words, shooting frantic glances across the carriage; Phoebe was elected to reply to his question.

"Of course the role is new to him, my lord, but he is doing as we expected of him."

That, of course, could mean anything, Will realized, as he watched Phoebe cross her fingers before tucking them under her skirts. So, Lord Langley was not providing for the sisters. He would be very interested to hear what Freddy had to say about the man when he returned, and if Will didn't like it then he would be next to visit Langley. It would be no social occasion and if he found that the man had mistreated Livvy or her sisters in any way there would be hell to pay. He remembered the marks on her breasts then. How had they happened? Dear God, if he found out a man had inflicted them upon her he would tear him apart with his bare hands.

"I find it stifling when I'm living here, yet when one returns to Twoaks it is a wonderful feeling, is it not, Livvy?"

"Yes, Phoebe, wonderful," Livvy said in a tone that held no emotion.

"Coming home is not something I will ever again take for granted," Will said as the carriage climbed the last rise to Willow

Hall and came to a stop.

"I can understand that," Phoebe added as he opened the door and then turned to help her down. "I sometimes think leaving your home makes you appreciate it more."

"That it does. And now I want to speak with your sister, Phoebe, so if you could give me a few minutes alone with her, I would appreciate it. Luke will bring your luggage into the house."

"I have nothing to say to you," Olivia said, trying to get out of the carriage which was impossible as he was standing in the doorway.

"However, I have something to say to you," Will said as he waited for Phoebe and Luke to walk up the path away from the carriage. Bracing his hands on either side of the doorway, he looked at her perched on the edge of the seat.

"If I didn't know you better I would say you were a woman who likes to tease men, Livvy Langley." Will placed two fingers beneath her chin and forced her to look at him. "But I do know you and know you do not have that behavior in you; therefore, it is something that has been forced upon you."

"Leave it alone, Will, please."

"No," he whispered, kissing her softly. "I will not leave it alone and after what we shared you cannot ask that of me."

"I can offer you nothing," she said, her eyes holding his, begging him to understand.

"You love me, Olivia Langley, otherwise last night would never have happened."

"No, you are mistaken, my lord, I—I love no one."

"Your eyes say the opposite to your lips, my love. When I return to Willow Hall tomorrow we will talk, Livvy, and you will tell me what troubles you. And while you lay in your cold bed tonight remember one thing. You are mine now and I will never let you go."

Leaning forward, Will kissed her softly, their lips clinging and holding until he eased away, leaving them both breathless. He then helped her from the carriage, his hands steadying her as she stumbled when her feet touched the ground.

"Tomorrow, my love," he added before climbing back inside.

Minutes later, Livvy stood at the edge of the path and watched Will's carriage until it had gone from her sight. She shouldn't feel the rush of joy at his words; it was wrong. They could have no future because of her cousin. Yet when he told her that she was now his, Livvy had wanted to yell that he was now hers, too.

"I saw that kiss, Olivia Langley!"

"Hello, Bella," Livvy said to the youngest Langley who was waiting inside the front door as she arrived. "Have you had a nice time since I was away?"

"Yes, Jenny's sister Helen is such fun."

"Well, now that you have greeted me perhaps we could step inside and close the front door so all the heat does not escape."

"Luke told me the weather was terrible in London and he was glad to be out of it when I enquired after his trip. He seems to be continually cross at the moment and I'm not sure why, Livvy."

"He's been away for five years, Bella. I should imagine it will take time for him to adjust," Livvy stated, stomping her feet on the mat.

"Perhaps you're right, and now I want to know why Lord Ryder was kissing you."

"Leave it be, Miss Bella. Your sister should be allowed her secrets," Jenny said, arriving in the hallway in time to shut the door.

Livvy looked at Phoebe and they shared a nod. They had

both decided to tell Jenny and Bella everything; there would be no more secrets between them.

"Will you and Bella come into the parlor, Jenny? Phoebe and I have some things we need to discuss with you both."

They were soon all settled in the chairs and Phoebe handed out the gifts to oohs and ahhs of delight and then the copy of 'La Belle Assemblée' was produced which actually got a round of applause. Livvy did not want to dampen the excited mood but knew what she had to say could not wait because she would probably run out of courage.

"I need to tell you both something, and it is not pleasant; however, both Phoebe and I believe you should hear it."

Phoebe sat on the arm of Bella's chair in case their little sister should need her support.

"What is it, Livvy? You look so serious."

"It is serious, Bella."

She nodded but said nothing further.

Livvy started with the death of their father and how he had taken his life.

"Poor Papa, he never was the same after Mother died," Bella said when Livvy had finished.

"Are you not angry with him, Bella? I was furious knowing he had left us alone with no support, especially after you also suffered in the accident," Phoebe said.

"I'm angry that you shouldered this alone, Livvy, and sad that he did not think to leave us with financial support, but I saw how he withdrew without Mother. His mind was not the same after her death and he left us long before he took his life. We have memories of what he meant to us and those are the ones I will hold on to."

Livvy had misjudged Bella as she had Phoebe; the youngest Langley was a lot tougher than she appeared.

"But there is more, isn't there, Livvy?"

Nodding, Livvy told the rest of her story, explaining about her visit to their cousin and his blackmail threats.

"Why that scoundrel! How dare he treat you that way when we welcomed him here and I made him my special bread and butter pudding?"

Livvy had to laugh when Jenny jumped to her feet, indignation and fury evident in every quivering inch of her ample body. "I escaped before he could do me any permanent damage, Jenny, and left him with a swollen jaw and a large bite mark on his hand."

"What shall we do, Livvy?"

"Run, Bella. Run as far as necessary, because there is no way I will ever let that man touch any of us again," Livvy stated. "If he is to blacken our names then he can do so, but we will not be here to listen to it. I am saddened that the good man our father was will be forgotten but there is nothing we can do to change what will inevitably happen when Lord Langley starts his campaign to discredit us."

"Livvy and I sent Lord Langley a note before leaving London and told him we would welcome his intentions and asked that he visit in January instead of December; therefore, we have a bit of time before we need to flee," Phoebe said.

"That is if he believes us, Phoebe, and is not harboring a deep anger over my treatment of him."

"He will believe it, Livvy," Bella said. "He believes he has us trapped. Furthermore, we are women without means. What could we possibly do but yield to his demands."

"Exactly what I said," Phoebe said with a smug look on her face.

"However, if anyone can think of another plan we are open to all suggestions," Livvy added, thinking of leaving Will and how much it would hurt.

They all spoke at once. Questions were asked and answered

and then Jenny said, "I say we kidnap him and send him on a long voyage. My cousin could organize that if we had enough money. He has his own boat which he smuggles goods from France to England on, I'm sure he would be able to take Lord Langley on a long journey somewhere."

The Langley sisters looked at Jenny, all wearing differing expressions. Livvy was thinking, Phoebe was in awe and Bella was nodding.

"What kind of goods does he smuggle?" Phoebe questioned, looking more interested than she should.

"It matters not what he smuggles, just that he can help us if we need him," Jenny said, giving Phoebe a look that indicated she was not happy discussing her nefarious cousin any more than was necessary.

Bella clapped her hands together. "I like the idea of that vile man being at the mercy of a wicked ship's captain."

"We don't have enough money, surely?" Livvy said, hardly daring to believe she was considering Jenny's words seriously. "And what if he returns?"

"When he is gone then we do to him what he was to do to us. We start spreading stories around about him, blackening his name so that by the time he returns no one will believe a word he says," Bella said with a calculating look on her face.

"It may just work," Phoebe said, looking out the window. "It has not snowed for a few days here by the looks of things and that means the roads will be passable by horseback. If we go out for a couple of nights this close to Christmas, we should be able to steal enough money to pay for his long voyage."

"I can't believe I'm considering this," Livvy whispered, feeling hope flutter inside her. "It is surely too farfetched and we have no hope of pulling it off."

"Dire times call for dire actions, sister," Phoebe stated.

"We do need more money for whatever we choose to do,"

Livvy agreed. "For now we will concentrate on obtaining that before deciding upon the drastic step of kidnapping a peer. And what if we fail?" she warned. "He could have us clapped in irons.

"We will not need to worry about his return because you will have married Lord Ryder by then and we shall be protected by both him and the Duke." Bella's face held a sly smile.

Livvy ignored the words, although she could not stop the swell of excitement in her chest at the possibility of marrying Will. Dared she hope?

***

Will wandered aimlessly along the lower floor of Rossetter. He had been back

for several hours and was due to look at the property that Freddy had found for him nearby. However, he was feeling less than enthusiastic about the prospect and, of course, that was due to a certain cinnamon-eyed woman. His thoughts were consumed with Livvy and how she had felt in his arms, the rightness of sharing his life with her. Never had he wanted a woman with such an all-consuming need. She was in his blood and he knew she would be there until he drew his last breath. He needed her to trust him, tell him what troubled her, but he was damned if he knew how to do that.

"'ill!"

Looking up at that shriek he found Joseph approaching with his son riding on his shoulders.

"You seem preoccupied, brother. Care to join my rascal and me in the conservatory where you can unburden your soul while he plays?"

Will didn't unburden to people. He kept his secrets and thoughts close to his chest. Yet wasn't that part of what had driven him and his brother apart, his inability to share his thoughts and troubles? Joe was also a wise man who would not pass judgment unless it was required.

"Lead on, your grace," he said, realizing he wanted to talk about Livvy to someone who understood how to love.

The conservatory was to the rear of Rossetter and comprised of a long, curved glass entranceway that opened into a huge round room with more windows that looked over the pasture and hills beyond. It housed hundreds of varieties of plants Will had never known the names of, and Greek statues. A raised fountain housed fish and was an instant attraction to Billy, who squealed and pulled his father's hair as they drew near.

"Hideous brat," Joseph said fondly as he lowered his son into his arms and let him look into the water.

The windows, even on a cold day, kept the room at a nice temperature and

Will wandered slowly around the room, touching leaves and smelling flowers and trying to remember the names of the statues as he and his siblings had when they were children and found themselves in here.

"Aphrodite, Athena and Zeus," he said.

"Poseidon," Joseph said, pointing to one tucked behind a large leafy plant.

"Hera and Ares," he then added, pointing to another two statues.

"I always felt sorry for Hera being stuck next to Ares.

"Why?" Joseph said, trying to stop his son from plunging head first into the water.

"Firstly because she is Zeus's wife and he's off romping with the goddesses of love and wisdom and secondly because she is the queen of marriage, women and that sort of thing and is next to the god of war," Will said, studying the statues before him.

"Perhaps she's enjoying the change," Joseph said, lowering

himself onto the seat beside Hera and Ares.

"I think that's highly unlikely as Ares would be spending most of his time off battling foes," Will said, joining him.

"And your point is?"

"True," Will grunted, stretching his legs out before him.

"So how was your trip to London?"

"Brief, successful, and frustrating."

"Come here, Billy, and I will remove your mittens if you don't tell your mother."

Eager to shred leaves and play in the dirt, the little boy came to his father instantly to have this hands freed.

"Start with the successful," Joseph said, pocketing the mittens.

The brothers discussed warehouses and ships and the town house Will had purchased for some time, and slowly he began to relax as Billy dashed around the room returning every few minutes with another gift that he handed either Will or Joseph. So far they had flowers, leaves and a small pebble.

"If there are any insects, prepare yourself. He loves them and they are the highest form of offering he can give a person."

"Excellent," Will said. "I shall hope that particular delight eludes him, then."

"Now tell me of the frustration, brother."

Blowing out a loud breath, Will thought about what he would say and then simply started with, "I think I've found the woman I want to marry, Joe."

"Olivia Langley."

"Yes." He was not surprised his brother had guessed.

Opening his arms Joseph caught his son as he ran to him and Will realized he wanted to do that to his own children, his and Livvy's children. He wondered if they would have red-gold locks like their mother.

"Why is loving Olivia Langley frustrating?"

"I didn't say I loved her," Will clarified. "Just that I want to marry her."

Ignoring his brother's snort he continued. "Something is very wrong in that household, Joe. Freddy and I encountered Phoebe and Livvy in Damply waiting for the stage to London."

"What! I hope you bloody well took them yourself. Christ, it doesn't bear thinking about all the things that could have happened to two women alone on a stage coach to London." Joseph shuddered.

"After a heated debate with Olivia, I managed to convince her that my carriage was her only option."

Joseph laughed. "I can imagine that debate. Olivia Langley is not a lady who would willingly take a backward step."

She wasn't and that was just something else he liked about her. Livvy would never let him have everything his own way.

"'ill," Billy said, reaching for his uncle. Hefting the boy into his lap, he was then rewarded with a throaty little chuckle as the boy held out something wriggly for him to inspect.

"Delightful," he said, taking the offering and hefting it over his shoulder while the boy wasn't looking. Yawing loudly, Billy stretched his legs onto his father's lap and settled his body into Will's arms.

"Freddy said that the Langleys only have one servant and that when he walked through the house, many of the paintings have been removed because he could see the darker patches of paint left behind.

"If they are indeed struggling they have hidden it well, because when Penny and I visited them at Thea's prompting everything appeared the same as it always had."

"Something's wrong, Joe," Will said, running his fingers through his nephew's soft locks. "Livvy was happy enough when we reached London. I took them around the warehouses and gave them gifts and hot chocolate and then I left for a few hours to go to an appointment. When I returned, everything had changed. Both she and Phoebe had been crying and told me they had to return home immediately.

"Who had they seen in that time?"

"Their cousin, Lord Langley."

"Sniveling little weasel. I never liked that man. However, I saw no indication that he was not supporting his cousins as he should, so Penny and I did not interfere. You believe otherwise, don't you?" Joseph looked at his brother.

"Yes, and Freddy is now digging as deep as he needs to, to find anything that may indicate what I suspect."

The brothers were silent, both looking at Billy who had pushed his dirty face into Will's jacket and was now snuffling happily in his sleep.

"I never thought much of children before him, you know. But he tugged at my heart from the first glance."

"It's because you share blood. Makes things more complicated," Joseph said. stroking his son's soft cheek. "When he was born, I cried like an infant and vowed from that day onwards to love and cherish him, even when he hands me worms."

Will sighed. "Love is a painful, uncomfortable thing, brother, and I'm not sure if I'm up for the challenge."

"Too late," the Duke drawled with a smug expression on his face. "I was thinking…" he then added.

"I'm shuddering."

"Christmas Eve is soon and we should invite the Langleys to join us for the burning of the Yule log and you could then coerce Olivia under the mistletoe after I have coerced Penny."

"I think that is a very sound notion, brother. Get Thea to invite them. They won't refuse her."

CHAPTER FIFTEEN

"Are you not wishing to tie us up and take our jewelry, too?"

"No, we just want your coins, thank you, Madam. Now please return to your carriage," Livvy said.

"But surely you need to search my sister and I to ensure we are not concealing anything of value," the woman persisted.

The Langley sisters had been surprised when the two elderly ladies had stepped from the carriage they had pulled over. Neither of them had swooned or cried. In fact, they appeared delighted with the turn of events. One had dived back into the carriage, returning with a large velvet pouch carrying a substantial amount of money if the size was any indication of what it held.

"We carry this in our carriage for just such an occasion," the woman had then said before throwing it at Livvy. "Your need is obviously greater than ours."

"We have no wish to inconvenience you further, ladies. Our purpose was to gather money to feed our family, nothing more," Livvy said, feeling the need to explain in the face of such generosity.

"Oh, well, in that case, we insist you take some of our jewelry, don't we Hester?" the woman said, beginning to remove her necklace.

"Dear God," Livvy whispered, her horror turning to laughter as the second lady started doing the same.

"Ladies, please! We have no wish to take your jewels and really must insist you return to your carriage. I would hate for you to get overly cold on such a night." Livvy could hear the tinge of desperation in her words as she struggled to stop laughing. Beside her, Phoebe was making noises behind her hand.

"Such a lovely thing to say, Hester, don't you think?" one of the ladies said, looking at Livvy once more.

"Lovely," Hester agreed.

"I have a gun pointed at you, my lady." Livvy felt she had to point out the obvious.

"Yes, but I'm a good judge of character, young man, and desperation is the only thing making you do this. Therefore, we will not hold it against you," the woman said, turning towards the carriage.

"Are you sure you don't want a necklace or two? They're quite valuable, I believe," Hester said.

"Positive, but thank you again for your generosity and allow me to apologize to you for any inconvenience," Livvy said, knowing that neither Jenny nor Bella would believe them when they recounted tonight's events. She hardly believed them herself.

It was as the women finally closed the carriage door that Livvy looked at the trees beyond and saw the man watching them from horseback.

"Ride, Phoebe. We are being watched!"

Turning Boris, Livvy charged after her sister, who was by now a few feet in front. Crouching low over his neck, she urged her mount on as she followed Phoebe, who was weaving in and out of the trees. The thunder of hooves told her that whoever was pursuing them was gaining fast.

Sending Boris a silent apology, she kicked him in the stomach which sent him leaping forward until she drew level with her sister.

"Split up!" Livvy called and then she veered left as Phoebe kept going straight. Seconds later, the sound of hooves told her that whoever was chasing them had elected to follow her.

Livvy knew the roads well and was about an hour's ride from Twoaks, so she would need to try to lose whoever followed her by changing direction frequently before she reached her home.

Urging Boris on, he sailed over a fence and then Livvy pulled hard to the right and headed back along the road. Whoever followed her was an excellent rider as her maneuver did not deter him. They rode at breakneck speed for a time until Livvy felt Boris slowing beneath her. Desperate now to lose their pursuer, she saw the forest ahead and charged recklessly into it. Branches tore at her hat and scarf but Boris kept going as she turned him left and right, until finally she dared to look behind her once more and saw that she was now alone. Pulling Boris to a halt, she ran a trembling hand down his sweaty neck and listened. There was no sound of hoofs or breaking twigs. She would stay here for a while until she was sure her pursuer had finally gone.

Livvy waited until her teeth were chattering from the cold before she urged Boris from the trees and back onto the road. She missed Phoebe's company as the darkness closed in around her and she tried not to look at every shadow and jump at every sound. It would not be fair to ride Boris hard again so soon, yet she longed to crouch over his neck again and race home. Urging him into a gentle trot instead, Livvy sang softly until she saw the welcoming light of her home.

"Livvy! Dear God, I thought you had been caught and I did not know what to do," Phoebe said, hurrying towards her.

"I'm all right, Phoebe." Livvy climbed wearily down from

Boris's back. Leading him to his stall, she unsaddled and brushed him down and then threw a blanket over his sweaty flanks before filling up his trough with food and water. "You did well tonight," she said, patting his cheek before shutting the stable door and leaving him to his much needed rest.

I was so scared," Phoebe said, following her up the path to the kitchen door. "I turned around to look behind me and found you had disappeared with whoever was following us behind you."

"We will talk inside, Phoebe. We need to warm up. My hands and face are so cold," Livvy said, hurrying towards the house. She then yelped as her feet started to slide on a patch of ice but she could do nothing to stop falling. Landing on her bottom, she slid several feet and came to a rest against the kitchen door. Turning the air blue with several choice curses, Livvy tried to regain her feet.

"Did you just cuss, Olivia Mary Elizabeth Langley?"

"Oh, and you've never heard those words before, Phoebe Jane Emily Langley," Livvy said, taking the hand her sister held out to her.

"Let go!" Phoebe cried as her feet started to slide, too.

"Ouch," Livvy grunted as her sister sat on her. "Get off me, you lump."

"Lump? I'll have you know I'm considered petite."

"By whom? Not those blind idiots you call admirers, surely?" Livvy hissed as she tried to push Phoebe to her feet.

Phoebe started giggling as she struggled to get off her sister, only to fall back into her lap. The aftermath of fear soon had Livvy joining her and in seconds they were both laughing hysterically. It was their youngest sister who found them minutes later rolling around on the icy ground laughing like two candidates fit for Bedlam.

***

Will was weary when he finally returned to Rossetter after pursuing the highwayman. Stabling his mount, he then made his way through the silent house to his rooms. A fire had been lit and the warmth was welcome as he shrugged out of his jacket. The scarf and hat he had tucked inside fell to the floor. The foolish highwayman had plunged recklessly into the thick forest in hopes of escaping him, and in doing so he had lost his belongings. Lifting them to his face Will sniffed. Frowning, he did so again and felt ice fill his veins.

Knocking on the front door of Willow Hall early the following morning Will's mood could be termed, at best, dark. He'd spent the night with visions of Olivia being clamped in irons and him visiting her in Newgate prison. Any sleep he'd got had been fleeting and he was feeling mean after a long, restless night. Maybe he was wrong about her being a highwayman, and he was willing to ask questions before he shook her so hard her teeth rattled, yet the gnawing anger inside him told him he was not

"Good morning, Mrs. Bell. I have called to see Olivia."

"She is in the stables, my lord. If you like to come inside, I shall fetch her for you."

"Don't trouble yourself, Mrs. Bell, I know the way," Will said, heading around the side of the house before she could refuse. Lengthening his stride, he walked down the path to the rear and then over the grass towards the stables. There had been no fresh falls of snow for several days now, and although it was still bloody chilly he was relieved to be outside without something icy dripping down the back of his neck. His boots made crunching noises as they walked on dewy grass and he could see the trail of Olivia's footprints to his right leading towards the stables.

The Langley estate was not huge but it had plenty of rolling hills and enough green pasture so that it was pleasing to the eye. However, all Will could think about was what he would say to the eldest Langley when he got hold of her. Entering the stables, he passed several empty stalls, one he noted held a carriage leaning drunkenly on its side which indicated the wheels were broken, yet more evidence that the Langley sisters were without funds.

The sound of humming reached him as he neared the end of the row. He stroked the black head of one of the only two horses in residence as he looked over the half door and studied the animal. There was no doubt to Will's mind that he had seen this animal twice before. The tightness in his chest intensified as a roaring sound filled his ears. Rage suffused him at the thought of what she had done.

"I'm sorry you had to gallop so hard last night, Boris. However, after the effort you put in I have come to realize you are a big fake for letting Harvey beat you all this time."

Will stood listening to Livvy as she talked to the horse. He was happy to let her incriminate herself further and then he'd show himself and tell her exactly what he thought of her foolish behavior. Just thinking about the speed she rode and risks she had taken last night plunged his stomach to his feet.

"I shall get you some fresh water, Boris."

Realizing she would see him as soon as she reached the door, Will stepped up to it and rested his hand on the top.

"Care to explain why you galloped your horse so hard last night, Olivia?"

She literally froze in a half-crouch position. Her knuckles quickly turned white as they clenched around the handle of the bucket.

"L—Lord Ryder!"

Her words came out squeaky and high-pitched and she looked like a cornered rabbit.

"Shall I repeat the question, Olivia?" Will couldn't believe he wasn't breathing fire and was even more surprised at how polite he sounded, although his hands were gripping the wood, the edges biting into his palms as he fought the urge to reach for her.

"I—I ah, took Boris out for a run yesterday and pushed him too hard. I was t—training for the D—Derby."

Will let her words hang in the air between them as he studied her. She wore an old dress and cloak with her sunset curls pulled back with a simple band at the nape of her neck. She looked like a young country maid and he wanted to grab her and shake her hard. What was she thinking, taking such risks? Even now she could be in a jail cell somewhere awaiting the hangman's noose.

"A training run," Will said, stretching the last word out for a few seconds. "Is that how you got that scratch on your face?"

Her hand crept up to cover the mark that ran the length of her forehead, an angry red welt that was no doubt received after she flew into the woods to escape him.

"Yes," she said, shooting him a look before dropping her eyes to her hands.

"Well, I think that proves you are not ready to ride with the men in the Derby, Olivia, if you cannot even manage a simple training run on a snail like Boris without injuring yourself."

"Boris is not a snail!" she said, defending her horse before herself.

She could have been taken from him last night.

"I have seen Boris and this other horse next door before but cannot remember where," he said, opening the latch and letting himself into the stall. Olivia, he noted, shuffled round Boris's rump to appear on the opposite side from where he now stood. "Did you buy him from someone local? Perhaps I have seen his sire somewhere."

"Why are you here?" she whispered, once again looking nervous.

"You know why I'm here, Olivia. To return the things you lost last night," Will said, urging Boris back a couple of paces until his rump nearly touched the wall. He then circled the front.

"What things?"

He saw the minute she realized what he had done. By moving Boris and approaching from the front, he had caged her in.

"These things." Will kept his eyes on her face as he pulled the hat and scarf from the inside of his jacket.

Her eyes widened as she looked at the items, and then she turned away. "Th—they're not mine."

"Yes, they are, and it was you who robbed me on my way to Rossetter House and it was you I chased last night!" Will snapped out the last word as his anger got the better of him. "Have you any idea how foolish you have been?"

She didn't yield or admit defeat, and Will could almost admire her courage as she faced him with her shoulders drawn back. She'd dropped the bucket and was now gripping Boris's tail tightly and her cinnamon eyes were wary, as if he was a four-headed creature and she was uncertain of its next move.

"Have you resorted to your old ways, my lord, and started drinking throughout the night?"

"No, and you will not help this situation by insulting me."

"W—well this story you have concocted is pre… pre…"

"…posterous," Will finished for her as he took a step closer.

"If you needed money, Olivia, you should have gone to my brother for help and if not he, then to me when I returned."

"You are speaking of things I have no knowledge of, Lord Ryder. Now please step to one side so I may freshen B—Boris's water."

Will advanced on Olivia until he had her back pressed to the wall and his hands braced on either side of her head. She grabbed his wrists and tried to move them and then pushed against his shoulders but he did not yield. Instead, he pressed his body into hers.

"Let me go!" She begged him.

"I chased you last night while you flew over fences and rode under trees at speeds which, had you fallen, would have broken your neck, Olivia Langley! Do not tell me to let you go! I want to bloody shake you until your teeth rattle!"

"Please, let me go."

"A highwayman! Could you not have stolen a silver tea service from a neighbor or something from my brother? He would never have noticed in that bloody great palace he lives in!"

"I have no idea what you are talking about," she said, clinging stubbornly to her story.

"You could have been shot!" Will roared, his temper now unleashed. "And I suppose your accomplice was Phoebe?"

She kissed him, threw her arms around his neck and pressed her body into his. Will was so surprised he didn't react and then he felt her, the soft sweet curves that were Olivia Langley. Fighting the need that was filling his body, he wrenched his mouth away.

"If you think one kiss can stop me this time from saying what needs to be said," he rasped, "then think again."

She bit his bottom lip and then licked it, and Will shuddered.

"Olivia."

She didn't heed his warning, instead kissing his chin. She then lowered her hands and ran them up his back.

Her innocence was provocative, each touch and kiss may be one of inexperience, but it drove Will wild in seconds.

Kissing her way back to his mouth, she opened her lips and once again placed them on his.

Will felt his anger turn to lust as Livvy touched and kissed him. Suddenly, he was aware of her breasts crushed against his chest and the feel of her fingers running over his back. He tried to push the sensations aside, tried to speak again, demand that she tell him the truth but as he opened his mouth, she pushed her tongue inside and he was lost. Cupping her face, he tilted her head and took control of the kiss, his anger making him take her lips with furious hunger. Teeth clashed as they struggled to taste each other. Reaching for her cloak, he pushed it aside and then cupped her breasts through her dress. Instead of shying away she arched forward, filling his palms.

"I'm going to take you here and now," he whispered, tugging the bodice down and freeing her flesh. Lowering his head, he took one hard nipple into his mouth and bit down. She moaned, so he did it again.

"I have carried the taste and feel of you since our first kiss." His words were harsh against the straining flesh.

Livvy opened his jacket and waistcoat, then pulled his shirt free from his breeches. Slipping her hands beneath she then touched his chest, running her fingers over the muscled plans of his stomach and Will could do nothing to stop the moan that left his lips.

"You're so warm," she whispered, stroking the flesh above the waistband.

"Christ, Livvy."

His eyes closed as she trailed her fingers over his skin then with fingers that trembled Livvy released the buttons and slipped one hand inside his breeches to cup the hot, hard length of him.

"You're killing me, love," Will rasped as she caressed him. "But what a way to die." He groaned as she ran a finger over the tip of his arousal. When he could stand the torture no longer, Will grabbed her wrist and lifted it to his chest. He then reached for her skirts and pulled them to her waist.

"Hold your skirts, Livvy." She did as he told her to, her eyes glazed with desire, cheeks flushed.

"Now, Will, please. I need you now," Livvy begged him.

Will kissed her swollen lips and then touched the soft, plump petals that shielded the secrets between her thighs. She was wet and ready for him, and was soon making small incoherent noises, urging him on as he stroked and caressed her heated flesh. Slipping two fingers inside her tight sheath, he felt her clench around him.

"Yes, sweetheart." She gasped and he knew what was coming so he kissed the cry that tore from her lips, and then as she leaned into him trying to draw a breath, he lifted her.

"Wrap your legs around my waist."

In seconds, he was driving up as he lowered her onto his length. It was heaven to be encased in her velvet heat again.

Livvy urged him on, taking each silken slide and thrust as he pushed her passions higher until she was sobbing his name over and over again. She kissed his jaw and then he claimed her lips as he thrust into her hard, again and again. It was rough and fierce and soon the pressure reached its pinnacle and they both cried out their release.

Will's chest heaved as he drew in a deep breath. Need had driven them to take each other with none of the tenderness they had experienced before and he felt no remorse as she had been with him through every thrust and moan. She lay boneless against him, her arms wrapped around his neck her breath brushing his skin.

"Livvy, we need to talk." Will ran his chin over her hair.

"I don't want to talk. I want to sleep."

He snorted, but lowered her gently to her feet. Readjusting her bodice, he then straightened his own clothes.

"No, love, not this time. This time I want the truth."

"What truth?"

Standing once again, he lifted her chin, forcing her look up at him. Her lashes were at half-mast and her lips rosy from his kisses and she looked lush and sensual and she was his, every last maddening inch of her.

"You will tell me, and now," he said in a voice that usually got him exactly what he wanted.

"Livvy!"

"It's Bella. Dear lord, she can't see me like this!" Livvy hissed, looking for somewhere to hide.

"Tell me, Livvy, now before your sister sees the flush in your cheeks and your kiss-swollen lips and I tell her what we have just been doing."

"You wouldn't. Please don't upset Bella, not now."

The pleading in her eyes was his undoing.

"Pick up Boris's hoof and pretend to inspect it," Will said. When she didn't move he turned her and then lifted the hoof and wrapped her hands around it.

Dropping to his knees, Will looked at her. Her eyes were still dazed and had anyone really looked at her they would have known instantly that something was not right.

"This conversation is not over, Olivia, so don't think it is. And if I hear that you have attempted to don the guise of highwayman again, my wrath will make you wish you had never been born. Do you understand?"

She remained stubbornly silent.

"Answer me, love, or I will tell Bella how responsive you are to my touch."

"You wouldn't dare!" Livvy gasped.

"Try me," he said, holding her eyes until she relented.

"Yes, I understand. However, I still do not know what you are talking about."

"It would not be wise for you to think me a fool, Olivia, or to think I will eventually give up." Placing a brief kiss on her lips, he added, "I will know the truth and it will be you that tells me."

"Livvy?"

"In Boris's stall, Bella!" Livvy called to her sister.

"Horrid Lord Langley has sent us another letter and Phoebe is threatening to open it if you do not hurry."

When Bella peered over the door, Will had his knife in one hand and was flicking nothing out of Boris's hoof. To give him credit, the horse played his part perfectly, especially after what he had been forced to witness.

"Oh, hello, my lord. I did not realize you were here."

"Hello, Bella," Will said, wondering what was in horrid Lord Langley's letter because Livvy had flinched when she heard his name.

"Do you wish to take tea with us, my lord?"

"Lord Ryder has no wish for tea, Bella," Livvy said. "However, I will come with you now," she added, placing Boris's hoof on the ground once more.

"After what Freddy told me about Jenny's tea tray, I would be a fool to refuse such a request." Will rose to his feet and took Livvy's arm as she tried to hurry out the door Bella now held open. He knew her game; she thought that surrounding herself with family would stop any further questioning on his part.

"Can you tell me more stories of your travels, my lord?"

"Surely between us, Freddy and I have told you everything we know," Will teased the youngest Langley as he turned to shut the stable door and ran a hand down the horse who had moved to look over the door, no doubt making sure they were leaving after disrupting him for so long.

"There is always more, my lord. I want to know about the food this time and the houses you lived in. And then there is life at sea, as Phoebe tells me you own ships," Bella said, limping along beside him.

"I think the weather may deteriorate, my lord. Perhaps you had better head for home after all."

Will didn't comment, just looked up at the clear winter's day. Livvy wanted him gone yet he would not leave until he was ready. In fact, he wanted to look inside the house and observe the sisters. His anger had stopped him from seeing the outside of Willow Hall on the way into the stables, yet now he noted the neglect. The stable door hung on an odd angle and several of the fences were listing slightly. The rear of the cottage was chipped and peeling and there was a crack in one window.

"We shall go round the front," Livvy said, trying to shake his arm free and direct him down the path past the back door which stood open.

"We are not so formal, Livvy, I have no problems with walking through Mrs. Bell's kitchen. After all, I'm sure I ran through it at some stage in my youth."

She frowned at the charming smile he arranged on his face. She wanted no part of him walking through her house or into any of the rooms she did not direct him to.

Ducking his head he entered and then sniffed loudly.

"I smell something sweet. Tell me that cake is fresh from your oven, Mrs. Bell, and I shall marry you at once!"

"Go on with you, my lord. 'Tis nothing but a gingerbread cake," the housekeeper said, shooing him through her domain behind Livvy and Bella.

"But it is my favorite," Will added.

He heard Livvy mutter the words 'glib tongue' and something even less complimentary as she stomped up the stairs.

"So heavy footed for such a slight woman," he goaded, following the sway of her hips.

"Manners, I believe, are the hallmark of a gentleman," she said, walking quickly down the hallway.

"Alas, then I am found lacking once again." Will looked at the walls and noticed the darker paint where paintings had once hung. They were struggling to survive, these women, but were too stubborn to let anyone see or help. Well, that was about to change and Olivia would just have to get used to the idea.

CHAPTER SIXTEEN

Livvy waved Will into a chair and then told Bella to get Phoebe.

"I can light that."

"No, you are a guest, Lord Ryder, and our servants have the morning off. Therefore, I will do it."

Silence hung in the air between them as Livvy fussed with the fire. She wondered how they had been as close as two people could be in the stables yet now there was a distance between them again. Admittedly, it was of her making, but how could it be any different when she was forced to lie to him?

"If you just talked to me, Livvy, I could help you."

Closing her eyes at his gentle words, Livvy shook her head. She couldn't, not until they worked out what to do with Lord Langley. If they decided upon kidnapping him, which she shouldn't even contemplate but couldn't help herself, it was such a risk and could have disastrous consequences if anything went wrong.

She should not have made love with Will again; every time he touched her it bound her closer to him. He was her love—that once in a lifetime, happily ever after love every girl dreamed of and Livvy feared it would destroy her to walk away from him.

"Promise me you will take no more risks, sweetheart."

He cared for her, really cared for her, Livvy realized as she looked down into the flickering flame.

"I would not be happy if something happened to you, Olivia."

Her eyes were drawn to him and their gazes caught and held. Livvy wanted to pull away before he saw it, her love, yet was not strong enough to do so.

"You will never guess who has come to visit!"

"Who, Bella? Livvy rose to her feet with a sinking feeling. Not many people visited the Langleys even in the summer months; therefore, if they were out and about in the colder weather that could not be a good sign surely.

"Mrs. Popplehinge. Phoebe has gone to greet her."

"Dear Lord!" Livvy groaned, tearing off her cloak and opening the wood basket and stuffing it inside. "Tidy my hair, Bella, quickly. That woman is always so perfectly presented she will make comment if I am not the same. Oh, this is a disaster," Livvy added. "Quick, Bella, hurry and intercept them before Phoebe turns Mrs. Popplehinge into a raging beast."

"Yes, Livvy."

When she had left, Livvy cast her eyes around the room checking everything was in place and then they landed on him.

"Here I sit, love, where you last saw me."

"Please don't call me that," she whispered, ignoring the flutter in her chest at the endearment. "And do not provoke or make any sweeping statements about… you know," she added, waving her hand around. "While that woman is here."

"Are you confessing, my sweet? Finally coming clean on your nefarious night time activities."

"Nothing of the sort. I am just hoping you will behave and not tease or… or…"

"Make outlandish statements about the Essex gang and infamous Dick Turpin?"

"I always hated your ability to find humor in every

situation," she snapped, bending to pick up a spark that had jumped out of the fire.

"You are very lucky that I am being humorous, Olivia Langley, because were I following my instincts, I would have dragged you into a room somewhere in this house and locked you in there until you told me what I wanted to hear."

She slowly straightened at his words. His gray eyes held a threat that she would be foolish to ignore. Swallowing, she tried to ease the sudden dryness in her throat.

"You're a vastly different man from the one who left England, aren't you, Will?

He nodded.

"When you speak now, people listen and obey you, don't they?"

"Everyone except you, my love."

Livvy felt heat steal into her cheeks at his words.

"Olivia, you will not believe who has honored us with her presence on such a horrid day. Why, it is Mrs. Popplehinge, our dear friend."

"Were there a hole, I would dearly climb down into it," Livvy muttered as Phoebe's words reached her.

"Chin up, love. I'm here."

And he was, Livvy realized. The man she loved was seated in her parlor and she may not have him much longer in her life. But he was here now, and for that she would be grateful, because there was little doubt to Livvy's mind that the next few minutes were going to be fraught with innuendo and snide comments.

"How lovely of you to visit us, Mrs. Popplehinge, and in such conditions," Livvy said as she swept into the room with as much ceremony as any courtier.

"Lord Ryder!" Mrs. Popplehinge cried, delight written on every line of her gaunt face as she ignored Livvy in favor of the large, handsome lord. "I am delighted to see you again. I was unable to attend the Twoaks Assembly, you see, as my dearest son and daughter-in-law were in expectation of the arrival of their first child."

Livvy watched as Will bowed deeply over the woman's hand. She wore a black wool coat and on her head she wore a tall hat that tilted as she curtsied.

"Ah, Phoebe, why have you not taken Mrs. Popplehinge's coat?" Livvy questioned.

"I will not be staying long, therefore I will keep it on," the woman said loudly, as if she was addressing a room filled with hundreds of people instead of four of them.

"May I compliment you on your hat and coat, Mrs. Popplehinge? They really are quite the most stunning examples of fashion I have seen outside London."

"A man who understands fashion, my lord, is a very rare man indeed," Mrs. Popplehinge gushed. "In fact, some women could take a lesson in style from you," she added, looking from Livvy to Phoebe with a curling lip.

"I hardly think you…"

"Yes, we are select group, Mrs. Popplehinge," Will interrupted before Phoebe could launch an attack. "And our stars shine brighter when surrounded by those displaying less sartorial elegance."

Phoebe snorted, Bella giggled and Livvy simply rolled her eyes. The man had Mrs. Popplehinge eating out of his hand in seconds and her sisters laughing, which in itself was a feat, especially when Phoebe's most hated person sat across from her.

Livvy excused herself briefly on the pretext of ordering tea and then slipped upstairs to read the letter that Lord Langley had sent. Picking up the heavy parchment, she stifled a shudder and ripped it open. Running her eyes over the loathsome black scrawl, Livvy quickly scanned the page.

'I am pleased to see that you have come to your senses, Olivia, and I forgive you for your behavior when last we met. I have great expectations given your character, of us both finding mutual enjoyment in what I propose, and under the right guidance we shall be happy with our new circumstances. I have found a suitor for Phoebe, who will treat her as her nature dictates and on the matter of Isabella, I will offer for her a few days after my arrival at Willow Hall, which I anticipate will be on December 23rd, weather permitting. I have felt the twinge of familial obligation since your delightful visit and wish to spend Christmas with my dearest cousins. Please have everything in readiness for my arrival. Your devoted cousin.

"You'll feel some kind of twinge by the time I've finished with you," Livvy said as she carefully folded the note and tucked it inside the bodice of her dress. The arrogant fool had believed every word of the letter she and Phoebe had sent him and that they would welcome him into Willow Hall with open arms. He would get a welcome, all right, but it would not be the one he was expecting.

They did not have much time to decide what action to take, but at least he was not due to arrive until after the Derby which was on the 21st of December, two days from now. That would give her time to win the race and secure the prize money.

"Livvy, Jenny has brought tea!"

"Coming, Phoebe," Livvy called, hurrying back down the stairs. She prayed there had been no blood shed in her presence.

"He is the cutest baby, you understand, my lord. I believe he takes after my side of the family."

"One hopes he has your fashion sense, Mrs. Popplehinge." Will sent Livvy a wink as she entered the room.

"What did they name him, Mrs. Popplehinge?" Phoebe questioned in a polite voice that made her sister stare at her. Mrs. Popplehinge and Phoebe were not usually on the speaking terms… well, any terms actually.

"Chadwick Hybernious Popplehinge."

To her credit, Livvy keep pouring the tea with a steady hand while Phoebe coughed loudly and earned a hard whack on the back from Mrs. Popplehinge that made her eyes water.

"Th—thank you," Phoebe rasped when she could once again breathe.

"It is a fine name, Mrs. Popplehinge, and I can see you are a proud grandmother," Will said, taking the cup Livvy handed him. She'd tried to avoid his fingers but they brushed hers nonetheless and she twitched, which made him smile.

"Do drink up, Lord Ryder. It is so cold outside and I know how much you love tea." Phoebe gave him a sweet smile.

"May I ask, Mrs. Popplehinge," Livvy said, taking a seat when there was nothing else for her to do. "Why you have graced us with your presence today?"

Livvy's question produced an interesting reaction in the woman. In fact she noted a flush filling her thin cheeks. There was little doubt she was uncomfortable, yet nobody filled the awkward silence.

"Well, I had hoped to speak privately with you, Miss Olivia," she said, looking uncomfortable.

"I'm sure you can speak freely here, Mrs. Popplehinge," Livvy said.

"I do not like the Bruntlys!" Mrs. Popplehinge blurted out to the surprise of all present.

"I don't think you are alone in those feelings, Mrs. Popplehinge," Livvy added.

"He—he abuses Mr. Popplehinge every Sunday when we see him at church and his wife told me that I was a busybody with very little to offer anyone!"

She hadn't expected that, Livvy thought.

"Well you are not the sole recipient of her vicious tongue, Mrs. Popplehinge," Phoebe said, fishing out her handkerchief and handing it to the woman as she sniffed.

"The major and his wife abused Livvy at the Assembly. They said nasty horrid things, but luckily Lord Ryder was there to stand up for her."

"Thank you, Phoebe," Will said.

"But how can we help you?" Livvy prompted Mrs. Popplehinge.

"You must win the Derby or at the least beat that man's horse, Olivia. You simply must!"

Once again, she had reduced the room to silence. Livvy wanted to laugh. Was she serious? Twoaks's most proficient gossip was championing her.

"I will, of course, do my best, Miss Popplehinge. However, I must point out that Major Bruntly does have a fine horse."

The woman clutched the handkerchief and, surprisingly, Phoebe's hand.

"Can I do anything to help you?"

"You just have, Mrs. Popplehinge, by believing in me."

"Oh, I…I…oh, thank you, Olivia, and I do believe in you, dear," Mrs. Popplehinge said, sniffing louder.

"Well, I will expect you to stand with my sisters and cheer loudly then, because there are not many who seem overly happy to see me there."

"You have more supporters than you realize, dear. It is just that most of us have no wish to upset the major."

"I had not realized the major was such a bully." All eyes turned to Lord Ryder who had been, until that point, sitting quietly and listening.

Mrs. Popplehinge nodded furiously. "I wish someone would put him in his place."

"Lord Ryder will find a way."

"Will I?" Livvy could see Will was surprised by her words.

"Yes, you are clever and rich, and that man is neither… well, maybe a little of the second," she added.

"I have actually already begun to look into the major and his affairs, Mrs. Popplehinge."

"Have you?" Surprised, Livvy looked at Will.

"After the way he spoke to you at the Assembly, I wanted to know everything about him."

Livvy flushed with warmth at his words. He had cared enough about her even then. She wanted to kiss him again and have him hold her, which was foolish because she would be leaving him any day now.

"I would be most grateful if you could do something about him, my lord." Mrs. Popplehinge looked hopeful.

"How can I refuse a woman who dresses with such style and elegance?"

Olivia watched Mrs. Popplehinge's hands flutter around her as Will complimented her.

"And if you and Mr. Popplehinge are not otherwise engaged, the Duke and Duchess would like to extend an invitation to you both, and of course the Langley family, to share the burning of the Yuletide Log with us at Rossetter House on Christmas Eve."

"Oh, yes, we would love that above all things, my lord!" Mrs. Popplehinge cried, leaping to her feet. "But before I leave to tell Mr. Popplehinge the news, I would like to give Olivia this," she said, producing a parcel from the depths of her coat.

Livvy took the parcel and placed it on her lap. She could feel all eyes on her as she opened it slowly. Lifting the purple satin sash, she held it up for everyone to see.

"It's… it's remarkable," she said when she could find her voice.

The sash was two hands width wide and had the name Langley stitched in bright yellow letters down the front.

"I noticed last year that you rode in a coat and breeches. I just thought this would give you a more feminine touch," Mrs. Popplehinge said, looking anxiously at Livvy.

"It certainly will, and it's beautiful and very thoughtful of you, Mrs. Popplehinge, I shall wear it with pride."

"Really!" Mrs. Popplehinge clapped her hands together in delight. "If this weather will just stay fine then we shall have a race, and I feel certain that with my sash and your skill we shall beat that horrid major."

"How can we not," Phoebe said, rising to her feet to escort Mrs. Popplehinge to the door.

"We are grateful for the invite of course, Lord Ryder." Livvy carefully folded the sash back into the wrapping as Bella closed the door behind Phoebe.

"And accept," Bella added before Livvy could refuse.

"Excellent."

Before Livvy could protest, he had gained his feet. "Then I will also bid you good day, ladies, and of course will see you all at the Derby," he added, bowing before he left the room.

"Thank you."

He had reached the front door before Livvy's voice stopped him.

"For what?"

She blew out a loud frustrated breath.

"Just about everything."

"You're welcome, although I cannot take credit for Mrs. Popplhinge's sash. That creation was hers alone."

She walked to where he stood and let him pull her into his arms. The kiss was one of the sweetest they had shared.

"We… this," Livvy said, pointing to him and then back to her, "cannot go on."

"Why can this not go on?"

"There are things I can't explain that will not allow this…" Livvy said, casting about for the words that needed to be said and coming up short.

"This will happen, my love, never doubt that," he added, brushing a curl off her cheek. "But now, Olivia, I want you listen very carefully to what I am about to say to you and I expect you to obey every word."

"I have no wish to obey your words."

"You don't know what they are yet." He touched her cheek. "Do not leave this house again at night because I shall know," he added, clasping her chin.

"I do not answer to you." Livvy pulled free of his touch.

"In this you do, my love."

Livvy watched him open the door, and in seconds he was gone.

***

Livvy woke early on the morning of the Derby. She was both nervous and anxious for the race to start so it would finish and she could collect her money and get back to Willow Hall to decide what to do with her family's future. The Langley sisters had talked long and hard about what they would do tomorrow, as this was the chosen date for their final decision due to their cousin's arrival the following day. They had left things 'til the last minute because of the Derby and the much needed prize money, and were hopeful that Lord Langley would not arrive early because Jenny had muttered something about poisoning him if he did.

"You're awake," Phoebe said, poking her head around the door and seeing Livvy sitting up in bed.

"Yes, and contemplating our futures."

"There are still only the two options open to us," Phoebe said, lifting the blankets and slipping in beside her sister. "Well, three actually if you take into account Jenny's idea of poisoning him, which sits comfortably with me. However, I know you won't choose that option."

"No."

"All right, so we either flee or kidnap him."

"You make the choices sound simple, sister," Livvy said, resting her head on Phoebe's shoulder.

"Whatever we choose to do, Livvy, we will do it together," Phoebe said. "We have stored everything we want Jenny to hide in the barn and Jaccob will come and get it tomorrow if we choose to run."

"All three of us will make the final decision tonight, Phoebe, no matter if I win or lose the Derby. I have counted our coins and there is enough to see us to Scotland, if that is our course, and between us we shall come up with a plausible story of why we are there."

"I've been thinking about that, Livvy. Perhaps we should call on Mr. and Mrs. Munford. I'm sure they will help us."

"Perhaps, but how do you discount my non-pregnant state and lack of husband?"

"Yes, that could be a problem," Phoebe mused. "I think if we said he had beaten you and you had lost the child and we were on the run that they would believe you."

Livvy snorted. "We shall think about it tonight, sister, but now I must rise and eat something or I shall not be fit to ride Harvey. We shall enjoy today with the people who have been a part of our lives for so long and worry about the future later."

"All right. Jenny has your clothes cleaned and boots polished, so hurry and dress and I shall see you downstairs." Phoebe planted a smacking kiss on Livvy's head before climbing out of bed.

Livvy washed and dressed and then plaited her hair so it rested between her shoulder blades. Pinching her pale cheeks, she then forced a smile onto her stiff lips and left the room.

Jenny placed a heaped plate of food in front of her as she

sat at the table and Livvy tried to not to think about this being her family's second to last breakfast in the only house she had ever lived in. There was no time for sentiment now; they all knew what must be done.

"Are they comfortable?"

Bella was looking down at the breeches Jenny had altered for her. They had been Jaccob's.

"Yes, very much so. It's amazing how much freedom they give you compared to skirts."

"Well," the housekeeper snorted. "I think that is enough on that subject as it is not likely that women will ever walk freely in breeches as men do. You eat up now please, Miss Olivia," she added. "You need a substantial breakfast."

Breakfast was porridge and then Jenny forced Livvy to eat a piece of bread and jam because she needed the extra strength. Livvy felt sad that this woman may not be in their lives for much longer. She had come to mean so much to the Langley sisters.

"I shall see you at the Derby," the housekeeper then said, shooing them from the room once their bowls were emptied to her satisfaction.

The sound of a knock on the door had Bella hurrying to open it to find Mr. Blake on the other side.

"I would be honored if you will allow me to take you all to the Derby."

"We had thought to walk beside Livvy and Harvey, Mr. Blake," Bella said.

"I shall escort your sister."

Livvy felt the breath catch in her throat as Will appeared in the doorway.

"Excellent! Bella, get your things. We are leaving now," Phoebe said, doing the same.

"And Mrs. Bell, would she like a lift also?" Mr. Blake said, looking in the direction of the kitchen.

"Yes, she would," Livvy said, turning on her heel to retrieve the housekeeper. Her heart still thudded from just seeing Will standing in her doorway and she needed the space to collect herself. She also liked to think that perhaps Mr. Blake would be there for Jenny when they left, and that in time, perhaps he could persuade Jenny to return his feelings.

"Jenny, collect your things. Lord Ryder has a carriage which he wants to escort you, Bella and Phoebe to the Derby in," Livvy said, deliberately not telling her that Mr. Blake would also be in there.

"Oh, now, that's nice." Jenny hurried to take off her apron.

Livvy watched her pull on her coat and hat and then the gloves she was never without and then followed her up the stairs to the front door.

The only indication that Jenny was unsettled with the presence of Mr. Blake was the flush of color into her cheeks, as she sailed past him out the door.

"We shall see you there, Livvy," Phoebe said, kissing her sister. Livvy accepted the gesture and returned her sisters' hugs with perhaps a little more desperation than was required, and all the while she was aware that Will watched on.

When the carriage had left, Livvy pulled on Jaccob's jacket and gloves. Her hair now had a black satin ribbon, courtesy of Bella, tied at the base of the plait and with fingers that were not all together steady, she placed Jaccob's hat on her head.

"Nice touch," he said, pushing open the door as she slipped the sash Mrs. Popplehinge had made over her head.

"Thank you," Livvy said politely as she followed him outside and closed the door behind her.

Will saw the tension in every inch of Livvy's body. Her chin was up, neck straight, shoulders rigid as she walked before him around the house towards the stables. She looked small and slender in the men's clothing. Somehow the fitted breeches and jacket made her appear even more feminine, and every muscle in his body clenched as he fought the urge to grab her and haul her back into the house so he could hold her close and make slow, sweet love to her. Will was not happy about the fact that other men would be looking at her long, shapely limbs or the sweet curve of her bottom as she rode her horse.

"It's going to be a long day," he muttered.

"Pardon?" She looked over her shoulder at him.

He waved his hand about, indicating his words had not been important.

"Where is your horse?" she then questioned.

"In the stables."

She bent before him and plucked a long stalk of grass from the ground.Will was presented with the lush curve of her bottom once more before she righted herself and jammed the stalk into her mouth. He felt an irrational need to wrap her in a blanket so no one else could lust after her as he was. Of course he knew she could not ride in the Derby in a dress, yet he did not want everyone to see the body that he knew intimately. In fact, he had the feeling he would spend the day having words with any man who did so.

"How do you feel?"

"Nervous," she whispered, which surprised him. He had thought she would brush his question off.

"As am I."

"Why are you nervous?" she questioned as they walked into the stables, now side-by-side.

"Because I will have to watch you charge around a paddock surrounded by unscrupulous men whose only wish is to unseat you."

"Jaccob is not unscrupulous!"

"Not in the normal course of events, no. But he, like the

others, have their sights set on that prize money."

"As do I," Livvy said, letting herself into Harvey's stall.

"I'll give you one guinea if you don't race," Will added, joining her to help saddle the horse.

She snorted but didn't speak.

"His name is Harvey. He is Phoebe's horse."

"Hello, Harvey." Will rubbed his hand down the long face. "I'll give you an extra bucket of oats and one guinea, which can go into your old age care, if you look after your mistress today and make sure she reaches the finish in good health."

"You don't need to be here with me."

"Yes, I do," Will said, taking the saddle from her and throwing it onto Harvey's back.

They didn't speak again as they finished preparing Harvey and Will tried not to think about what he and Livvy had done in the next stall just two days ago. When they were finished, he took her hands and pulled her into his arms. He kissed her forehead then her nose and lastly her lips.

"Promise me you will take care." Cupping her face, he looked into her eyes.

"I promise, Will, please don't worry," she whispered against his lips.

He stood still as she touched him, running a finger down his nose and along his chin, It felt as if she was memorizing every inch of his face. Emotions flickered behind her eyes and then he saw the moment she had come to some kind of decision.

"Livvy?"

"I have no right to say this to you, Will, yet I must. When last you left and my anger had finally gone I realized that were you to die away from me then you would never have known how I felt about you."

"Livvy-"

Rising on her toes she kissed him into silence.

"I love you, Lord Ryder. I love the man you were and the noble, honorable man you have become. Please forgive yourself for leaving your family and absolve yourself of any guilt you may still carry. You are home now, here with the people who love you the most and I assure you all is forgotten and forgiven, Will."

Will felt a swell of emotion as he looked at her. She was his life now and the love she had given him filled the last of the dark corners deep inside his soul.

"You have asked that I promise to take care and in return I would ask that you promise to forgive yourself,' she added.

"For you, my love, I will try," he whispered, humbled by her words and that she had finally told him what he had known was in her heart. Reluctantly, he released her as she pulled away.

"And now we must leave or I shall miss the Derby."

Will threw her into the saddle. "I'll kill any man who dares to look at you in those," he growled as he caught and eyeful of her delightful bottom once more.

"I shall burn them after this race."

"I would never stop you from riding in the Derby, Livvy, yet I'm pleased to hear that this is to be your last race," Will said as he retrieved his horse.

"I know you would not," was all she said and when he looked at her she had turned away.

It was cool and clear and Will let his leg brush Livvy's whenever the opportunity presented itself and had they not been making their way to the Earl of Dobberley's lands where his future wife would attempt to not break her neck, he would have been a happy man. She loved him. Lord, that felt good. And maybe he could begin to forgive himself now that his heart was full and he felt finally at peace.

They rode together over the bridge and down into town. Carriages, horses and people filled the streets as everyone made their way to the Derby, eager to get a good place to view the race.

"Good luck, Miss Olivia!"

"Thank you, Miss Ogilvy."

Livvy smiled and touched her hat as some of the people of Twoaks acknowledged her. She rode beside him like a sentry, tall and proud, her purple sash fluttering in the breeze.

"I love you."

CHAPTER SEVENTEEN

"What? I mean, pardon?" Livvy said, turning to face him.

"I'm not going to repeat it, Olivia."

Her body was suddenly warm; her heart seemed to fill her chest entirely. Will loved her. She looked through Harvey's ears but saw nothing. Her thoughts were in turmoil.

They walked through the tall stone gates of Silverton Manor a short while later. Climbing up the slope to where the spectators and other riders had gathered, Livvy felt her stomach roll as she looked at the scene. Jenny's porridge was suddenly not sitting well. The start, finish line was festooned with flags that she was sure would put every horse present into a state of hysteria and the Earl was standing on a raised platform behind which a musical quartet were performing loudly.

Many had tried to get the Earl to change the race to a warmer month of the year, yet he would not budge. It was a tradition his family had upheld for years and, therefore, it would be run, as it always had, on the 21st of December. Oddly enough, there had only ever been one cancellation of the Derby and that was due to a blizzard that had swept England in 1703, but for the most part, the weather always seemed to clear for the Twoaks Derby. It was not a ride for the faint hearted, with the course starting with an incline and then a long stretch of flat, yet there was a portion through the woods which often determined who would win or lose. This part was unseen by any guests and most riders applied their whips and feet to which ever rider was near in the hopes of unseating a rival before they broke clear of the trees. Livvy had been kicked in the thigh last year and bore the bruise for days after.

"He certainly goes all out to make sure this day is a success."

Livvy looked at Will's handsome profile as he studied the scene before him. He loved her and she loved him and suddenly she knew with a certainty that she couldn't leave Twoaks now, not when they would both suffer for it. She would have to speak with her sisters, but Livvy would do whatever needed to be done to stay here and have a life with him and no one was going to take that away from her. Could she trust him with her secrets? Would he turn from her? No, not Will. He would be angry, but he would never walk away from her again. Yet she could not make any decision without talking to Phoebe and Bella first. It was their future as well.

"You are a disgrace to dress as you have, Olivia Langley!" Major Bruntly roared, storming towards her. "Your sash would be better colored scarlet, seeing as you dress like a harlot"

Before she could react, Will had thrust his reins at her and dismounted. In a few strides, he had rounded her horse and rammed his fist into the major's nose. The man fell backwards heavily onto the ground.

"Will, stop!" Livvy cried, getting off Harvey.

"Problem?"

She felt the breath refill her lungs as the Duke suddenly appeared beside his brother.

"He called Olivia a harlot." Will reached for the major to haul him to his feet so he could pummel him again.

"Did he now?" the Duke said, wrestling the man out of his brother's grasp and planting his fist in his stomach.

"I have been hearing some very distasteful things about you of late, Major," he then said. "Today, I have spoken with many locals who have mentioned shoddy business dealings and the purchase of shares you made them buy in ventures, which have yielded no returns. You have blackmailed some and stolen from others, Major, and I am only saddened that I was not aware of any of this until now. In short, Sir, you are not the upstanding gentleman you portray to the world."

The major wheezed but managed to straighten, although blood now trickled from his swollen nose.

"I have called for the magistrate, who I believe is at present awaiting you at your house. In fact, if I know Josiah Francis, he will be inside your house searching your records."

Major Bruntly didn't speak. He merely stumbled backwards several steps and then turned and ran.

"Idiot," the Duke muttered, following Bruntly with his eyes. "He actually believed me when I have not even had a chance to talk with Josiah. Are you all right, Will?" he added, now looking at his brother.

Livvy took the hand Will had used to thump the major and inspected the knuckles.

"I'm all right, love, I promise," he said, squeezing her fingers.

"Then I must join the riders as the race is due to start." Livvy kissed his knuckles, uncaring that half the villagers were watching.

"Be careful, Livvy, please," Will said, as he lifted her onto the saddle.

"I promise." Gathering the reins with a last smile for him, she then went to join the others.

Livvy nodded to the other riders as she made her way past the Earl who stood on his dais, acknowledging each rider as they reached him.

"I want to hand you the prize money this year, Miss Langley, so do not let me down."

Livvy took the hand he offered her. Like the rest of him, it was big boned and dwarfed her fingers.

"I will do my best, Lord Dobberly."

"I like the sash," he added as she moved on.

Moving to the start line Livvy took a deep, steadying breath. Harvey was already prancing, eager to be on his way.

She watched as people started making their way up the hill to get a better view of the race.

"'Tis four furlongs, remember," Jaccob said, moving to her side. "Try and make for the front or the rear when you reach the woods for the first time, then you will not have riders on either side of you. It's narrow. Use your whip or boots, if need be."

Livvy nodded. He had given her the same speech last year.

"Ely Grange did not ride last year but is entered this year. He's a right nasty piece and is none too happy about you being here."

"Point him out," Livvy said quietly.

She followed Jaccob's gaze and located a small man seated on a big-boned gray horse. He was looking her way and Livvy tried not to shudder at the hatred in his eyes.

"Try and stick with me."

"No, Jaccob, you look after yourself." Livvy did not want him throwing the race to protect her.

"Take your place for the Twoaks Derby!"

The Earl's words had the riders jockeying for position, and then he raised his hand from which a white scarf fluttered.

Mindful of Jaccob's words, Livvy moved away from Ely Grange and tucked in behind him and another horse. The spectators were beginning to call out their favorites' names in encouragement and she heard a few 'Miss Langleys.'

"Let the Twoaks Derby begin!"

Livvy felt Harvey surge forward beneath her and she immediately crouched low over his neck. The thunder of hooves drowned out all noise and she kept her eyes between his ears rather than looking around her. He was a brave horse who would run until he had nothing left in his legs, but this was not a distance that should tax him overly because she and Phoebe had been working on his training for months now. Slowly, he found his rhythm and soon began to make his way through the field until only two riders were in front of her. The woods were just up ahead. She needed to make it through them without incident the first time and then, if possible, be in the clear for the second pass. Once through the forest, there was another straight and then a wide turn and then they headed back the way they had come. Making sure her whip was in position, she urged Harvey into the trees.

"A woman should not ride in the Derby!"

Livvy looked into the angry face of Ely Grange as he pulled alongside her.

"Or a boy!" Livvy yelled, lifting her arm to protect both her and Harvey as he swung his whip at her. She did not cry as the leather bit into her sleeve. Instead, she kicked her foot free and lashed out at his thigh. It connected and Grange fell sideways, allowing Livvy to urge Harvey forward once again. She saw the light ahead. Just a few more feet and she would be out of the trees and once again in the open.

"Bitch!"

Grange drew beside her once again, only this time she was waiting for him.

"Cur!" Livvy screamed, lifting her whip and slashing it at him. He moved out of range, but she shivered at the look in his eyes. He was not finished with her yet.

Will watched Livvy come out of the trees in second place with another rider closing in on her. Exhaling the breath he had been holding, he made several heated promises to whoever was listening that if she made it back safe he would not sin for at least a month.

"She'll make it, Will, but I would suggest that you forbid her entry next year."

"She has already made me that promise, Joe," Will said, watching as Harvey thundered along the course with Livvy crouched low over his neck.

"She's good though, you must admit that."

Will grunted, but kept his eyes on that purple sash.

"Of course, Jaccob will win. He's riding the horse I purchased specifically with the Derby in mind," Joseph added.

"Livvy will win."

"Jaccob is perfectly placed."

"Yet Livvy will win," Will said, flinching as another horse bumped into Harvey as Livvy turned him to start the run home.

"Care for a small wager?"

"You will personally move my bed into my new house and place it in my new bedroom," Will said. "Then you'll make it perfectly, no creases, and with the edges turned down."

"Done, and you have to spend the entire day with great Aunt Hildeth who is about to return from Italy."

Will hesitated. Aunt Hildeth could out talk Mrs. Popplehange. "Done."

"May I place a small wager also?" Lord Levermarch said from behind Will.

"So, you made it." Will shot his friend a quick look before refocusing on Livvy. "Joe, introduce Finn to everyone."

Will heard the rumble of Joe's voice as he introduced Lord Levermarch to Phoebe, Thea and Isabella.

"Is that a woman riding? Good Lord, what's the world coming to?"

Ignoring Finn's horror, Will urged Livvy on. "Come on, sweetheart," he whispered as that same horse crowded into Harvey again.

"I take exception to that ridiculous statement, Lord Levermarch. A woman has as much right to ride in the Derby as a man, if not more so given our intelligence."

Will would have laughed at Phoebe's attack on Finn if he wasn't so bloody terrified.

"Who the hell is that bumping into her?

"Ely Grange, Lord Ryder. He rides for Major Bruntly," Mrs. Popplehinge said, appearing beside him.

"I'll kill him if he unseats her," Will growled as the bastard bumped into Harvey again.

"They will head for the woods for the second time and then home. Therefore, I suggest we make for the finish," Joseph said.

Will watched until she had disappeared into the woods and then made his way down the hill with the other spectators.

"Someone is deliberately checking her."

"I saw that, Luke," he said, joining him at the finish line. His stomach ached, it was clenched so tight.

"Here they come!" Bella cried as Joe put her back on her feet after carrying her down the hill. Beside her, Thea screamed her encouragement.

She was in the lead, but Ely Grange was once again closing. All around him, people were yelling their encouragement but Will kept his eyes on Livvy. She wouldn't put him through this again, ever. He was a churning mass of anxiety.

"She's going to do it! Come on, Olivia!" Mrs. Popplehinge squealed as she jumped up and down with Phoebe.

The other rider was gaining once more and Harvey's ears were flat to his head which indicated to Will that the horse was not happy. He watched as Livvy urged her horse on, bending low over Harvey's neck.

"No!"

Bella screamed as the other rider raised his whip as Livvy reached the line and he slashed it onto Harvey's rump. Will watched them cross the line seconds later and then Harvey bucked his hind legs in protest and Livvy went flying over his head.

"No!" This time it was Will who roared as he ducked under the railings to try to reach her before she fell. He couldn't stop her landing in a crash of limbs, but he threw himself over her body as the other horses charged over the finish line. The air around him came alive with the sound of hooves as he bridged his body over Livvy's still form. Clenching his eyes shut, he waited for the impact.

Joseph, Finn and Luke arrived first, turning the air blue with a startling array of foul words, followed by the Langley sisters who were silent with fear.

Realizing he was not about to be crushed by several hundred pounds of horse flesh, Will pushed to his knees and reached for Livvy. Her eyes were closed and she lay sprawled in a tangle of bent limbs. Pressing his fingers under her jaw he felt a steady pulse and nearly wept as relief flooded through him.

"She's knocked out," Joseph said, kneeling beside him.

He didn't speak because he couldn't, so Will concentrated on straightening her legs and arms and checking for anything broken. Removing her hat, he ran his hands softly over her head but found no blood.

"Is she all right?"

He heard Joe begin to reassure Phoebe and Bella as he checked on her injuries.

"Will?"

"Yes," he said as Livvy opened her eyes. "Hold still, love."

Her eyes searched for her sisters, who were both now crying. Instinctively, she tried to reach them but pain forced her back to the ground.

"What part of 'hold still' did you not understand?" Will growled, bracing a hand on her chest, thereby immobilizing her.

"I hurt," she whispered.

"Not surprising, considering you just fell to the ground while your horse was galloping."

Will felt her pain as she looked at him, but he could do nothing to ease her suffering.

"D—did I win?" she then whispered, her words unsteady as she struggled against the pain.

Will had been keeping his emotions under control until that point. In fact, he was rather proud of the fact that he hadn't raised his voice or located the man with the whip and killed him with his bare hands; however, those three words instantaneously released his rage.

"You nearly broke your foolish neck and you are worried about winning!"

"Steady, Will," Finn said softly.

"I want the prize money," she said, unwisely to Will's way of thinking, because that merely inflamed him more. The fact that she needed money so badly she had risked her life to get it tore him apart. He had money, sacks of it, and would give it all to her if only she had asked.

"Joe, tell Luke to bring the carriage close. Now!"

"I will as soon as he's finished carrying out a bit of retribution on your behalf, brother."

"What?" Will snapped.

"Luke is pummeling the man who hurt Olivia."

Will grunted his approval.

"He seems to have made his point, so I shall tell him to bring the carriage now," Joseph said minutes later.

"Bella will accompany you and I shall ride Harvey home," Phoebe said as Will lifted Livvy into his arms.

"I shall escort you home, Miss Langley," Finn added.

"I do not need an escort!"

"Yet you will have one," Finn said.

Nodding, Will started after his brother ignoring Phoebe's vehement protests.

Livvy hurt everywhere. Her head throbbed; in fact, there was nowhere on her body that was without pain. Looking up at the man that carried her, she noted his clenched jaw. He was angry and she knew it was because she had frightened him when she fell.

"Will, I—"

"Not one word," he said in a cold, hard voice.

Turning her face into his chest, Livvy remained silent and closed her eyes.

"Thank you, Luke, for what you just did," she heard Will say as they reached the carriage.

"Is she all right, Will?"

"Yes, I believe so, just bruised and sore. If you can take us to Willow Hall now, I would be grateful."

Livvy thought he would place her on a seat inside the carriage. However, he simply stepped inside and sat with her on his lap.

"Are you all right, Livvy?"

Bella's worried voice reached her from the opposite seat so she moved to get up.

"Let me sit up, please."

The arms momentarily clenched, and then he helped her into a sitting position.

"I'm all right, Bella, just a bit stiff and sore."

She was rewarded with a small smile of relief from her sister. The rest of the journey was carried out in a strained, uncomfortable silence. When the carriage finally reached Willow Hall, Livvy's head was throbbing and she wanted the comfort and solitude of her bed and to get away from the angry man beside her. His jaw was clenched and his face appeared carved in granite. Gone was the gentle man who had declared his love to her just a short while ago.

"Th—thank you, Lord Ryder, for the ride home," Livvy said, reaching for the door as the carriage stopped at Willow Hall.

"I'm coming inside as there are a few things I want to say to you."

And then she was in his arms again and he was striding up the path and into the house. He took the stairs two at a time.

"Which is your room?"

"I don't think…"

"Tell me now, or I will say what I want right here with your sister and Luke listening."

"Third door."

He opened it and then slammed it shut with his booted foot. In seconds she was sitting on her bed. Livvy couldn't help the small moan that escaped as her body protested the movement. It seemed to be the sign he was after because suddenly she was under attack.

"You promised to take care," Will snarled, moving back from the bed, almost as if he needed to put some distance between them.

"I did what I needed to win the race," Livvy said in her own defense.

"Tell me what drives you to rob innocent people and then nearly break your neck today in that foolish race. What drives you to live this façade where you have one servant but pretend you have more, that your house is made up of one room that looks as it should and the rest of it is in need of repair!"

Livvy had thought the pain in her body was the worst she would experience today, yet his words were like tiny daggers lancing her soul. How had he noted so much in such a short time?

"A viscount's daughter who is behaving like a common criminal," he roared, reaching for her.

"Stop!" Livvy cried as he started unbuttoning her jacket. His hands were determined and his eyes were banked with the embers of rage and she could do nothing to stop him.

"Wh—what are you doing?"

He wasn't rough but he would not be deterred as he removed her jacket and then opened her shirt and eased it off one shoulder. He turned her, then, so her back was facing him.

"This is the final proof, Olivia, this wound is from Luke's knife," he said, releasing her and stepping backwards once more. "He could have killed you, do you understand that?

Livvy pulled the shirt around her and only then turned. His anger seemed to fill all the spaces in her room.

"Talk to me, damn you!"

"I… I love you, Will, and I will tell you everything. Just not now," Livvy pleaded. "I must talk with my sisters first."

He stalked to the door and turned the key in the lock and then dropped it into the pocket of his jacket. Wrapping his fingers around the back of the only chair in her room, he then dragged it towards the bed and sat facing her.

"Don't talk to me of love and then tell me nothing. Don't talk to me of love and then make me watch you fly through the air and crash in a tangle of limbs onto the hard ground and wonder if, when I reach you, you will be alive or dead!"

"I'm sorry," Livvy whispered, seeing the anguish she had put him through written clearly on his face.

"Sorry is not enough, Olivia. Neither of us will leave this room until you tell me the truth… all of it. Every last bloody word and only then will I unlock that door. I'll not live with any more of your lies hanging over us. We can have no life together if you do not trust me and I will not wait around while you plunge recklessly into more danger and risk your life all for the sake of a few secrets. You will tell me now."

Livvy felt the sting of tears but held them at bay. She needed time to think, to decide what must be done.

"I—I'm cold, can one of my sisters tend me, please."

He looked at her for several seconds and then, taking the key from his pocket, he opened the door and closed it behind him. Livvy heard the key turn in the lock once more and then she was alone.

Was he walking away from her? Fighting back the tears, Livvy fell sideways into her pillows. She had no strength to follow him, even to bang on the now locked door. Would she survive losing him a second time? Closing her eyes, she had no idea how long she lay there feeling lost and alone, the pain in her heart mirroring the pain in her body. She buried her face in the pillows as the key once more turned in the lock; Livvy did not want her sisters to see her distress.

"Sit up."

Lifting her head, she watched Will walk in carrying a tray which he lay on the foot of the bed. She didn't move; in fact. she couldn't. Even lifting her arms was a gesture beyond her reach now.

"You are stiffening up, Olivia. We need to get you washed and into bed now."

He sounded impersonal, as if he was addressing an acquaintance, not the woman he supposedly loved.

"I do not want your help."

"Yet, you need it."

She watched him move to her drawers, going through the contents until he found what he wanted and then returning to her side with one of her nightdresses clenched in a large hand.

"I can do that," Livvy said, but he ignored her and started

pulling her boots off her feet. He lifted her upright then, his hands gentle but determined even though he radiated anger. Slowly, he began to remove her shirt and chemise, then her breeches. He was too strong for her to fight so she suffered the indignity, biting her lip as pain snaked through her body. When she was naked, he wrung out a cloth and washed her.

Livvy was desperate for some distance between them, but the fierce expression on his face kept her quiet.

He lifted a small pot off the tray and scooped the contents into his hand. "Jenny said this will soothe your aches."

"I can…"

"No, you can't," he said, rubbing the ointment into her body.

Will watched Livvy bite her lip to stop crying out as he touched her. She lay silently as he cared for her, tormented and hurting, and he could do nothing to ease her pain, only give her comfort. But that he would not give until she told him the truth.

"Lean forward now," he directed when he had finished. Bruises were beginning to darken her pale skin, and seeing them compounded his anger. Taking the nightdress he had found, he dropped it over her head and eased her arms through the sleeves. Propping a few pillows behind her, he then lay her back and drew the covers to her chin. Clenching his fingers, he fought the urge to brush a hand over her head. Retrieving the cup of tea Mrs. Bell had given him, he then handed it to her.

'If you love her you'll put a stop to all this nonsense now, Lord Ryder,' the Langley housekeeper had said when he'd tracked her down in the kitchens. Bella and Phoebe had looked at him with big, fearful eyes but had remained silent as he prowled around the room waiting for the water to heat.

"Can you drink without help?

She nodded and Will retrieved the second cup. Moving to

the chair, he then once again sat.

"Now talk."

She sipped the tea and then briefly closed her eyes. When they opened, he knew he had won. He had buttoned her white nightdress to the neck and her hair hung in a long dark plait, still tied with the black satin ribbon. She looked very young and fragile sitting against a pile of pillows, but Will wasn't fooled. The love of his life was about as fragile as a battalion of soldiers.

"I would ask you to listen to me fairly and without interruption and to know that I did what I believed needed to be done to secure my family's future?"

"However misguided," he added, before taking a large mouthful of the hot water with lemon and honey the housekeeper had made him.

"Have you never made choices that were wrong, Lord Ryder, choices forced upon you when you had no other option?"

"This is not about me, Olivia, it's about you," Will said softly.

Her sigh was loud and the glare she directed his way was spoiled by a yawn.

"The carriage accident that hurt Bella and killed Mother also injured my father," she said. "And slowly, the pain of losing his arm and my mother began to destroy his mind until some days he did not even recognize his own daughters. One day, I took him his lunch and he was dead, lying back in his chair staring sightlessly at me as I ran towards him."

Will didn't speak. He wanted to. He wanted to tell her that she was here safe with him and that he would always care and protect her and her family from this day forward, yet he did not. He needed to hear everything and to do that he had to watch her closely. Only then would he know if she was hiding anything from him.

She looked down into her cup before speaking again.

"I found a bottle of poison and a note and quickly put them into my pocket before my sisters arrived."

My God, how could her father have done that to her?

She told him the rest then, about how they had been left without any money and how they had sold things to survive but that the money had not lasted long. She spoke of trying to keep up appearances so her sisters would have a future, and then becoming a highwayman and the guilt associated with her actions. Her strength amazed him, the courage she had shown to keep her family safe and their reputations untarnished.

"When you saw Phoebe and me awaiting the stage to London, we were going to see my cousin, the new Lord Langley."

"Why did you need to see him?"

She told him about the letter and Lord Langley's intentions of throwing them out of Willow Hall.

"Did he hurt you, Olivia? Was it he who left those marks on your breasts?" Will watched her eyes lower. "Everything," he said, feeling the anger that had begun to subside rear its head again.

"He knew about father, had found the note and poison bottle. I—I had not destroyed them, you see. I hid them until I could and then forgot to do so."

"What did he do to you?"

"He told me he would marry my lame sister, as no one else would, and he would treat her like a lady if I b—became his courtesan."

"I'll kill him!"

"No," Livvy whispered as he said the words.

"Did he touch you, Livvy?

"Yes, a little, and he tried to… you know," she whispered. "But I punched him in the jaw and then bit him hard."

"Good girl," Will said, thinking that what Lord Langley would get from him would leave him with more than a sore jaw.

"Are you still angry with me?" she whispered.

"Yes."

"I'm s—sorry."

He heard the tremor in her words and saw the glisten of tears on her cheeks.

"You're crying now? After what you went through at the Derby and what you have just told me, it is my anger that makes you weep?" Lowering his cup, Will moved to the bed and looked down at her.

"I—I know you are disappointed and angry with me and I fear my actions have lost your love," Livvy said, holding his eyes. "B—but, Will, I—I would not change what I have done because I believed it was the only course open to me."

"We will address your penchant for reckless behavior another time. For now, I want to know why you think I no longer love you. Do you believe that I am so fickle that I can stop caring in a few hours just because you've angered me?"

"I've lied to people, stolen money from others and my father killed himself. Can you not understand how these things tarnish me?"

"You are the bravest, most beautiful woman I know, Olivia Langley." Will needed to hold her close, so lifting her he then re-settled them both on the bed, resting her on his lap. "Only a strong woman could have done what you did, love, and no matter how I feel about the choices you've made, I cannot blame you for them. You did what you thought was necessary to keep your family safe."

"I thought I had lost your love," Livvy said, gripping his shirt tight.

"Never, Livvy. I could sooner stop breathing than loving you."

"You were so angry with me."

"I'm angry because the woman I love was in danger and I was not there to keep her safe. I'm angry that you confronted your cousin alone and he frightened and could have hurt you and I would not have known. But more importantly, I'm angry that you believed I would care about how your father died or that his suicide would in any way impact how I felt about you or your sisters."

"But how was I to know how you would feel about Father's death? I no longer knew the man you had become. How could I trust you when you had left me before?"

"Perhaps in the beginning that was true, but later, after we had made love and you knew my feelings, you should have told me then."

Will took the sting out of his words by kissing the top of her head. Cupping the back of her neck, he began to knead the muscles he knew must be aching.

"You broke my heart when you left, Will. Just waking up every day took so much effort for weeks and weeks. Hiding it from my family and your family was even harder. The pitied looks and pats on the shoulders.

"Had I stayed, I would have broken it anyway, my love. I was a man bent on destruction and I would have taken you with me."

She thought about those words and realized they were true; he would not have settled for marrying her had he stayed.

"Tell me that you trust me now, Livvy, and promise me there will be no more secrets between us."

Tilting her head back, she looked up at him, saw the doubts on his handsome face.

"Yes, I trust you with my life and that of my sisters, Will, but you have to understand that for so long I have dealt with this alone, frightened that someone would see what we took pains to hide. To trust another with our secrets, even you"—she added as he opened his mouth to speak—"was not something I took lightly."

"I love you, Olivia Langley." Will closed the distance between them. He kissed her softly, a slow meeting of lips and souls. "And I hope you can trust me to deal with everything now."

"We will deal with it, Will. I'll not be pushed aside, not when I have been the head of this family for so long."

He traced her features with a finger. The fine, feathered brows, the line of her nose and curve of her check, the fullness of her lips.

"*We* will deal with it then,"

He held her, lying quietly with her in his arms, feeling peace for the first time in days. Will inhaled the scent of his woman. She was here, safe with him, where she would now always be.

"Love me, Will," Livvy whispered, lifting her face for his kiss.

"Forever," he said, pulling her close and framing her face with his hands. "I believe I have always loved you, Livvy Langley, yet only now since my return have I come to realize how much."

Livvy closed her eyes as he kissed the tears from her cheeks.

"Five years ago, when Thea told us you had left, I felt as if my world had crumbled. I was devastated that you had gone without a word or a note and it was not until I saw you that day in the cemetery that I realized your feelings had not been the same as mine," she said, placing one hand on his chest.

"I did care for you, love, very much, yet I carried so much anger and confusion inside me and I knew that I had to leave or it would destroy us both."

Livvy stroked a hand down one of his cheeks. He was such a strong, powerful man, yet beneath the surface lay vulnerabilities, just like the next person.

"I still loved you then, Will. With me you were always gentle, even when you were teasing me."

Capturing her hand, he placed a kiss on the palm.

"Of course I was gentle. You could punch harder than any man I knew." Will sucked one of her fingers into his mouth as he finished speaking and felt her shiver.

"Marry me, Olivia Langley. Let me sleep with you in my arms and wake you with my kisses. Only with you can I truly be the man I want to be. You fill all the places inside me that have been empty for so long and you take away the pain of who I once was and the people I hurt."

"Yes, Will. Oh, I long to marry you. But what of my cousin? He is to arrive shortly"

"I have had my suspicions about him since your visit to London, Livvy, and have had Freddy investigate him. As it turns out, your cousin is not a very nice man."

"Really?"

"Really, and now we shall open that door and bring your sisters in before they break it down," Will said, lifting her from his lap and placing her gently beside him as he regained his feet.

"But what will we do?" Livvy said, trying to follow him, only to moan loudly as her body protested the movements.

He braced his hands on either side of her head before speaking.

"Do you trust me?"

Livvy nodded.

"Then know that what I am about to do is the best thing for your family, love. Allow me to share your burdens now. You are no longer alone, Livvy."

CHAPTER EIGHTEEN

"Lord Ryder said you were to stay in bed until he returned, Miss Olivia," Jenny said as she helped Olivia down the stairs and into the front parlor.

"Yes, Livvy. Will was insistent in this. He said you would try to override his orders and we were not to let you," Bella said from behind them.

"I will not receive the Duke in my room. It is bad enough that none of you will help me change into a dress," Livvy snapped, and then hissed as some other part of her damaged body protested.

"You'll lie on the sofa and have a blanket pulled up to your chin before Lord Ryder returns or we will all be in for it," Jenny added.

Livvy didn't say anything further as she was now seriously regretting her intention to face the Duke in the parlor. Her head swam as Jenny lowered her onto the seat.

"Pinch her cheeks, I hear a carriage," Phoebe ordered Bella as she hurried to the windows. "She looks like a bloody ghost and we shall be in for it if Lord Ryder walks in and she's fainted.

"Please, I can take no more of your tender care, sister," Livvy said as she tried to fight off Bella's hands.

"It takes a lot to intimidate me, Livvy, but when he stormed into the kitchen after locking you in your room, I swear I have never seen an angrier man. His eyes were narrowed and his fury seemed to fill the room, even though he was speaking to Jenny politely."

"You should have shared a carriage with him." Bella shuddered. "He sat with his fists clenched on his thighs the entire journey and his eyes never moved from Livvy.

Rather than feeling intimidated by her sisters words, Livvy felt warmth fill her. He would never hurt her, she knew this; his anger was because he loved her.

"Perhaps you should slap some color into her cheeks," Phoebe said, returning to Livvy's side.

"Witch!"

"I thought I told you to keep her in her bed!"

Livvy could do nothing to stop the foolish smile that lit her face as Will stormed into the room, over coat flapping around his heels, head bare. He frowned at her which only made her smile more.

"Pray, enlighten me. Why you are smiling?" he said, dropping to his knees beside her.

Livvy grabbed a handful of his coat and pulled him towards her.

"Because I love you and finally I feel hope."

The scowl fell from Will's lips. "You humble me, love." Kissing her, he then stood once more to make room for his brother.

"I'm sorry you have been brought into this, your grace," Livvy said as Joe bent to take her hand. "It was never my intention."

"We are to be family, Olivia. In fact, I believe I am to inherit three sisters when my brother marries and family must always stick together, sister."

Will watched Livvy as tears filled her eyes. "You always were a silver-tongued sod."

"I inherited my nature from our mother, unlike you," the Duke added, taking the seat next to Bella.

Will snorted, but said nothing further; he had never loved his brother more than at that moment.

"If you'll allow me, I will tell Joe your story now, Olivia, Phoebe, Isabella." They all nodded, and so briefly he told his brother what Livvy had told him.

"Good grief, you robbed people to survive?"

"Yes, your grace." Will watched Livvy blush.

"Lord Ryder was our first robbery," Phoebe added. "The second was Major Bruntly, and the third, two women who seemed rather pleased with the experience."

"They do not need to hear that, Phoebe," Livvy said softly. "What we did was wrong, no matter the outcome."

"Good grief!" Joe said again.

"I almost wish I'd been there to see you robbing Bruntly," Will said softly.

"I understand you must be horrified over what we have done, Your Grace, but I felt we had no other choice," Livvy rushed to add.

"You did what you thought needed to be done, Olivia, however misguided," the Duke said, mirroring his brother's words. "I have no right to judge you because of it."

Livvy sent Will a look when he snorted.

"However, I wish you had come to me for help when your father died and the subsequent years after, but I understand pride as both my brother and I have plenty of it."

"A horse is coming," Phoebe cried, running to the window. "It must be Jaccob alerting us that Lord Langley is near."

"Perfect timing," Will said, taking a large bite of Jenny's fruit cake.

"But what will we say?" Livvy tried to rise, her face pale with worry and pain.

"Trust me, Livvy?" Will said, reaching for her and lifting her to her feet.

"I do, Will."

"Then let your sisters button you into a dress. Then I shall carry you to a chair in here and we shall await your cousin."

"Should she not be resting?" The Duke questioned.

"If she is not in the room, she will be standing outside of it listening at the door," Will drawled.

Forty minutes later, Livvy was sitting in a large, comfortable chair with Will sitting on the arm at her side. The Duke was sitting in another slightly further back. They had discussed what needed to be said and Will had told Livvy she was to keep her mouth shut. He had little hope of her obeying, but he had asked anyway.

"Oh, dear, he is here," Livvy whispered, grabbing his hand.

"He can't hurt you anymore, love, remember that."

Nodding, she let his hand go with a final squeeze and tried to look calm.

Lord Langley walked into the parlor and then stopped upon seeing Will standing beside Livvy and the Duke at the rear.

"What are you doing in my house?"

Neither of the brothers rose to their feet.

"Waiting for you, Langley," Will said calmly.

Olivia's cousin looked foolish, dressed in lavender breeches and matching waistcoat with a neckcloth that was tied in so many folds he looked like a puppy. He was fat and sweaty and the thought of him touching the woman he loved had him clenching his fists.

"Easy," Joseph whispered.

"I demand to know the meaning of this!"

"I don't believe you addressed me correctly, Langley," the Duke said. He, like Will, had a dark, implacable gaze leveled on the man. Langley must have seen something that gave him pause because he quickly slipped into a clumsy bow.

"Your grace, pardon me. I was merely surprised to see you here."

This man had dared to touch Livvy, threaten her and her sisters, and were it not for the lecture about winning this battle with words that Joseph had given him just moments ago, he would have planted his fist in the man's face by now.

"You will listen to what I have to say, Langley, and not speak," Will said. "You need not concern yourself over your cousins any further as they are no longer your worry and are now under my care."

"I care for my cousins!" Langley declared, taking a step closer to Olivia.

"Step back, Langley," Will said quietly. Something in his voice had the man doing just that.

"I have heard disturbing things about you this day, Langley, things about murdered girls, gambling debts, bungled investments, and more."

"T—tis untrue, Lord Ryder!"

"I think not, Langley," Will said. "In fact, my man is, as we speak, on his way to London to buy up every one of your markers."

"What? Why would you want my markers? They can be of no interest to you," Lord Langley said, darting a look from Will to Livvy and then finally, Joseph.

"You will be indebted to me, Langley, for some time, if not the rest of your life," Will added. "And make no mistake that I am bluffing, because I am a very wealthy man and your debts will cause me very little discomfort and a great deal of control."

"Why?" Langley asked again. He was clearly baffled by the animosity in the room. "What have I ever done to either of you?"

"The Langley sisters are very, very good friends of ours,

Langley. It is my belief you have not treated them as a family member should have." Will climbed to his feet and walked closer to the man. "You have neglected to care for them and left them to fend for themselves."

"'Tis untrue! Would you believe their word over that of a nobleman? If she has spoken against me, it is slander, I tell you, and jealously that I inherited and she did not," he said, pointing at Olivia.

"Liar," she hissed. "You are a weak, gutless man who failed in his familial obligations and, furthermore, you suggested vile, horrible things to me when I visited you in London."

"Be quiet, Olivia," Will said.

"I will not. He is an abhorrent, perfidious man who deserves a thorough thrashing, and I want you to give it to him, Will!"

Will heard Joe cough to cover his laughter while he struggled to keep his features calm. She was fiery, his beloved, and he couldn't wait to have all that fire centered on him.

Lord Langley's eyes bulged and his fists clenched as he took a step towards her, which foolishly put him in Will's path.

"I tell you, those bitches lie if they have slandered me. They are the worthless daughters of a man who took his life and I can prove it. You will not want to associate with them when I produce proof!" Langley cried. "She propositioned me in London, came calling and begged me to take her. She's nothing but a little slut!"

"You can't stop me, Joe, no one can," Will said calmly, taking a step forward and reaching Langley. Gripping the man's collar, he shook him like a bed sheet.

"Just the one, Will, and not the face," the Duke said from behind him.

Will planted his fist in the man's soft stomach and forced him backwards into the door he had recently entered. Hauling him to his feet, he then shook him again.

"Never again speak of my fiancée, do you understand, Langley, nor her sisters. Were we alone I would frighten you like you did her, you gutless coward."

Dropping him to the floor once more, he took a few steps backward, putting himself out of striking range. He felt Livvy's hand slip into his and then she was leaning against him. Lifting his arm, he tucked her into his side.

"It's all right now, my love," he whispered.

Langley floundered about on the floor like a landed fish while he tried to haul in a breath.

"Here is what will happen, and if you do not comply with what I say, Langley," Will said when he knew the man could once again hear him, "I will have you before the magistrate for the deaths of those two innocent girls your name is linked to. "You'll be leaving England for America on the next available ship, coincidently owned by me. Someone will escort you to London and retrieve any and all evidence you have on the Langley family and then they will help you pack and take you to the docks to meet your ship."

Will looked at the man and thought of the pain he had caused Olivia. He had never wanted to hurt someone so much before. This is what love did to a person.

"You will sleep at Rossetter House in a room that locks from the outside. There will also be a guard stationed outside the door so there is no possibility of escape, Lord Langley. Do I make myself clear?" Will added.

"Yes." He was a beaten man and Will was happier knowing that fact. They were safe from him now, Livvy was safe.

***

Livvy watched the Duke light the Yuletide Log in the hearth with the embers from last year's log. The Popplehinges stood arm in arm, Mrs. Popplehinge resplendent in deep forest green with matching red trim on her hat and coat. Bella stood chatting with Thea and Penny, while Luke, Freddy and Jenny stood at the rear. Phoebe was having a heated debate with Lord Levermarch about the correct way to shoot a pistol.

"Are you happy, my love?"

Livvy's smile was full of love as she turned to the man who was responsible for the joy inside her.

"So very happy, Will, and it is because of you."

He looked down at her for long seconds and then a slow smile spread over his lips.

"Will you spare me a few minutes of your time, Miss Langley?"

Nodding, she let him lead her from the room and out towards the front doorway. He bundled her into warm clothing and then they were outside. Pulling her into his side, they walked slowly down towards the lake.

"It's so beautiful out here, Will."

He didn't speak, just led her down to where the willows stood silently. Tugging her beneath, he then kissed her. Livvy melted against him, seeking his warmth and the magic of his kiss.

Lifting his head he looked at her.

"I first kissed you here, love, under these trees and I remember thinking that no other woman had touched me as you did that day."

"Oh, Will."

"I promise to cherish and love you until I draw my last breath, Olivia Langley," he said, framing her face with his hands. "Marry me, sweetheart; only with you can I truly be someone I'm proud of."

"No, Will, you always had the man you are today inside you. It just took time for you to find him," Livvy whispered against his lips. "Let me hold you close now, my love, and I promise to never let you go."

"Yes," Will sighed, drawing her closer. He was home, finally, and this is where he would always stay.

EPILOGUE

Will looked down the aisle at the assembled guests and then across to where Livvy stood. She looked beautiful in pale blue, with her hair woven in matching satin ribbons. The worry was gone from her eyes now and he saw only happiness and love every time she looked at him, as she was now.

"Dearly beloved, we are gathered here today to marry this man to this woman."

As the Reverend started talking, Will felt his chest fill with love. Around them were friends and family, all here for this special day, people that he had never let into his life before, yet now he could not live without. Their people, his and Olivia's. Giving her a final look, which she answered with a soft smile, he then focused on the service.

"Do you, Frederick Stanley Blake, take Jenny Elizabeth Bell to be your lawfully wedded wife?"

The bride cried softly beneath her veil and managed to say yes when the question was put to her a few moments later, while the groom looked down at her with love shining in his eyes.

Will looked at Livvy as he heard her sniff. In one month, this would be them. They would marry and then they would live out their days together and that day could not come soon enough for him. He wanted to spend hours talking with her and when they weren't talking then they would be making love. She had breathed life into him. Her love had made him finally believe in himself and that he was someone worthy of that love.

Will watched Freddy lift his new wife's veil and seal their union with a kiss. The new Mr. and Mrs. Blake would take up residence at Willow Hall as now the Langley sisters all resided at Rossetter house while Will finalized the purchase of the house they would all then relocate to.

Will swallowed his smile as Phoebe glared at Finn as he held out his arm so they could follow Freddy and Jenny from the church. Luke and Bella came next, and then Will held out his arm to Livvy.

"Come, sweetheart."

Together, they followed the others out of the church and into the cool, clear winter's day.

"I can't remember a time when I have felt this happy, Will."

Wrapping an arm around her waist, he pulled Olivia close to his side.

"And your happiness has only just begun, my love."

"Our happiness," she corrected.

"Our happiness," Will repeated, and then together they went to congratulate the married couple.

THE END